UNMASKING THE THIEF

Pleasure Garden, Book 5

Mary Lancaster

© Copyright 2022 by Mary Lancaster
Text by Mary Lancaster
Cover by Dar Albert

Dragonblade Publishing, Inc. is an imprint of Kathryn Le Veque Novels, Inc.
P.O. Box 23
Moreno Valley, CA 92556
ceo@dragonbladepublishing.com

Produced in the United States of America

First Edition March 2022
Trade Paperback Edition

Reproduction of any kind except where it pertains to short quotes in relation to advertising or promotion is strictly prohibited.

All Rights Reserved.

The characters and events portrayed in this book are fictitious. Any similarity to real persons, living or dead, is purely coincidental and not intended by the author.

ARE YOU SIGNED UP FOR DRAGONBLADE'S BLOG?

You'll get the latest news and information on exclusive giveaways, exclusive excerpts, coming releases, sales, free books, cover reveals and more.

Check out our complete list of authors, too!

No spam, no junk. That's a promise!

Sign Up Here

www.dragonbladepublishing.com

Dearest Reader;

Thank you for your support of a small press. At Dragonblade Publishing, we strive to bring you the highest quality Historical Romance from some of the best authors in the business. Without your support, there is no 'us', so we sincerely hope you adore these stories and find some new favorite authors along the way.

Happy Reading!

CEO, Dragonblade Publishing

Additional Dragonblade books by Author Mary Lancaster

Pleasure Garden Series
Unmasking the Hero (Book 1)
Unmasking Deception (Book 2)
Unmasking Sin (Book 3)
Unmasking the Duke (Book 4)
Unmasking the Thief (Book 5)

Crime & Passion Series
Mysterious Lover
Letters to a Lover
Dangerous Lover

The Husband Dilemma Series
How to Fool a Duke

Season of Scandal Series
Pursued by the Rake
Abandoned to the Prodigal
Married to the Rogue
Unmasked by her Lover

Imperial Season Series
Vienna Waltz
Vienna Woods
Vienna Dawn

Blackhaven Brides Series
The Wicked Baron
The Wicked Lady
The Wicked Rebel
The Wicked Husband

The Wicked Marquis
The Wicked Governess
The Wicked Spy
The Wicked Gypsy
The Wicked Wife
Wicked Christmas (A Novella)
The Wicked Waif
The Wicked Heir
The Wicked Captain
The Wicked Sister

Unmarriageable Series
The Deserted Heart
The Sinister Heart
The Vulgar Heart
The Broken Heart
The Weary Heart
The Secret Heart
Christmas Heart

The Lyon's Den Connected World
Fed to the Lyon

De Wolfe Pack: The Series
The Wicked Wolfe
Vienna Wolfe

Also from Mary Lancaster
Madeleine

Prologue

Returning to England after almost a year, Francisco de Salgado y Goya was in no mood to tolerate his instructor's rudeness. Once, he had been amused to be summoned so urgently, only to be left kicking his heels while His Arrogance finished writing his document or reading a report or just staring into space, deep in thought.

Today, Francisco had neither the patience nor the time. He wanted to go and get drunk with his friend, Ludovic Dunne—it had become something of a homecoming tradition—and then do nothing. *Nothing* was calling him.

So, despite the fact that his instructor continued to write with provoking precision, Francisco dropped his letter, which landed on the desk, right beneath His Arrogance's hovering pen.

"What is this?" His Arrogance inquired without looking up.

"My resignation," Francisco said happily. "Feel free to read it at your leisure. Goodbye, sir."

Turning on his heel, Francisco walked jauntily to the door. At least he appeared to have stunned his instructor at last, for no sound at all came from the desk behind him. That gave him some satisfaction.

"But you can't," His Arrogance said at last.

"On the contrary, sir, I have." Francisco didn't even pause, except to reach for the door handle.

"Wait. Please, sit."

Francisco debated whether or not to keep walking. But the man had never said please to him before, so he supposed one civility deserved another.

He sighed but returned to the desk and sat opposite his instructor. The pen was in its stand.

His Arrogance held the letter by one corner. "Why?"

Francisco blinked away the image of the dead face beneath the waves, which had become somehow unbreakably connected to older, much more devastating visions of death. "I'm bored."

The instructor stared at him. "Are you? But I need you. No one else is available for the next several weeks, and the matter is urgent."

"Dear me," Francisco remarked. He flicked a speck of dust from his cuff.

"Do this one, simple thing for me—one evening's worth at a pleasure garden—and I will accept your resignation."

Francisco stared at the ceiling and counted to ten. In several languages. Perhaps the instruction would be *so* simple that he could still go and get drunk with Ludo.

"With full fee?" he asked.

A long-suffering sigh rent the air. Anyone would think it was *his* money. "Very well."

Francisco lounged back in his chair, already bored. "Instruct me."

CHAPTER ONE

"HAVE YOU EVER been to Maida Pleasure Gardens, Miss Matty?"

The innocent question was thrown at the governess by her one-time pupil, Miss Catherine Dove, who sat at the other end of the sitting room deep in whispered conversation with her friend Hope Darblay.

Matty, on the window seat, mending one of her pupils' stockings while lost in her own none too pleasant thoughts, glanced up warily. "No. Maida Gardens are bad ton, and full, besides, of vulgar people and pickpockets and worse. You would not find it comfortable." Matty knew better than to say Mrs. Dove, her employer and Catherine's mother, would not allow it.

"Oh, I know *that*," Catherine replied. "Hope and I were just discussing it because although it's such bad ton, both our sisters have been there."

"Well, then," Matty said mildly, resolving to keep a rather closer eye on Catherine, "I suggest you ask Lady Wenning or Lady Dominic for a description. It would certainly do your consequence no good to be seen there."

"My sister Grace will be home, soon," Hope said happily. "And then life will be much more fun."

Matty frowned at her over the spectacles she wore for close work. Hope had never been her pupil, officially, but a fondness for books and study had forged a bond between her and Catherine well before their come-out, and Matty had tried to fill the gaps left by Hope's somewhat ramshackle education. Such as the rules of polite behavior.

Hope's sister, the Countess of Wenning, had been a leader of the fashionable set, before accompanying her husband on his diplomatic posting to Constantinople. Although Hope had shown little desire to follow in her sister's tonish footsteps, she was a pretty little thing, and Matty doubted she was short of suitors—despite the Darblays' well-known financial difficulties.

But Catherine, much to Matty's surprise, appeared to have fallen in love, or at least infatuation, within the first two weeks of her launch. Mrs. Dove was ecstatic, for the young man showed her pointed attentions, and he was the heir to a respectably wealthy baron.

For a sensible, bookish girl to fall in love so fast made Matty uneasy. But she had her own problems to deal with. And despite their eccentricities, neither young lady was foolish.

Matty finished mending the stocking and put it away in her basket before leaving them to their private conversation. It was almost time for them to change for dinner and then on to the next party. While Matty could write back to her mother and tell her she had no intention of coming home.

She would certainly have been considerably more worried had she overheard the discussion that followed her departure.

MISS HOPE DARBLAY did not take her first London Season seriously. She accepted gentlemen's declared admiration with a hefty pinch of salt, well aware that had it not been for her brother-in-law Wenning's money propping up her dowry, they would not have come near her at all.

Catherine, of course, was in a different position. As the next best thing to penniless, she was entitled to believe in the honesty of her swain, Mr. Granton. Or, at least, to expect it.

"What reason could he have for going to Maida?" Catherine worried.

"Just a lark, I'm sure. Rollo used to go sometimes. Maybe he still does."

"Yes, but *Rollo*," Catherine said significantly.

Hope accepted this perfectly reasonable criticism of her brother in the spirit with which it was meant. "Well, yes, he's not respectable, and neither is Maida. But the point is, no one goes there to be serious. Your Mr. Granton will dance and perhaps even flirt in a lighthearted manner—"

"As he does with me?" Catherine interrupted, her expression ominous.

"Of course not. That is my point. Maida is a lark. You are his serious interest. At least, I imagine that's the case. You certainly should not start imagining he is the biggest libertine since the Duke of Dearham—or Rollo!—just because he chooses to go to a Maida Gardens masquerade."

Catherine looked stricken. "I don't really know him at all, do I?"

"After two weeks, a few dances, and a drive in the park, no," Hope said bluntly. "How could you possibly? You only know what you see and what your heart tells you."

Catherine's breath caught and held. "We could go to Maida and see for ourselves."

"Spy on him?" Hope said dryly. "I hardly think that will endear you to him. Nor will his discovering you there, for it will make him think you a hoyden, and your reputation would be bound to suffer."

"You're right about the latter," Catherine admitted. "But as for spying… Doesn't it seem to you we are expected to go into marriage blind? No one tells us anything until we are married, so any unsavory details are kept from us."

"I think we're supposed to rely on our menfolk to keep the

wolves from us."

"Like Adrian," Catherine said wryly of her own brother.

She had a point. Adrian was a schoolboy. And besides, Hope was adventurous by nature. "I suppose we *could* go, just for an hour or two, and keep out of his way, just ensure he isn't entertaining his mistress at Maida."

"Oh, God, do you think he is?" Catherine broke in.

"Of course not. But if it takes an hour to set your mind, it would be worth it." Hope frowned. "Only we don't want to stand out at all. And two young females without a male escort will certainly attract too much notice. Which will be unpleasant for us and, worse, may even attract Mr. Granton's attention."

"I never thought of that," Catherine said, wriggling back discontentedly on the sofa. She brightened. "Perhaps Rollo would take us!"

Hope looked appalled. "Of course, he would not! He may be a shocking rake, but he would never let me go to a Maida masquerade, with or without him."

"Didn't he take your sister once?" Catherine asked.

"Well, yes, but that was *Grace*, and she was married, and there was a good reason. Forget Rollo. He won't do it."

"Adrian would," Catherine said wistfully. "If only he wasn't at school, we could have made him look older and…"

Hope's eyes widened. Her heart began to beat faster, with mischief, excitement, and pure fun. "We don't need our brothers. We just need their clothes."

FRANCISCO WAS TIRED, irritable, and not best pleased to be at Maida Gardens in pursuit of some shadowy goal he expected to dislike. He still needed a rest, a holiday, a change in the direction of his life. But for the moment, all he could do was swill wine and gaze moodily around the dance floor and the tables surrounding it.

He had been to the Gardens before, in his youth, when he had met some charming and generous women who had given him some very memorable nights. At least they had seemed memorable at the time, even though he could not now remember their faces with any clarity. Well, it had been a long time ago, and he was not here to entice women to his bed.

More recently, he had come here as a favor to his friend Ludovic Dunne, to persuade a very nasty and dangerous man into loose-tongued confession. Even then, he had found the place tawdry and vulgar—which, considering many of the gutters in which he spent his time, was saying something. Perhaps he had just grown up.

Not before time. I am almost thirty years old with damn all to show for my life of adventure. And yet here I sit, watching for a young man in a red mask to give a large ring to a lady with a red corsage. All with the aim of preventing a few poor people asking for a better chance at life.

Francisco had done some distasteful things in his life, but he had always seen the higher cause. This was…

Someone brushed past him, her voice strumming his memory as she said with perfect clarity, "Isn't this all quite deliciously vulgar?"

From old habit, he almost answered her before he realized that, of course, she was not addressing him but the gentlemen on either side of her. She had not even seen him. Which was just as well. Behind the mask, she looked as beautiful as ever, her body swaying with just that touch of slow, sensual swagger that had once driven him wild.

It wasn't doing a bad job now, he realized, hauling his gaze away from her and casting it swiftly over her companions—another fashionable young matron and four gentlemen, all but falling over themselves to seat the ladies to their own advantage. Another set of rich, bored aristocrats amusing themselves at the expense of the vulgar.

Francisco moved unobtrusively away. Even if he had not

been working, he had no desire to encounter Emma Carntree again. Still, the stab of lust had shaken him from his normally cool observations, so much so that he almost missed the odd young couple sitting near the door.

She wore a red tulip threaded through the fastenings of her pink domino cloak. And her swain, wearing a red mask, sniffed dubiously at the contents of the glass set before him. The girl beside him giggled.

Christ, was this what he had been reduced to? Pursuing children at a party just to make sure the poor stayed poor and power remained in the hands of those who had always had it? If Francisco had been tired and disillusioned before, he was seething now.

Tomorrow, I shall most definitely resign, with or without permission. I'll buy an estate in the country—I don't care which country—and devote myself to the land and rural pursuits. Whatever they are.

In the meantime, he propped his shoulder against the nearby pillar and tried to keep the savagery from his eyes as he regarded his prey. As the young man twirled the glass in his fingers, he reached out to the girl, laying his other hand over her arm and directing her attention to the front of the ballroom, where, among other people, his old lover, Emma Carntree, was preparing to dance with one of the gentlemen from her party.

Francisco was more interested in the large, opal ring gracing the boy's left hand. That appeared to remove any doubt that they were his villains of the evening, God help them. His best plan would be to wait until the boy slipped the girl the ring, then steal her reticule. Or if she was silly enough to wear the thing, then he would dance with her and distract her with flirtation while he slipped the ring from her finger.

But frankly, the whole matter left a nasty taste in his mouth, and he just wanted it over with. Cursory observation told him the girl was an innocent, probably of good family, judging by her posture and her wide-eyed, troubled perusal of the dance floor. What a stupid place for them to meet just to pass a message, however important. It made no sense to Francisco, who just wanted his task done so he could go home to bed and resign in the morning.

On the thought, he strolled across to the couple, offered them a brilliant smile, and pulled out the chair opposite them. "May I?"

Since he already had, there was little they could do except gaze at him through their mask slits like a couple of wide-eyed children caught in some naughtiness.

"Do we know you, sir?" the boy asked. Judging by his voice, he was even younger than Francisco had guessed.

"Oh, everyone is a friend at Maida." Francisco hid his fresh burst of shame and anger in his best reassuring and yet intriguing smile. Without conscious thought, his speech had slipped into the accents of a Spaniard speaking good English. He stopped a harassed-looking waiter and ordered a bottle of wine with fresh glasses. "I hope you will be my guests," he added to the couple, "rather than risk whatever dubious substance you have before you."

The boy let out a hiss of laughter. He was ridiculously young. Francisco doubted he had ever even shaved. More interestingly, he appeared to be wearing a wig, for although his eyebrows were fine and dark, his hair was fair, long, and tied behind his head in the old-fashioned style. He really *was* in disguise, Francisco mused with his first hint of humor this evening.

The pair seemed slightly bemused by him as he explained how to be served the decent wine at Maida. The girl's attention kept slipping to the dance floor, perhaps wondering if she should dance with her companion in order to receive the ring, since Francisco had made a discreet gift impossible.

"Ah, here is the wine." Francisco poured a glass, passing it to the young lady with an inclination of the head, before pouring a second, which he pushed across to the table toward the youth's left. As he'd hoped, the boy wrapped his left hand around it uncertainly.

"That is a very handsome ring," Francisco observed. It was also too big for the slender finger it adorned. Casually, he reached out and grasped the hand the young man was already withdrawing in an instinctive rush. Not a working man's hand, it felt smooth and childish, almost girlish to the touch—a schoolboy's, perhaps, or a clerk's. Francisco didn't much care.

He ran his finger over the valuable opal, thinking how little of this case made sense, while he smiled at the startled girl and asked her to dance.

"D-dance?" she repeated in dismay.

Francisco's lips twitched. "It is a ball," he pointed out.

The girl's wild gaze sought her companion's.

"Even masked," Francisco pursued, keeping his voice low and blatantly seductive, "you are easily the most beautiful lady present. I would count it the chief pleasure of the evening."

Predictably, the boy sprang to his feet. "Unfortunately, the lady has promised the first dance to me," he said firmly.

Francisco, his hand resting over the ring on the table, inclined his head. "Then I must wait my turn," he said graciously and watched with amusement as the pair almost scuttled past him onto the dance floor.

Francisco didn't wait to see them dance. He slid his hand back to his own side of the table and slipped the opal ring into his pocket before standing, abandoning his wine, untouched, and strolling out of the pavilion.

ON THE DANCE floor, after a brief period of confusion as they worked out whose hand went where, Hope, in her brother's clothes and an old wig, glanced around to be sure they were nowhere near the Granton-like gentleman dancing with the beautiful lady. The last thing they needed was to be recognized. She just hoped the annoying intruder would be gone from their table.

"Hope, your ring!" Catherine hissed.

Hope blinked at her left hand holding Catherine's. There was no ring there. "Drat, I knew it was too loose to wear! Come on, we'd better find it, or Rollo will murder me."

To the best of their ability, they retraced their steps across the floor, weaving between couples. Of course, it could have been kicked by any number of dancers and be anywhere by now.

"At least *he* is gone," Catherine muttered as they moved toward their now empty table where a bottle of wine and three glasses still remained. There was, fortunately, no sign of the stranger.

Hope recalled his insolent grip on her hand as he examined the ring, even while he made eyes at Catherine, inviting her to dance.

Hope's jaw dropped. "He was distracting me by flirting with you. He thought I'd be jealous enough not to notice when he stole my ring. And I didn't!"

***

FRANCISCO RETURNED TO his discreet rooms in Covent Garden and threw his black mask and domino cloak on the armchair. Then he took the opal ring from his pocket and sat down at his desk, looking for the catch that would open it. Close examination revealed no such thing, nor any sign of interference with the setting.

Annoyed all over again, he took a small tool from his desk drawer and set about prying the opal free of its setting. It was a large stone, handsome and no doubt valuable, but it was solid, covering no hidden compartment, no place for any note of names, contacts, or intentions.

It was just a ring.

"A broken ring," Francisco said aloud, tossing the bits across his desk. It appeared he had just stolen from a perfectly innocent pair of young strangers. "Which really just rounds off my day."

CHAPTER TWO

MISS MATILDA MATHER, Matty in her childhood and again to her charges in the Dove household, abandoned her letter for the third day running. Since it was Sunday, there were no lessons, and she was able to devote her whole day to it. So, she took herself to the deserted library, hoping a change of scene would help. But the words merely tied themselves in knots before her eyes. She would have thrown the wretched thing in the fire, except paper was expensive, and Mrs. Dove was already generous in her allowance of its use.

The impossibility of the task pressed down on her. There was nothing she could write that could possibly help the situation. She could not in sincerity congratulate her little sister on her betrothal to a man who could not be trusted. Nor could she advise against the marriage. For one thing, she did not want to explain exactly *why* Sir Anthony should not be trusted. She was not even sure it would be right to do so if her sister was happy. And perhaps Sir Anthony had changed, though she doubted it.

She could not ask *why* he had offered for Marion either, not without provoking a storm, for Marion was a pretty, if suddenly wealthy, young lady, and it was no doubt as abundantly clear to her as to their mother and all the neighbors exactly why Sir Anthony Thorne had offered for her. Obviously, it was nothing to do with Marion's money. Clearly, he was in love with her.

And perhaps he was. After all, he was eight years older now, and Marion was not Matty. But Matty had good reason not to trust Sir Anthony, and she didn't want her sister's trust betrayed either.

Perhaps she should simply obey her mother's summons and go home. Not forever as Mama demanded, now that Marion was about to marry an important man. There was no way on God's Earth that Matty would be beholden to Anthony Thorne, let alone live in his house. But she could stay long enough to persuade Marion and their mother against the match.

And if she had to explain…

The eruption of Catherine and Hope Darblay into her private hell was a welcome relief. They were talking together so animatedly that they almost fell through the door of the book room and for several moments did not even notice Matty's presence.

"I could swear it was not in the ballroom," Catherine was saying.

"Of course, it wasn't," Hope said impatiently. "*He* took it! Everyone says the place is *full* of thieves."

"Will Rollo notice?"

"Notice what?" Matty asked, mainly to point out her presence to the young ladies.

They both swung on her with almost identical expressions of surprise and alarm.

Oh dear, thought Matty, replacing her pen in its stand with something approaching relief.

The girls glanced at each other, and Catherine closed the door.

"What have you done?" Matty asked with resignation.

"I borrowed my brother's ring," Hope said. "Not *exactly* with permission. And I lost it. That is, we think it was stolen."

Matty regarded Hope's slender hands and thought of Mr. Darblay's large person. "What in the world did you want with a man's ring that wouldn't even fit your thumb?"

"We were dressing up," Catherine said uncomfortably.

"But not with your sisters," Matty guessed. She waved them to the sofa and turned her chair to face them. "You had better tell me everything."

Catherine shifted uncomfortably beside her friend, seeming to struggle for words, much like Matty with her letter.

"It's about Mr. Granton," Catherine said at last.

Matty nodded. "The gentleman who has been showing you attention and whom you are inclined to encourage."

Catherine blushed but did not deny it. "Well, at the theatre party last week, I overheard some talk about him attending one of the masked public balls at Maida Gardens. And someone else said people only go there to…misbehave."

"We know that isn't necessarily true," Hope spoke up. "Because my sister has been, and so has Viola. But then so has my brother Rollo, and he pretty much misbehaves wherever he goes. So, we decided to see for ourselves. Incognito," she added, as though that were a matter for congratulation.

Which it might have been, although Matty doubted it. "You went last night, didn't you? When you had cried off Lady Marshall's ball."

Catherine nodded in a defensive kind of way. "Hope wasn't going to the ball, and this seemed more fun."

"Since Mr. Granton was not to be at Lady Marshall's," Matty said pleasantly.

Catherine blushed.

"I see I need not even begin to point out how wrong you were to deceive your mother and Hope's over this or anything else. I hope I need never be ashamed of you again. So how exactly were you disguised?"

Both girls had the grace to look stricken with guilt at this scolding, though Catherine roused herself enough to answer the question. "With a mask and my oldest evening gown from before the Season. And a very enveloping domino cloak."

Matty's gaze shifted to Hope. "Forgive me, but where does

Mr. Darblay's ring fit into all this?"

Hope blushed. "I wore my brother's old clothes and an old wig from the dressing-up box."

"So, it would look as if I had a gentleman's escort," Catherine explained.

Matty refused to let her eyes close as they wished.

"I thought Rollo's ring would complete the picture," Hope said, "but it was far too loose. Even so, I'm sure someone stole it."

"Is it valuable?" Matty asked.

"I don't know, but he must like it, otherwise he'd have pawned it along with everything else." Hope frowned. "I need to get it back."

"I've said we can buy it back with all my pin money," Catherine said. "Only we're not sure that would be enough, and in any case, we've no idea how to find this man again."

"Or if he's sold it already," Hope added. Her eyes began to brighten. "I think we have to go back to Maida and hope to see him there. Only this time, I'll have to tell Rollo and make him escort us. He won't be happy, but if you came, too, Miss Matty—"

"He won't do it," Matty interrupted. "And even if he went alone, Mr. Darblay does tend to draw the eye, if not a good deal of trouble. Tell me *exactly* what happened and why you think this particular man stole the ring."

Matty listened to their tale. In any other circumstances, the mingled shame and relief in their expressions might have amused her. But the relief was clearly due to depositing the youthful mess in the lap of a supposed adult who could solve the problem. It was as well they didn't know she couldn't even write a letter to her family to prevent her sister from making a disastrous mistake.

In many ways, Hope's ridiculous dilemma was a blessed, if guilty, relief. Matty could focus on a problem that was not her own, right someone else's wrong, and save reputations. If she could only find the culprit.

"How would I know this man?" she asked. "Did he stand

out?"

"Oh, yes," the girls said at once with such fervency that Matty raised her eyebrows.

"He had only one eye? A wooden leg, perhaps?"

"No, but he was foreign. He spoke with an accent that might have been Spanish." Hope, becoming aware of Matty's gaze, explained, "Rollo had a Spanish friend. This man spoke English in much the same way." She frowned. "Actually, he sounded almost gentlemanly in speech, but I expect that was the fault of the accent, for he certainly didn't behave in such a way."

"Spanish," Matty repeated. "Was he tall? Short? Thin? Fat?"

"Not fat," Catherine said. "And I don't think he was short, but we never stood beside him, so it's hard to tell." She frowned. "He seemed to have a kind of...*presence*."

"Threatening?" Matty asked sharply.

"Oh, no," Catherine assured her, then looked less certain. "That is, I didn't see him as such until we worked out what he'd done."

Matty let that go. "Was he dark or fair?"

"Dark," they both said at once. Catherine continued, "Very dark. Black hair. And I think his complexion was dark, too. His hair was wavy, almost curly, and he wore a black mask and domino."

Matty sighed. "I wish he did only have one eye. I'd have some chance of recognizing him. But perhaps *I* have more chance of being noticed by *him*. What exactly were you wearing, Catherine? And when is the next wretched masquerade?"

"An old pink domino."

"With a red tulip," Hope added. "And the next ball is on Tuesday evening. But if he connects you to us, will he not rather avoid you?"

Matty nodded thoughtfully. "Perhaps. But maybe so obviously that I will notice."

"You can't go alone, Miss Mather," Hope said. "You would not be safe."

"I shall be perfectly safe," Matty said robustly. "I have my governess's repelling stare. As a matter of interest, was Mr. Granton present?"

"Yes, with a party of his own." Catherine frowned, then smiled apologetically. "I'm not even sure why I was so eager to go now. I find I care a good deal more for the return of Rollo's ring."

Well, that, Matty supposed, was something.

THE LETTER REMAINED unsent. In fact, so far as possible, it remained unthought of as Matty planned her avenging trip to Maida. To the pooled money of Catherine and Hope, she added the savings she had to hand and prayed it was enough. At least together with the threat of informing the management of the Gardens against the thief. She had heard somewhere that Maida's owner was not a man to be crossed.

Of course, guests had their pockets picked all the time there, by all accounts, but she was quite prepared to imply a connection between herself and the owner, and pray the thief did not have a better one. Her main difficulty, she suspected, would be in finding the right man. And she had no guarantee he would even be there.

In the meantime, she threw herself into teaching the younger girls and taking the family's enormous dog for walks.

"It's a pity you can't take Pup to Maida for protection," Catherine said with regret as she and Matty left him in the schoolroom on Monday afternoon. "Now that he behaves so well, he could just sit beside you and look huge and threatening."

"He would certainly draw attention to me," Matty admitted. "But sadly, he has become rather well known as the Dove family dog."

"I have been thinking," Catherine said in a rush. "I am going to tell Dominic everything and ask him to go with you. Viola might even go, too."

"Lord Dominic is a friend of Mr. Darblay's, and I think we should try and do this quietly. If I fail tomorrow evening, then we will just have to confess all and let Mr. Darblay take whatever action he considers necessary. But Catherine? If I have not said it before, please never do anything like this again."

"I won't," Catherine said fervently. "I promise you!"

ON TUESDAY EVENING, once dressed for her own party, Catherine rustled into Matty's chamber. She helped thread a red tulip through the domino fastenings, as she had worn it, then pressed her hand in thanks.

"I don't like to think of you there alone," Catherine said, clearly still troubled.

"I shall be perfectly fine," Matty said impatiently. "The greater danger is that I will achieve nothing, and you and Hope will just have to confess to her brother. Now go and forget about it, and I shall see you when we both return."

An hour later, the hackney dropped her at the gates of Maida Gardens, and she no longer felt quite so bold. The masked people clustered about the gate were undeniably vulgar. She suspected at least one of the women gathered there, she of the particularly penetrating, screeching laugh, was drunk.

It took more courage than she had expected to walk past them, even with her face masked and her hood up, and buy her ticket. Ignoring their ribald comments, she walked through the gates and up the lantern-lit path.

Nervous and determined as she was, she could still acknowledge the enchantment of the gardens, lit by the stars and myriad lanterns and flaming torches. Here and there, water glistened from ponds, streams, and even waterfalls. She caught a glimpse of a fairytale castle on a hill and a Grecian temple between the trees. Distant music filtered through the noise of mingled chatter and laughter. Just as she began to think it was not so very bad, she saw a couple kissing against a tree and hastily averted her eyes.

The pavilion Catherine had described came into view as she rounded a corner. As she approached, two masked young women ran giggling across the path in front of her into the trees beyond, hastily pursued by three men.

No, Maida was not at all the thing. And Matty began to realize she was not really much less sheltered than Catherine. However, she was older, wiser, and very determined. Throwing back her shoulders, she sailed into the pavilion and paused to look around her.

The place was well lit, and the orchestra, playing constant waltzes, was really quite good. There were all sorts of people here, from all walks of life and all types of character. A microcosm of the outer world.

Remembering her purpose, she walked slowly around the edges of the dance floor, looking for any signs of the man Catherine and Hope had described. Black domino, black mask, black, waving hair. She noted a couple of doubtful possibilities, although they lacked the gentlemanly posture the girls had described. But the thief, no doubt, was some kind of flim-flam man who could adopt whatever character suited his purpose. No doubt he had spotted Catherine's quality—whatever he had made of Hope in disguise—and suited his approach accordingly.

Well, if his preference was for fleecing gently born ladies, she would do her best to be seen. She began a second circuit of the dance floor, this time weaving around the tables, keeping her searching gaze cool and glancing, never meeting anyone's eyes.

"Perhaps you'd care to dance?" a voice asked beside her.

She turned her head to see a man with straight brown hair and a blue domino. "No, thank you." She passed on, realizing from his astonished expression that she had probably broken one of the unwritten rules. Certainly, at a private or even subscription ball, it was considered rude to refuse an invitation to dance. No doubt it was the same here, but she could not afford to waste time dancing.

Of course, her quarry might be out in the gardens, picking the pockets of the lustful and scantily dressed…

Well, she was not brave enough or stupid enough to go wandering the paths of this place alone and unprotected. Surely, if he was here at all, he would visit the pavilion eventually.

Coming upon a flight of stairs, she climbed them and discovered a dining room with many booths, a few of them curtained off for privacy. At the center of the room was a very large table laden with food of all descriptions. Several of the platters were already almost empty. But although it seemed likely to be a long evening, she was too nervous to consider eating.

As she toured the floor, she saw no one resembling her quarry, and none of the booths were closed to her view—time to return to the ballroom.

But as she reached the staircase, someone slid around in front of her, blocking the way. A fair man in a scarlet mask, smiling at her in a manner she supposed was meant to be engaging. "Allow me to escort you."

"Thank you, there is no need," she replied distantly.

"There is if we're to dance together."

"But we are not. Excuse me, sir, you are blocking my way."

"Don't be like that, my beauty." The man took her hand as though to place it on his arm, and when she instinctively jerked to free it, he held on tighter.

She gazed up at him with her governess's stare. She wasn't used to using it on adults, and behind a mask, it was surely diluted. But after a moment, his gaze faltered and fell, along with his hand, and he stood aside, slinking past her back into the dining room.

And revealed the man who had been waiting patiently behind him on the stairs. A tall man with black, waving hair, a black mask, and a black domino cloak.

CHAPTER THREE

THE DARK EYES glinted through the slits of his mask. His lips curved in clear amusement. "I am impressed. Like my grandmother, you can kill a strong man with one basilisk-like glare."

At last. He even spoke with a foreign accent. "I, however, am not so impressed by being compared to anyone's grandmother." Let alone a basilisk.

"She was beautiful," he offered.

"Too late," Matty said flippantly. "The damage is done. Your pardon, sir."

"Granted, though I see no reason."

"I mean," she said patiently, "I would like to go downstairs." She could only hope he would follow her, for she could not hold this conversation where any passerby could hear.

He turned, offering his arm. "Madam."

Her heart lurched, for this was really too easy. Nevertheless, after making him wait only a moment, she laid her hand on his sleeve and walked downstairs with him into the ballroom.

"May I bring you wine? Or perhaps you would prefer to dance?"

Matty hesitated. She positively did not want to dance, and yet waltzing would provide the opportunity to talk with more privacy than at any of the available tables that she could see. And one could be just as threatening on the dance floor as across a table.

"I believe I would like to dance," she said as though she were given the choice every day.

"I rejoice," he assured her.

It struck her that he might well be mocking, but since she didn't really care about such trivialities, she merely allowed him to lead her onto the dance floor. Then he took her hand in his, placed his other hand on her back, and began to dance. And suddenly, nothing was trivial at all.

With new trepidation, she gazed into his masked face and found, too late, that his dark eyes were unreadable, profound, and…something else. Something she recognized but could not name. Her whole being tingled with awareness.

His face around the mask was sharp boned and lean, his mouth, smiling faintly, and yet equally unreadable. He did not hold her too close, though his grip was firm, his dance steps sure.

A thief who preyed on innocent, vulnerable, if foolish, young people, *her* young people. And yet suddenly, she could not despise him. He might have been all those things and more, but what wiped away the last of her superiority, what rendered her speechless, was the sudden recognition that he was *unsafe*.

He was dangerous.

The dark gaze left hers, dipping unhurriedly over her face and lips to her throat. "What a pretty way to wear your flower," he observed.

Matty swallowed, reminding herself she still had a task to complete and no time to waste. "I got the idea from a young friend of mine," she said boldly. "She attended the last ball held here."

"Did you?" His gaze returned to hers.

"No. But I think you did."

His eyes did not change, but neither did they leave her own. "What gives you such a thought?"

"The knowledge that you could not have stolen my friend's

brother's ring had you not been here."

Still, his steady eyes gave nothing away, though his lips quirked upward into a half-smile. "You shoot straight, madam. I admire that."

"You do not deny it," she noted.

"I never argue with a lady. The question is, what do you wish to do about it?"

"I want you to return the ring to me."

His fingers caressed hers, depriving her of breath. "It would never fit you."

"I mean, as you know perfectly well, to return it to its owner."

"He won't thank you for it," the thief remarked.

That was true enough. With any luck, Rollo Darblay would not notice its absence, never mind its return. "I'm prepared to risk that. Do you still have the ring?"

He seemed to think about it. "Yes."

"Here? Now?"

He smiled. "No."

No, that would have been too simple. "Well, if you bring it to me tomorrow morning in...in Barclay Square gardens, I will pay you a guinea."

This time, the amusement gleamed briefly in his eyes. "A whole guinea," he marveled. "It is worth rather more."

"Not to a man whose life is about to become as difficult as I would ensure yours did."

Now, he looked genuinely intrigued. "How will you do that?"

"Speak a few words in the right quarter. To the magistrate. To the Maida management. Even if you escape arrest, a guinea will surely be better than no income at all."

"You strike a hard bargain," he said gravely. "Perhaps you had better give me two days."

"One."

"Well, if you insist, but if you want it tomorrow, you'll get it back in bits."

She frowned. "Bits?"

"I broke it. But perhaps I *could* give you it back, repaired, still for a guinea. Just not until the day after tomorrow."

She stared at him, baffled. She could not convince herself she had frightened him into submission, and yet he was quite politely offering her more or less exactly what she had come for.

The insidious temptation of curiosity pushed her on.

"Come now, sir," she mocked. "Are you telling me a man of your considerable if dubious talents is not capable of having the ring repaired for a whole thirty-six hours? I will give you until *ten* o'clock. Tomorrow morning."

For a moment, she forgot to breathe, for laughter danced across the visible parts of his face, dazzling her and, she suspected, surprising him.

"You drive a harsh bargain, madam," he observed, a beguiling smile in his voice. "But I cannot work quite so hard for a mere guinea. You must give me something else. Will you tell me why you want the ring back so desperately that you come here alone to do so?"

A flush of fear surged through her. At least, some of it was fear. "No," she managed. "That is not your concern. I merely want what you stole returned to my friend."

The fathomless eyes considered her. "You understand it is merely an opal set in gold? There is nothing…unusual about it. Nothing that makes it unique."

It was hard to think while his thumb idly caressed the side of her hand, while she was swamped with awareness of the large, elegant body controlling her every movement. She could not understand whatever point he was making, so remained silent.

He danced her backward, his thigh brushing hers as he turned her. Now, she was too close to him, and if her mind knew to be frightened, her body seemed to rather like it. What on earth was the matter with her?

He bent his head nearer her. "Do you still want it back?" he murmured.

"Of course," she managed, making a huge effort. "Tomorrow, at ten of the clock."

"As I said, I can't do it for a mere guinea," he said regretfully.

He smelled of woodland and cinnamon and clean, male skin, which helped no one. "Can't or won't?" she snapped.

"Won't," he admitted, still holding her gaze. "But I will do it for a guinea and a kiss."

She jerked in his hold, and his grip clamped on her fingers, on her waist, holding her in place—and even closer than before. She could feel the heat of his body, his breath in her hair—when had her hood fallen back? His strength was terrifying, and yet that wasn't what frightened her.

Between her teeth, she said, "I do not deal in such coin."

"If you did, the kiss would have no value."

She stared at him, fright fading into the electrifying butterflies playing in her stomach. "I am not so foolish as to go anywhere alone with a thief." The barb might have worked better had her voice remained steadier.

As it was, a gleam of amused understanding lit his eyes. "I would not ask that of you," he assured her and bent his head.

Only then did his blatant intention enter her head. Gasping in outrage, she balled the hand on his shoulder into a fist and pushed at him. "Don't you dare! You cannot kiss me in public!"

"Darling, it's Maida, not Almack's. Do you want the ring tomorrow or not?"

She stared into his unreadable eyes, fascinated to find little flames of amber glowing there. He was right. No one at Maida cared for propriety. No one knew who she was or who he was, and she would never, ever come here again. And she did want the ring back as soon as possible. Nagging at the back of her mind was a terrible anxiety that she was using the ring as an excuse, for God help her, she had begun to like the heated tumult in her veins, and she could not help wondering, shamefully, what his kiss would feel like.

One mere moment, and I am free of him and will have secured the return of the wretched ring. If he keeps his word... There were no guarantees, of course, but she would have to take the chance.

He was waiting with apparent patience, his eyes mocking her struggles. She uncurled her fingers and slid them back to his shoulder.

"Very well, but be quick. And I expect you to..." As she spoke, his lips curved into a smile and parted, causing wild confusion in the depths of her stomach, and then, obliterating her words, he covered her mouth with his and kissed her.

She was wrong again. It didn't take one mere moment. That might have covered her shock, the period of his lips brushing against hers with cool, tantalizing promise, teasing her awareness, tempting her to some sin she couldn't quite grasp. And then his mouth sank and sealed, and her bones melted to liquid heat.

Somewhere, she was aware they had stopped dancing, that couples moved around them, and the music continued its relentless, energetic rhythm. But that was all on the fringes of her consciousness. All she could focus on was the silken sweetness of his mouth, firm and yet soft, warm, tasting, and persuading.

Sensation battered at her. Wonder held her captive in his arms against his lean, powerful body. Without meaning to, she leaned into the kiss, opening her mouth and her person to his onslaught. His tongue dipped over her lips, arousing, seducing. And time ceased to matter.

His mouth left hers, and she gazed, utterly dazed, into his glittering eyes. For the space of a heartbeat—or perhaps three since her pulses were galloping—they did not move.

And then his lips quirked. "Damn. I believe I'd forego the guinea."

Reality rushed on her, along with humiliation and not a little shock. "Tomorrow, at ten," she said harshly, breaking free largely because he let her.

If she had a plan, it was to walk sedately off the dance floor and out of the pavilion without looking back. She had not bargained on the ribald comments from the other dancers or the male hands reaching out to her.

Panicking, she dodged one hand, and another plucked at her arm. Before she could pull free, the importuning hand was gone, and her own was tucked in her erstwhile partner's arm.

"This, too, is Maida," he said ruefully. "I had better take you home."

At least they were off the dance floor, and he made no effort to redirect her steps as she made for the main door. "Under no circumstances," she managed in a clipped, harsh voice that she only hoped covered everything else. "You have done quite enough."

He did not answer.

A few guarded glances to either side showed her they appeared to have left the insults on the dance floor. Her companion opened the door, and she stepped outside into welcome chilly air.

She dropped his arm immediately. "Good night," she said carelessly, to prove her only problem was with the vulgarity of the other guests.

"Until tomorrow," he replied. He might have bowed, but she did not look, merely walked on alone toward the main path to the gates.

Please, God, let there be a hackney.

At least the fresh air and her brisk walk restored some semblance of reality. She even felt a breath of laughter shake her. *Well, I got more than I bargained for there! But I believe I might actually have won back the ring for a mere guinea and a brief dent in my pride that no one need ever know about. Well done, Matilda.*

Perhaps her posture was now thoroughly repellant, for no one addressed her, let alone accosted her as she strode toward the gates. She was relieved to see two hackney carriages waiting at the stand and realized with a surge of relief that the hardest part of her mission was complete.

Only after she had given the driver directions and climbed into the carriage did she notice the masked figure watching from the shadows on the other side of the gates. A tall man with black hair, a black mask, and black domino.

Had he been seeing her safely into the carriage? Or merely following her?

FRANCISCO WATCHED HER departure thoughtfully and with a hint of unaccustomed shame. Kissing her was hardly the worst crime he had committed in the service of his adopted country, and it had certainly been more pleasurable than most.

He had wanted to see how much she knew and how far she was prepared to go in order to retrieve the ring, but he had also just wanted to kiss her. Because she was out of the ordinary. Because she was pretty and spirited enough to dispose of unwanted admirers with no nonsense and had a withering stare quite as worthy of his formidable grandmother as he had told her. And because she hid the fact that she was struggling, well out of her depth, and was determined not to give in.

Such determination intrigued him on a professional level but also on a personal one. Even masked, he had liked looking at her. And when he had touched her, attraction sizzled through his veins, taking him by surprise. As for the kiss…

Inside her carriage, she turned her head to look out of the window. Francisco resisted the urge to step further into the darkness. He thought of bowing, but fortunately, the hackney moved off, and he could no longer see her. She would probably have thought it more mockery instead of the apology he *probably* meant.

He could follow her, he supposed. Find out exactly where she lived. But it seemed rude somehow, for he doubted she was anything to do with his mission. She was simply looking for the ring he had taken in error. Which really exonerated her from having anything to do with the message-bearing ring he still had not found and was now unlikely ever to do so. On one hand, he was not particularly sorry. On the other, he never left things unfinished. And so, he would be in Barclay Square tomorrow to ensure he was correct about Miss Basilisk and her youthful friends. And then, he would need another talk with his instructor.

As he walked out the gate, he squashed something underfoot. Bending, he picked up the red tulip that had been threaded into the frogs of her domino. Red like the younger girl's, worn, perhaps, to attract his attention. Which it had.

Another memory flitted in from nowhere. At Saturday's ball, Emma Carntree had worn red flowers, too. Stupidly, he had been too determined to avoid her to notice. Or to appreciate, now he thought of it, that the boy whose ring he had taken was, in all likelihood, a girl.

He let a hiss of laughter escape him because, actually, the whole messy situation was funny.

His hackney was far enough behind hers that he could not have followed her if he had wanted to. As it was, he went home to bed and rose early enough to rouse his favorite goldsmith at seven in the morning.

By ten, he was sitting on a bench in the center of Barclay Square, watching the nursemaids play with their charges or tow them around the square. A very large dog walked past with two adolescent girls. It was a pleasant, sunny spring morning, and he stretched his legs out in front of him, crossing them at the ankles in a pose of supreme relaxation.

In fact, he was not relaxed at all. Every sense was alert for attack, sneaking or otherwise, whether because someone knew what he was or wished to punish him for his disrespectful behavior to a lady last night. He thought the latter unlikely since if she had had male protectors, presumably she would not be the one going alone to Maida Gardens to retrieve the lost ring.

He was also looking for her in every young woman he saw. A dark-haired, dark-eyed lady with a swan-like neck and soft, full lips, shapely and ripe for kissing… Though, remembering *that* was not the best way to stay alert.

He wondered what she would look like without the mask, who she and her bizarre, even younger friends actually were.

In the end, he almost missed her because she wore an old, straw bonnet with a dull ribbon and an unprepossessing grey wool cloak, and in his mind, she was full of color. But he could see a lock of almost-back hair trying to escape the bonnet, and her lips…her lips were exactly as he remembered them. And as she walked toward him, she gazed directly at him.

Chapter Four

Matty was not surprised to receive a late-night visit from Catherine.

"I couldn't possibly sleep without knowing you were home safe," the girl exclaimed in clear relief, closing the bedchamber door behind her and sagging against it. "What happened? Was it awful? Did you find the miscreant?"

"Yes, I found him," Matty said with a pretended coolness she could not yet feel. "Or at least, I suspect he found me. The tulip was an excellent idea, for I do think it caught his attention and reminded him of you."

"Did he say so? To be honest, I was afraid he stole from so many that he would not remember me!"

"Oh, I think he did. The good news is that he is prepared to give us the ring back for a mere guinea."

"Oh, you clever thing," Catherine breathed, launching herself across the floor to sit on the bed beside Matty. "How? When?"

"Tomorrow at ten o'clock in Barclay Square. Which is the bad news. He says he broke the ring, but he will have it repaired. Also, I'm not entirely convinced he will do as he says."

"Why not?"

"I'm not sure," Matty said, frowning at her hands, "that he is the sort of man to whom a guinea means very much."

"But you must have threatened him, too, to have got such a

low price!"

"Yes," Matty admitted. "But again, it didn't seem to trouble him unduly."

"Then why did he agree?"

"That is what I don't know, and why I'm not perfectly certain he will come to Barclay Square."

"Well, we can worry about that if it happens," Catherine said, squeezing Matty's arm. "Thank you for this. I don't know where I'd be without you."

"In Rollo Darblay's black books," Matty retorted. "And your mama's. It hardly seems worth mentioning my own."

"Well, you can't go alone," Catherine said decisively, ignoring Matty's last words. "I'll fetch Hope, and we shall come with you. What's more, we'll take Pup."

"Good Lord, you can't possibly come with me," Matty scolded. "It will undo every effort to keep your escapade secret if he even gets a *hint* of who you are! None of you are to go anywhere near Barclay Square tomorrow morning. Even Pup is far too easily recognized to be seen near me."

Catherine blinked, looking anxious and uneasy. "I suppose you are right."

"And really, what harm could become of me in daylight in Barclay Square?"

Catherine smiled with some relief. "That is true. Especially when you have already braved the public ball at Maida Gardens alone!"

"I have, and I won't pretend the anxiety was not tiring. Off to bed with you, Catherine, and let me fall into mine."

MATTY'S HEART DRUMMED, and her stomach seemed to be tied in knots as she entered the gardens in the square. At first glance, there was no sign of him, only a few small children with their nurses and a lady with a pug on a leash.

Matty walked on toward two gentlemen deep in conversation, neither of them the right shape or coloring to be her thief. And then, emerging quietly from one path to another, she saw him.

He had removed his hat—a decent beaver which sat on the bench beside him. He seemed quite relaxed, long, elegant legs stretched out in front of him, crossed at the ankles. His clothes—blue coat, buff pantaloons—*could* have belonged to a gentleman of quality, although he lounged on the bench, his face turned up to the sun in a quite ungentlemanly posture.

Her heart gave a funny little lurch, for as she walked determinedly toward him, she saw that without the mask, he was almost ridiculously handsome. In a dark, saturnine kind of way. He had a thin, aquiline nose, broad cheekbones, and a strong chin beneath the thin yet almost sculpted lips she remembered all too well.

A small, fearful part of her wished he hadn't come at all, although, for most of the morning and the previous night, that had been her greatest fear.

She tried to look straight ahead so that she only saw him on the periphery of her vision. She could hear no one behind her, and there was no one in front. And the unsafe *thief* who had kissed her uncoiled his limbs and stood, bowing before her.

"Miss…Smith?" he hazarded, humor lurking in his dark, profound eyes.

"Why not?" she conceded while a pulse jumped in her throat.

"Shall we sit?" he suggested, indicating the bench.

Why didn't he just give her the dratted ring and let her be on her way?

Because their meeting should look natural.

She moved abruptly and sat beside the hat. He folded himself onto the bench on the other side of it, and she was glad of the barrier, however small.

"Do you have the ring?" she demanded.

"I feel like the groomsman at a wedding," he said flippantly. "Do you have my guinea?"

"I do."

He delved into his pocket and, without even glancing about to check that they were alone, opened his hand to reveal a masculine ring with a large, fine opal in an engraved gold setting.

What on earth was Hope been thinking about to wear such a thing? It would have been ridiculously loose on her dainty fingers, drawing attention to their femininity. And, of course, easily pilfered by the likes of Matty's present companion.

"There is very slight damage to the setting *there*," the thief pointed out, touching the outside edge, "but I don't think it's noticeable. It was the best my goldsmith could do."

She reached out, and his fingers closed around the ring once more.

"My guinea," he said with reproach.

Mocking reproach, for his eyes gleamed with humor, inviting her to share the joke. Really, he was a very odd thief. She opened the faded reticule on her lap and took out the coin. She placed it in the brim of his hat between them.

Gravely, he dropped the ring on her side of the hat brim. She snatched it up and placed it in her reticule, drawing the ribbons tight. He was slower to retrieve the coin, and when he did, he turned it in his fingers, his gaze on her face as she sat on the edge of the bench, poised for flight.

"You are not what I expected," he observed.

"I'm incognito." She knew she should stand up and leave, but none of this made any sense. "How did you come to break the ring?"

Of all the questions she could have asked, she wasn't sure why this one spilled out, but she couldn't take it back.

"I pried the stone loose of its setting."

"Why?" she asked blankly.

"To see what was underneath."

"And what was?"

"Nothing," he replied with apparent regret.

She frowned. "What did you expect? Surely not a love letter?"

His eyes gleamed. "Close, but not quite. I suppose you won't tell me who were your young friends."

"You suppose correctly."

"Two young ladies kicking up a lark," he said steadily. "A rather dangerous lark. And *you* should not go to a public ball alone."

"Not even with my basilisk stare?" she asked politely.

He smiled. "Not even with a loaded pistol. May I see you home?"

"No, you may not."

"Why not?" he challenged.

She stood. "Because I know nothing about you except that you're a—"

"Would you like to?" he interrupted.

Her eyes flew to his face as warmth surged into hers. Where was that basilisk stare when one needed it? He had risen when she did, and they stood facing each other almost as close as in last night's dance.

As she tried to summon a flat "No," he astonished her all over again by conjuring a flower from his coat pocket. A slightly wilted red tulip with a crushed stem.

Her eyes widened, and that denial remained unspoken.

"You dropped it last night," he said, holding it out to her.

Over his shoulder, she saw an elderly couple approaching with a child. In a panic that was not all to do with being seen together, she snatched the battered tulip from his hand with a muttered thanks. Only as she tried to stuff it into her reticule did she realize she also held a cold coin, which dropped into the bag along with the flower.

Once again, her baffled gaze rose to his.

His lips quirked. "Perhaps, one day," he observed obscurely as he picked up his hat from the bench. "But then again, perhaps not." He bowed slightly. "Good day, Miss Smith." And he sauntered off down the path.

FRANCISCO, HAVING DISCHARGED his duty and being as sure as he could be that no plots or political protests were likely to be planned by either his spirited young lady or her even younger friends, left the square and headed toward Bruton Street.

All the same, he was conscious of a tug, like an invisible thread, drawing him back to the dully dressed lady. There was as much regret as attraction in that pull, but he had no inclination to consider such foolish reactions. Even incognito, if that was true, she was not the sort of lady he could touch, and he was certainly not the sort of man *she* should touch. And so, duty and honor satisfied, he moved on to the next line of his investigation.

Emma Carntree, the most memorable of his former lovers, who had worn a red corsage on the night a message was to have been passed to such a lady.

He was clutching at straws, of course, because he had been lured so foolishly to the wrong people that night. But he had been abroad for a long time. He had no idea where Emma's restless interests had drawn her, and he was both curious and reluctant to find out.

It was not yet eleven of the clock when he knocked at the Carntree front door, but he hoped by persuading the servant to take his card immediately to her ladyship, he might catch her before her surprise had worn off.

Accordingly, when the liveried footman opened the door, he presented his plain, white card, on which was engraved G. Francis, Esq., and beneath it an Albany address that he rarely visited.

"If her ladyship would see me now, I should be most grateful," he said pointedly.

But before the servant could say or do anything, a startled

voice from the depths beyond exclaimed, "Francis? *Francis!*"

A lady walked briskly into view. "Let him in, George," she commanded, and as Francisco removed his hat and stepped inside, she approached him with blatant delight, both hands held out. "What a lovely surprise!"

"Isn't it?" Francisco agreed, allowing the servant to take his hat so that he could take her hands and bow over them. "How are you, Emma?"

"Horrendously bored, of course, which makes me doubly pleased to see you back in London. Come upstairs. George, we'll have tea in the blue salon." She turned to him, smiling, "How long have you been in London, Francis?"

"About a week, I suppose." He followed her across the landing and into a tasteful, bright room with blue curtains and wallpaper.

"A whole week, and you have only now got around to calling on me?"

She seemed genuinely outraged, which almost made him laugh. He regarded her for a moment, waiting for the inevitable rush of lust that had stayed with him long after mere liking had died. It didn't come. Her beauty, he thought dispassionately, although definitely eye-catching, was somehow obvious, almost vulgar.

Compared with whom? he mocked himself. *A plainly dressed lady in grey with eyes that could annihilate at twenty paces?*

"One has things to attend to," he said vaguely, taking the chair opposite her own. "I am trying to cultivate a sense of duty before pleasure."

"You, Francis?" she teased. "Never."

Which bore witness to the strength of his mask. If only she knew.

"Actually, I thought I saw you at Maida Gardens the other evening," he murmured.

Her reaction was almost imperceptible. If it hadn't been for the hand smoothing her skirts, pausing for the tiniest instant, he might have missed it.

"Maida?" she repeated in mock outrage. "You went to Maida days before you called on me! Why didn't you speak to me there?"

"I was with another party. And besides, I wasn't sure it was you. It seemed a very unfashionable place to find Lady Carntree."

She wrinkled her pretty nose as a different footman entered with a tray. "One can see why it is unfashionable, not to say vulgar. Thank you, Alan," she added as the servant deposited the tea things on the table in front of her. "You may go. But my dear Francis, it would have been a much more enjoyable party if you had joined us. All I had for company was Lizzie Betshaw and Harry Granton. Oh, and the Finchley brothers who are not quite as scintillating as they imagine they are. What about you? Did you have a pleasant evening?"

"Not particularly, though who knows where it will lead?" He accepted a cup of tea from her with a murmur of thanks. "So, what is the talk of Season, Emma? What is your latest enthusiasm?"

She gave a theatrical shudder. "Enthusiasm, sir? I believe you were my last. Now, I am merely paralyzed with ennui. As for talk...the Wennings are apparently due back in town, and the world is speculating if they still speak to each other after two years in each other's company, which is foolish. After all, there are as many ways to avoid each other abroad as there are in England, are there not?"

"I'm sure you are better placed to judge than I," he said mildly, referring to her married state. He sipped his tea.

For the first time, a frown of annoyance marred her brow. "How can you say so when you fled the country to avoid me?"

She really was the most self-centered creature he had ever tangled with. In any capacity. Once, he had been intrigued to see how far her selfishness went, to discover what lay beneath. By the time he had discovered that nothing very much did, she had convinced herself and her very best friends that he was madly in love with her.

Physically, he probably had been enslaved for a while—the pang he had felt on seeing her in Maida the other night had been an echo of it—but family matters had sent him to Spain, and several assignments thereafter had kept him in Europe. Not a broken heart. Regarding her now, he could not summon even a memory of desire.

"You cannot believe that I would ever avoid you," he said. "In fact, I would rather know where I might find you for the next few weeks."

She fluttered her eyelashes. "I'm going to the theatre to-night..."

MATTY DISCOVERED CATHERINE and Hope in the schoolroom, distracting the girls from their work. Admittedly, this was not difficult, for neither were as bookish as Catherine, and they did not have their sister Viola's excuse of reading difficulties.

Matty, having removed her cloak and bonnet, entered the schoolroom wearing a frown of disapproval that caused the younger girls to subside immediately and provided an excuse to summon Catherine and Hope to the other side of the closed door.

Before either could speak, she shoved the ring into Hope's hand. "There is very slight damage, but I can't see it. I don't imagine your brother will. But, ladies? No more, or I will be forced to tell your parents."

They both hugged her, which she pretended to endure, although she was secretly touched, and then they ran off, calling to Mrs. Dove that they were going to Darblay House. It was interesting, Matty reflected, that Catherine no longer mentioned Mr. Granton, the reason for them going to Maida in the first place. She supposed Catherine was of the age to fall easily in and out of imagined love. But for the first time, it struck her that both the girl's fixation on a man no more than unexceptionable in most people's opinion, followed by the risky adventure at Maida, had the same cause. Boredom.

And the Season was not so far along that a debutante should be tired of its delights. Catherine did not possess her older sister Viola's dread of society, but her interests were more intellectual, her conversation more mature than the vapid chattering of most girls her age. The thought stayed with Matty, so when she had released the younger ones from their learning torture, she went in search of Mrs. Dove.

This rather vague lady was discovered in the drawing room, supervising the removal of furniture to one of the reception rooms downstairs.

"Oh, there you are, Miss Mather. Do you think this room is large enough for a few couples to dance?"

"Oh, I think so. Once you have taken out most of the furniture, I'm sure eight or ten couples could stand up easily here."

"That is what I thought," Mrs. Dove said anxiously, "but now I look again, I am not so sure."

"But you plan to open the connecting doors to the dining room, do you not?"

"Yes, that is the plan. The dowagers and people not dancing may chat or play cards in there while still keeping an eye on the young people. And a light supper will be served in the morning room across the hall. Do you really think it will work?"

"I see no reason why not. Unless you have invited half the ton. In which case, it will be pronounced a shocking, if literal, squeeze and be counted one of the great successes of the Season."

"It's all very well for you to laugh," Mrs. Dove said morosely. "But I have Catherine to think of. We don't have the space here to hold a ball, although the Gorses did offer to let us hold it in their house."

"I think Catherine is happier with a smaller gathering."

"I thought so, too, but it is more difficult getting the numbers and the mix of people just right."

"Have you invited Mr. Granton?"

"Yes, but I'm starting to think that is a waste, for at Celia Maybury's soiree last night he seemed to be all over that Carntree creature." Mrs. Dove scowled. "I wish I hadn't invited her either, but she does have a fashionable cachet. The others are mostly the younger set. Plus Viola and Dominic, of course, and the marquess. And the Darblays, which I hope doesn't put anyone off, for Rollo isn't quite the thing, is he? At any rate, they may not come, for apparently, Lord Darblay is under the weather."

"Oh? Hope said nothing about that."

"They probably keep it from her. My trouble is, people keep asking if they may bring other people, and I can hardly say no, so now I'm afraid there will be too many."

"Perhaps not if the Darblays don't come," Matty soothed.

Mrs. Dove brightened. "That is true! Miss Mather, are you busy this afternoon? Would you mind overseeing this? I'm just not as organized as I should be, and you are so good at such things… And I feel I do need a lie down if I am to take Catherine to the theatre this evening."

CHAPTER FIVE

ALTHOUGH FRANCISCO REFUSED to join Emma Carntree's party at the theatre, his reason for going was certainly to watch her. From his seat in the pit, he kept an unobtrusive eye on her box to see who visited her, as well as to discover if she had any obvious acquaintances among the lower orders seated below with him. He half-suspected it for a fool's errand, for he could not imagine Emma involving herself with the plight of the poor or powerless. Until he sauntered into her box during the first interval and found himself face to face with Sir Anthony Thorne.

It gave him a nasty moment, which he was far too experienced to show, merely allowing his amiable gaze to skim over him to Emma.

"Francis," the lady exclaimed from the center of her admiring throng. She really did appear pleased to see him, throwing out her hand to him in a manner that cast several young men aside at once. "You came after all."

As he approached, it struck him that a faint flush stained her cheeks. Of course, the candles and the number of people in the box made it too warm, but he suspected it had something to do with Thorne, which was interesting. Was Thorne her true interest? Was she embarrassed to have greeted Francisco so enthusiastically in front of the other man?

He bowed over her hand. Her smile was more restrained

now, her gaze flickering from him to Thorne.

"Do you two know each other? Sir Tony, my old friend, Mr. Francis. Francis, Sir Anthony Thorne. I know you'll have heard of him at least, for he is quite one of the leading lights of the cabinet these days."

"My dear Lady Carntree, you flatter me," Thorne said in tones of amusement. He offered one languid hand. "How do you do?"

At least Thorne had a proper grip rather than the limp two-fingered shake of some self-important acquaintances. Thorne was not self-important. Confidence and intelligence shone out of his good-natured yet serious eyes.

"Francis has recently returned from…somewhere or other," Emma said with a careless wave of one hand. "So he may not have heard of you."

"You malign us both," Francisco said with a faint smile. "Of course, I have heard of Sir Anthony's firm and decisive views."

"You don't agree with those views?" Sir Anthony asked with equal amiability.

By silent consent, they sat.

"I think holding back reform is a mistake," Francisco admitted, poking the tiger just to see what would happen.

"Then you have missed my point. Reform is absolutely necessary. But it cannot be by mob rule, or we risk a revolution here like the one we spent decades fighting in France. Once the country is quiet, then is the time for serious, even radical reform of everything from representation to poor laws and taxes."

"Is the country *not* quiet?" Francisco asked with a hint of bewilderment.

"There is unrest all over, in the northern cities, in the countryside, even here in the capital. If you have been abroad, perhaps you are not aware of the seething turbulence."

"I'm not," Francis said bluntly.

Thorne smiled. "I can see you are something of a liberal by nature."

Francisco lifted one eyebrow. "I don't have a horse in that race. I am not remotely political. By nature."

Thorne leaned forward, boyishly confiding. "I'll tell you a secret, Mr. Francis. I am both political and liberal by nature. But reform must come from the top to be sustained."

"If you say so."

"Why are you talking politics at the theatre?" Emma demanded.

"Habit," Thorne said with a grin. "Forgive us such ill manners."

"But it is a timely reminder that the play is about to resume," Francis said, rising and bowing to Emma. As he sauntered away, his gaze landed on one of the men who, he was sure, had accompanied Emma to Maida. He wondered if that was interesting or not.

Returning to his own seat in the pit, he considered Emma and Thorne. He could imagine Emma attaching herself to the man's rising star, except she was married already, and had there not been something in the papers about Thorne's betrothal to an heiress?

At the next interval, he watched Emma, escorted by Thorne, enter a box on the other side of the theatre. In it were a dowager, a debutante, and a handsome couple he was sure he knew. Well, he knew the male half. Lord Dominic Gorse, to whom his old friend Ludovic Dunne had once introduced him. Ludo had proved the man innocent of the murder of which he had been wrongly convicted.

Emma did not stay long. She held a polite conversation with the mother while Thorne engaged the debutante, who had a rather lovely smile and seemed vaguely familiar. Emma moved on to Gorse, but only briefly. Other people entered the box, and Emma and Thorne left to be seen a few boxes on, visiting someone else. Rather like a couple.

Interesting…

THE FOLLOWING MORNING, Francisco walked round to visit his old friend Dunne. Once, they had studied law together. Since then, they had traveled in different directions, with Ludovic, a practicing solicitor, although he would have made an excellent barrister, too, and Frances pursuing more adventurous goals. But they retained their mutual love of puzzles and mysteries. It was notable that they both spent a lot of time investigating.

Dunne was now a family man, with a lovely wife, a stepson, and a baby daughter.

Without comment, the butler showed him immediately into the breakfast parlor, where the couple sat at table with young Tom. Since this was not Francisco's first visit since returning to London, he was greeted with casual grins and an invitation to join them in breaking his fast. Which he did.

"What do you know," he asked without much delay, "about Sir Anthony Thorne?"

Ludovic shrugged. "Nothing much. Good family, eldest son, but not a lot of wealth. Shrewd politician and apparent friend of the Prime Minister. Why?"

"I'm not sure," Francisco admitted. "He bothers me. Do you know a family called Dove?"

"Yes, they're Dominic Gorse's family by marriage. Viola, his wife, is the eldest daughter. There's also a son at school and, among the younger daughters, one making her come-out this Season. Why?"

Francisco encouraged some egg on to a piece of toast. "I believe there is some sort of party there this evening, and I would like to attend. I was hoping you could oblige me."

While he ate, Ludovic held his gaze. "Why?"

"Someone I wish to keep an eye on will be there. But I am not acquainted with Mrs. Dove."

Ludovic set down his coffee cup. "Is your interest personal or professional?"

"Professional," Francisco admitted.

Ludovic's brow twitched, a rare sign of unease. "I would not like you to upset the Doves. They are rather a charming family with nothing about them to interest you. They are not wealthy, and I suspect Viola's marriage settlement keeps them afloat."

"My interest is not the Doves, per se. Or at least not yet. I will be discreet, Ludo, and do my best not to upset your pets. Are you going to this party?"

Ludovic glanced at his wife.

"No," Rebecca replied. "It will be primarily for Catherine's sake, so we are of little interest. Yes, Tom, you may leave the table, but not until you've wiped your mouth with the napkin."

Tom grinned, jumped to his feet, gave the speediest bow ever executed, and bolted out the door.

"I'll take you round to Gorse on my way to the office," Ludovic sighed. "I'm sure he and his wife will be going."

Gorse received them in an untidy but rather pleasant library. He wore no cravat, and his hair stuck up slightly, but he welcomed them with casual amiability and waved them to chairs.

"I can't stop," Ludovic said. "But I shall leave Francis with you. He wants to ask a favor, and I only came to vouch for him. If he makes me regret it, you may kill him. Slowly. I will absolutely defend you."

"HOW WAS THE play last night?" Matty asked Catherine when they met over luncheon the following day. Luncheon was served in the morning room since that was where the dining table now stood.

"Oh, it was excellent," Catherine replied with a spark of enthusiasm. "I do enjoy Shakespeare."

"Mr. Granton paid us a visit," Mrs. Dove said. "Paid particular attention to Catherine."

"He paid particular attention to Lady Carntree in another box entirely," Catherine said wryly.

"It's a fashion," Mrs. Dove said with a shrug. "When Viola came out, the same kind of attentions were being paid to dear Grace Wenning, and we *know* there was nothing untoward in that."

"Perhaps we could be at the party, too," Arabella suggested. "After all, I'm almost sixteen, and if it is a small affair—"

"It isn't that small," Mrs. Dove said firmly. "You will not attend. And you will not make Miss Mather's life unbearable by pestering her or trying to pull the wool over her eyes."

"We *couldn't* pull the wool over Miss Matty's eyes," Susan said gloomily.

"Then there's no point in trying. Oh, and you must keep Pup out of the way. He can't stay in the kitchen, or he'll cause havoc, so he must stay in the schoolroom or your bedchamber until our guests have departed."

"We'll try," Arabella assured her mother. "But, Mama, why can't Miss Matty attend the party?"

Matty almost choked on her soup.

"Because clearly, she needs to keep watch over you." Mrs. Dove patted Matty's arm. "Not that you wouldn't be an asset to the party, my dear, but the fact is outweighed by the horror of these two and Pup invading the drawing room." She fixed both her youngest daughters with a glare. "This is to a civilized party for Catherine, not a fairground circus!"

In an effort to prevent any such fairground events, Matty declared a long walk for Pup as the main event of the afternoon. Fortunately, Viola, now Lady Dominic Gorse, arrived to help her mother with the preparations, so Matty marshaled the younger girls off with Pup for a march around the parks.

They were almost at Hyde Park before she realized that Catherine had joined them. "I thought you were helping your mama."

"Viola will keep her calmer, and I need to walk."

Matty relinquished Pup's leash to Arabella and fell back beside Catherine. "Is something wrong?"

Catherine cast her a lopsided smile. "Something else? No, nothing is wrong, and I have committed no further follies, to my knowledge. I have just been overwhelmed by the…the shallowness of all this. I know the Wennings, Viola and Dominic, even Lord Sedgemoor, and my mother are all making sacrifices so that I can enjoy a Season, but the thing is I don't think I *do* enjoy it."

"In what ways?" Matty asked. "I thought you liked to dance and go to the plays and meet new people."

Catherine tugged impatiently at her bonnet ribbons, seeming to struggle for words to explain her feelings. "Meeting new people is interesting. Or at least it was. But they don't seem to matter. At home, I knew everyone, and they will always be friends. Here… People notice you and then forget you. They are not interested in me but in the possibilities of my connections and whether or not those would make up for my small dowry."

"Some might think like that," Matty allowed. "There are self-serving, greedy people everywhere. But you also know people who are *not* like that. Lord Dominic, for example. You just aren't well enough acquainted with the ton to sort the wheat from the chaff."

"Is Mama?"

"Perhaps," Matty said diplomatically. "But Lady Wenning is also due in London any day. And other friends like Lord Dominic and Mr. Darblay will at least know who *not* to trust. Is this about Mr. Granton?"

Catherine shook her head. "No. Well, sort of. Mama and I both had hopes of him as a suitor, which is why Hope and I went to spy on him at Maida. At least, I thought that was why we went. But in truth, I barely noticed him there. It was the adventure with Hope that was fun. At least until that awful man stole Hope's ring. And later, when I saw Mr. Granton flirting with Lady Carntree at the theatre, I suddenly realized that not only did

I not care, but I was actually relieved. I don't want to marry Mr. Granton. In fact, I don't think I want to marry *anyone* I've met in London or am likely to meet."

"Then don't. You are seventeen years old, Catherine. You needn't make such decisions yet. This is a Season to meet people, not to catch any old husband."

Catherine regarded her thoughtfully. "I'm not sure Mama sees it that way."

"Your mama wants you to be happy. She wants opportunities for you, not to palm you off on someone you don't like."

"Opportunities," Catherine repeated, considering. "Perhaps that is a better way of looking at things. But there are opportunities other than marriage, even for young ladies. Like you, Miss Matty. I think I would make a better governess than a wife."

"Well, you are interested in learning," Matty allowed with a hint of unease. "But you must not assume every family taking on a governess is as kind as yours. Before I came to you, I was not always well treated. I was despised and overworked and... Well, I need not go into that. And you need not consider such a fate either."

Catherine's gaze was unexpectedly sharp. "Why *did* you become a governess, Matty?"

"Because I had no choice."

"You are clearly a lady. Did you have no chance to marry?"

With an unpleasant jolt, Matty recalled the letter she still had not answered. She would rip up the rambling nonsense and come straight to the point. And she would stay in her position for as long as she was needed.

"Almost," Matty admitted. "I was flattered, for he was considered the catch of the neighborhood—handsome, clever, ambitious, from an old, respected family."

"What happened?"

Matty smiled. "Nothing, of course. I didn't understand that he needed to marry money, and I didn't have any."

"So he was just trifling?" Catherine said indignantly. "I think we should send Dominic to seek him out and—"

Matty laughed. "Don't be ridiculous. I would have made him a terrible wife. And more to the point, I would have hated to be married to him. One can be misled by one's own feelings, especially in youth."

"Like me with Mr. Granton. He was never serious, was he?"

"Probably not for more than a few dances. You are very pretty and appealing, my dear, but you would be wasted on the likes of Mr. Granton."

"As you would have been wasted?"

"Exactly."

Catherine laughed and took her arm. "Look, Arabella has unclipped Pup's leash. Be prepared to run."

Matty hoped their talk had helped Catherine. Unexpectedly, it had helped her, too. As soon as they returned from Pup's long walk since there was no point in even trying to begin new lessons with the girls, Matty shut herself in her bedchamber. She seized the letter she could never quite bring herself to send and tore it into tiny pieces.

She was almost nine-and-twenty years old. She was not going to wheedle and equivocate or allow her sister to walk blind into the same trap she almost had.

My dearest Mama,

I could not be happier for Marion's good fortune, all the more welcome, I am sure, for being so unexpected. I, for one, fully expected Great-Aunt Horatia to leave all her money to the orphanage!

Although we must always regret my great-aunt's passing, I rejoice that this legacy has given Marion the greatest of gifts: the ability to choose the direction of her life. Obviously, the choice is not mine, but since you ask me, I would advise unequivocally against her accepting Sir Anthony Thorne's offer of marriage. As you point out, the man was once all but engaged to me, so you must allow me to know his character. Please consider the timing of his courtship, so soon after Marion inher-

ited Great-Aunt's legacy and recall that he has already run through his late first wife's fortune.

Never imagine this advice as my "sour grapes." Like you, I care about my sister's happiness.

Please also thank Marion for her offer of companionship. But I made my choice nearly ten years ago, and I will not be leaving my position with Mrs. Dove, whether or not Marion accepts Sir Anthony.

I look forward to your next letter.

Your loving daughter,
Matilda.

She read it over once, sanded it, then folded and sealed it before neatly inscribing her mother's direction. Then, with a light heart, she went to join the family for tea.

CHAPTER SIX

FRANCISCO FOUND LADY Dominic Gorse quite unexpected. Shy but quick to laugh, quiet but perfectly, affectionately comfortable in the company of her outspoken husband and the acquaintance thrust upon them.

"Thank you for allowing me to join you," Francisco said as the carriage tooled the few streets to the Dove party.

"My mother will be delighted," Viola replied. "If surprised."

"Surprised?"

Her gaze was direct. "You do not appear to be a man of unsophisticated tastes."

Lord Dominic emitted a crack of laughter.

Francisco smiled with some amusement. "I can be as unsophisticated as the next man. But I am perfectly house-trained."

The lady flushed. "I apologize. I phrased that poorly. I used to stop myself saying exactly what was on my mind, but Dominic talked me out of it, and now I occasionally offend people."

"I am not remotely offended. And I doubt anyone else is either. You are much too delightful."

"Now there, he is right," Lord Dominic said. "And here we are. Prepare to meet the children, not to mention—"

"The children are banished for the evening on pain of dire retribution," Viola interrupted as a footman dashed from the carriage in front to let down the steps.

The house on Bernard Street, on the edges of fashionable London, was modest from the outside and unpretentious inside. Since Lord Dominic was acting as nominal host, they were among the first to arrive and were greeted by Lady Dominic's mother and sister at the drawing room door.

Viola hugged them, sparing an encouraging grin for her younger sister. Lord Dominic kissed their hands and cheeks and introduced Francisco.

"Here is Mr. Francis, whom Viola promised you this afternoon. Francis, my mother-in-law, Mrs. Dove, and Viola's sister, Miss Catherine Dove."

The older lady was gracious if a trifle flustered. The younger… Now she was interesting. Although pretty enough, she had not quite got over the awkwardness of some young debutantes, and her smile was slightly reserved, unlike the one she had given to Lord Dominic. On the other hand, her eyes were clear, expressive, and probably intelligent.

More importantly, judging by her eyes and mouth, the shape of her face, and the color of her chestnut curls, she closely resembled the female half of the couple whose ring he had stolen in Maida.

"Thank you for inviting me, especially at such short notice," he said easily. "You are very kind and welcoming to a stranger."

Mrs. Dove seemed pleased with his civilities.

Her daughter, with a hint of humor, said, "Dominic always has such interesting friends."

"I shall endeavor to be so," Francisco said, allowing his eyes to twinkle, which inspired a responsive smile in the girl who, fortunately, showed no signs of recognition. No doubt, his perfectly accented English and more diffident air helped.

Since guests were coming in behind him, he followed Dominic further into the room and challenged himself to find the "male" half of the couple.

This turned out to be remarkably easy. As he made conversation with the matronly young Lady Rampton, Dominic's sister-in-law, he watched the new arrivals. A sulky, very young man greeted his hostesses and slouched across the room, nodding curtly to an acquaintance. He sat down alone, gazing about him as though angry with both his presence and his fellow guests.

Behind him came another debutante, dramatically dark and pretty, together with a carelessly dressed young man who could only be her brother. In fact, Francisco recognized the brother—one of the wilder young rakehells to be found in London during the Season, wenching, drinking, and kicking up larks for ridiculous wagers. Darblay. Only son of Viscount Darblay.

Catherine greeted them both with the ease of old friendship and embraced the girl. Both young ladies were chattering the whole time in the time-honored tradition of close female friends. Darblay left them to it, strolling across the floor in search, presumably, of congenial company. He and Lady Rampton exchanged distant bows and murmured inanities, and then, as the lady's attention was taken by someone else, Darblay threw himself into the chair beside Francisco's.

"Devilish, ain't it?" he said cheerfully, offering his hand. "We've met, haven't we? Darblay."

"Francis." Francisco's gaze dropped to the proffered hand. A large opal ring glared at him. His lips twitched as he gripped the hand. "Glad to see you again."

Darblay's sister tripped past them, arm in arm with Catherine.

One mystery solved. Now all he had to do was find the lady to whom he had returned the ring. And that was a much more exciting prospect.

CATHERINE, BEING A good-natured girl, dragged her friend toward young Mr. Archibald Holles, who was sitting on his own, scowling in the far corner.

At least he stood as they approached him, banishing his scowl by an apparent effort of will, although he still didn't look exactly glad to be honored with their company.

"Mr. Holles," Catherine said brightly. "How are you enjoying the Season?"

He made a sound very like a groan. "I'm not."

"Oh," Catherine said. "Well, at least you have joined us this evening."

"Only because my father made it impossible for me not to."

"Clearly, he made a mistake," Hope said sweetly. "He should obviously have kept you at home and taught you some manners. Come, Catherine."

Hope flounced away, but the young man at least had the grace to blush and actually caught Catherine's arm to prevent her following.

"Wait. I apologize. That was unforgivably rude and entirely uncalled for. I'll go, if you like."

"That would probably make you much too happy," Catherine observed. "And, therefore, does not count as punishment. But I'll let you go quietly if you tell me why the evening is such an ordeal."

"It isn't, of course. I'm merely angry."

"With your father? With me?"

His face relaxed into a smile. Surprisingly, he had a very nice smile. It was almost...charming. "Of course, not with you. With my father a little, though I know he means it for the best. Mostly, I'm just angry with the whole concept of the Season, when all we scions of the rich and powerful get together to over-indulge even more than usual, while those less fortunate die in the streets unnoticed."

She blinked and sat down. "It's a worthy thought. But I don't believe *not* going to parties will solve the problem of the poor."

"It would if we bent half the attention to the problem that we put into arranging extravagant balls and dinners and card parties."

"What would you do?" she asked, not expecting an answer

beyond platitudes and floundering.

"I'd give more people a say to begin with. Plough money into building decent, low-rent housing, which would also help with unemployment. In the long term…"

There were few platitudes here, only ideas—not necessarily new ones, but well-researched and thought out and delivered with a passion she had not thought him capable of. She drank his words in, fascinated and not a little impressed until he broke off with a rueful smile.

"I'm sorry. I must be boring you rigid and keeping you from your dance partner besides."

"Dance?" The hired violinist had indeed begun to play. The older people had wandered off into the other room, and the younger were forming a country dance set. "Oh, goodness. I don't have a partner."

"Would you care to dance with me?" he asked with unexpected diffidence. "I promise not to prose on about politics and the poor. Of course, if you would rather not…"

"I'd love to," she replied, surprised to discover it was the truth.

His charming smile appeared again as he stood and conducted her onto the dance floor.

PUP BEHAVED WELL until Viola slipped into the schoolroom to see them. Even though he had seen her earlier in the day, the dog lunged at her with all the joy of a decades-awaited reunion, and it took the combined efforts of Matty, Arabella, and Susan to keep him off her delightful silk and gauze evening gown.

Viola only laughed and ruffled Pup's ears until he calmed down.

Her little sisters bombarded her with questions. "What's happening? Did everyone come? Is Catherine dancing? Is Mama happy?"

"Several guests brought guests of their own—including ourselves!—so it's a bit of a squeeze. Very fashionable! Yes, Catherine is dancing, and Mama appears to be happy. But I'd better not stay away from her for long."

"Who did you bring?" Susan asked curiously. She grinned. "Mr. Napper?"

"No, though I would like to see him stand up with Lady Carntree! We brought a friend of Dominic's who seemed to be at a loose end and in want of company. A Mr. Francis."

"Is he young and handsome and rich?" Arabella asked eagerly.

"Young-*ish*, very handsome in a piratical sort of a way, and I have no idea," Viola replied. "But if you are thinking of him replacing Mr. Granton in Catherine's affections, I doubt there is the need. I'd better go back down, but I'll try and sneak you up some choice morsels from supper."

The girls grinned at her.

"Don't forget Pup when you do," Susan reminded her.

"I never forget, Pup. Good luck, Matty!"

When Viola had slipped out again, Pup sniffed disconsolately under the door, whining. Although the girls tried to play with him, Viola's visit seemed to have unsettled him, and he kept breaking away to pace and whine at the door. He even ignored the ball Matty threw for him.

Eventually, he reared up to his full, massive height, his front paws scrabbling at the door.

"Oh dear," Matty said uneasily.

Arabella looked at her. "I think he needs to go out."

"Well, he'll just have to wait," Matty said. "He never has accidents now, so I'm sure he'll manage."

Pup let his claws slide down the door until his front paws were back on the ground. He woofed encouragingly and nudged the door with his head.

"What if he ate something nasty in the park?" Susan said.

Matty shuddered. "Don't. I'm sure he'll settle down if we just ignore him. He knows there are strangers in the house, and he wants to investigate them. That's all."

Pup, however, did not give up. He marched up to everyone, in turn, getting their attention and then galumphing to the door and whining with increasing agitation."

"It might have been very nasty," Susan pointed out.

Matty groaned. "Find his leash, and we'll take him into the garden by the back stairs. But we'll have to hold on to him because if he trips one of the servants laden with glasses or supper, the consequences will be appalling!"

Matty arranged it like a military maneuver. Susan, on reconnaissance, led the way while Arabella held the dog on a short leash. Matty, for extra strength, kept hold of his collar as they descended the back stairs. They held him back successfully as a maid and a footman bolted up with trays from the kitchen to the first floor. They then crept on past the landing and down to the ground floor, where a short passage led between the kitchen and the servants' hall to the back door.

Matty breathed a sigh of relief for half the task was almost complete. Only then, she blundered.

Since Susan could not quite reach, Matty let go of Pup's collar in order to take the key from the high ledge. And Pup bolted.

Knocking Arabella against the wall, he lunged back the way he had come, yanking the already dazed girl off her feet. She spread her length on the passage floor before the leash was dragged out of her hand. Susan leapt over her, skirts flying, and rushed after the dog.

Matty paused only long enough to make sure Arabella was unhurt before yanking her to her feet and haring off in pursuit of Susan and the dog.

Fortunately, the servants were used enough to Pup to have immediately slammed the kitchen door, so the household was spared one disaster. Pup didn't waste time on it. In fact, he appeared to be on a different mission entirely, for he galloped past the servants' hall, too, and flew up the stone stairs.

"Oh no!" Susan cried, for it was quite clear the dog was making for the baize door that separated the servants' area from the main part of the house.

"Pup, *stay!*" Matty commanded in the voice that had tamed many a wild, disobedient child.

It even penetrated Pup's determination, for at the top of the steps, he did turn his head to spare Matty a glance. However, the door was right in front of him, and three of his favorite people were chasing him. Obedience never stood a chance.

He even seemed to grin at them before he battered his way through the baize door. The following thud, a female squeal, and the crashing of crockery felt inevitable.

"Oh, no," Susan said, pushing open the door a lot more gently and not without dread.

The maid, sitting in the midst of messy disaster, her cap askew, merely pointed across the hall toward the main staircase.

"We'll help as soon as we've caught him," Matty gasped, leaping over the mess, both girls at her heels. Music and many-voiced chatter drifted down, but so far as she could tell, only from the drawing room and dining room, so they still had time. They flew across the hall in the dog's wake and up the staircase almost to the half-landing, where Matty wrenched to a halt.

Both girls bumped into her, but she barely noticed. On the half landing sat Pup, wagging his great tail while he gazed adoringly up at the man on the step above. By some miracle, he was the only guest in the vicinity. But it was not gratitude that closed up Matty's throat and held her paralyzed. It was recognition.

The thief looked even taller than she remembered him and considerably smarter in immaculate evening dress with his unruly hair brushed into submission. He frowned down at the dog, although his eyes gleamed with rather wicked appreciation.

Matty's heart hammered.

"Oh, well done, sir," Susan approved. "Dominic's the only other person he will stop for in full flight!"

Hastily, Matty bowed her head and picked up the trailing leash from the floor.

"You must be Lady Dominic's sisters," the thief said, causing Matty to frown as she turned, tugging at the leash.

"Yes, I'm Arabella, and this is Susan. And this—"

"This is Pup," Susan interrupted, much to Matty's relief as she tugged harder on the leash to drag the wretched dog back downstairs before the thief could glance at her face.

"That is not a pup," the thief stated. "That is a pony. At the very least."

The girls laughed with evident delight, while in Matilda's breast, bewilderment warred with rising anger. For the man spoke perfect and very gentlemanly English, without a trace of a Spanish accent.

"And this is Miss Mather, our governess," Arabella said.

"Unmasked, madam," the thief murmured, causing Matty to jerk a glance over her shoulder at him.

It was a mistake. He *had* been talking to her, and the wicked laughter in his eyes assured her that she was recognized and caught. She and Catherine and Hope Darblay could all be in trouble now.

"Perhaps, sir, if you were to walk downstairs with us?" Susan suggested. "He might be more easily distracted from all the people upstairs, and from there, we can tug and bribe him back up the servants' stairs. What do you think, Miss Matty?"

Matty opened her mouth to veto the plan, but before she could speak, a large masculine hand brushed against hers, closing on the leash. She snatched her fingers free as though burned.

"Allow me," the thief said mildly.

Pup, the traitor, trotted downstairs at his heels, good as gold. Arabella's eyes widened and met Matty's in admiration. Matty almost groaned, for the girls, inevitably, were skipping downstairs with Pup and the thief.

Reminding herself to move, Matty hurried after them, grasping for her wits.

"You have not introduced yourself, sir," she said coldly. "Who are we to thank for preventing further disaster?"

He halted at the foot of the stairs, dragging his gaze from the servants frantically clearing up the mess by the baize door to Matty's face.

"My name is Francis," he said blandly. "And I am at your service."

Chapter Seven

So, she was the governess. Francisco's delight was out of all proportion to the importance of the discovery. It explained her connection to, and her protectiveness of, Catherine Dove and her friend. But more than that, her place of importance in this eccentric household seemed curiously right.

Of course, she was in charge of this monstrous if amiable hound, and of course, her lively human charges had adopted her to the extent of addressing her comfortably by nick-name.

And he was so pleased to have discovered her, even by accident, that he did not even care he had spoken in the wrong accent and given away something of his own masquerade. He even liked that they held each other's secrets.

She really had extraordinary, dark eyes, and he had always been intrigued by the softness of her mouth, even though it spoke so sharply. Her clothes were awful, of course. Old, dowdy, and dull. He wanted to see her in colors, in silk and lace that emphasized rather than hid her figure and alluring femininity. Not that the dowdiness really hid her beauty. Just veiled it slightly. If one troubled to look, her features were refined and pleasing, almost...enchanting.

Even when she was glaring at him as though he had somehow crawled onto the sole of her shoe.

"Are you?" she uttered, and he recalled that he had claimed to be at her service.

He smiled and was gratified to see that rattled her. A flush seeped along her delicate cheekbones, and her glare melted into something much more flustered.

"Of course," he said. "May I take this pony to its stable—or wherever it resides?"

"He resides in the house," Susan, the younger of the adolescent girls, informed him. "We had him trapped in the schoolroom during the party, for he can be a great nuisance, especially to ladies with fragile dresses, but he seemed to need to go out."

"And now we don't know if he just wanted to go after Viola," Arabella added. "What do you think, Miss Matty? Should we take him into the garden anyway?"

Miss Matty dragged her gaze free of his own to look at the dog, who sat down and wagged his tail at her. She sighed. "I suppose we should, or he will merely try the same trick again in half an hour. But there must be two people holding him while the door is unlocked. Sorry, Neil," she added to the footman who had been helping clear up the mess by the kitchen door and was now hurrying past them to the stairs.

The footman cast a quick, lopsided grin at her and the girls, though he gave the dog a wide berth. A sharp knock on the front door caused him to swerve, slightly harassed, to answer it.

"Is this not rudely late?" Susan asked.

"It's probably Rollo," Arabella said dismissively.

"Mr. Darblay?" Francisco guessed. "He is already here." He smiled at Matty. "He escorted his sister."

Reprehensibly, he had hoped to make her blush by the implication he had spotted Catherine's "male" partner in crime from Maida. But a sound that was almost a snort escaped her, just as a flash of laughter glinted in her eyes. And Francisco couldn't breathe.

Then she turned to the children. "Come, let's get him outside. Susan, you had best scout ahead."

Francisco said, "Allow me to—"

"Francis, isn't it?" came an amused voice. "Are you taking up dog walking? Or is the animal a new fashion at parties?"

His whole reason for being here had finally arrived, and here he was trying to flirt with the wretched governess. He turned to face Sir Anthony Thorne.

"A mere touch of foolhardy chivalry," he said. At his side, Miss Mather seemed to have frozen. "Besides, I'm not convinced it *is* a dog."

Tension seemed to be rolling off the governess in waves, so much like fear, that he shifted his gaze to her. Even in candlelight, she was pale. "What do you think, ma'am? Since we do not have time for introductions, shall I just take the beast about his… er… duty?"

Her distraught gaze flickered to him. Already she was turning away toward the baize door.

"Oh, I don't believe introductions are necessary," Sir Anthony drawled. "A little changed, perhaps, but still unmistakably Miss Mather."

Because of his position, to say nothing of his sharp-eyed interest, Francisco saw her eyes close for the merest instance. Then, with what he sensed was a huge amount of courage, she fixed a distant smile on her lips and turned to face Thorne.

She did not offer her hand. "Sir Anthony? How do you do? I didn't realize you were acquainted with Mrs. Dove."

"It's a scraped acquaintance." He did not say who had done the scraping. "I came to take you home."

At that, her shoulders twitched, and to Francisco's relief, the frightened governess gave way to the lady who annihilated with a mere glance.

"Then you have a very odd idea of your place in the world," she snapped.

"Don't be a little fool. I am here at your mother's command, and even you must know this is hardly fitting." He reached to catch her hand, and Francisco knew he had to step in.

The trouble was, he needed to keep Sir Anthony on friendly

terms. Yet he could not let Miss Mather be harassed any further. The girls were already looking uneasy. And the dog... Of course! The dog.

Francisco gave it a quick, surreptitious flick of the lead and allowed himself to be dragged between Thorne and Miss Mather. Thorne jumped back in clear alarm. Another flick of the lead had the dog pulling toward the baize door.

"I believe matters have grown urgent," Francisco threw over his shoulder with a tolerant grin. "Ladies, you must show me the way..."

Fortunately, Miss Mather elected to take the escape he had arranged and charged ahead to the door. "Susan, see if the way is clear."

Susan strode past her to ease open the door. "I don't like him."

"No one likes him," Miss Mather muttered.

"Pup didn't," Arabella said. "Did you hear? He was *growling*. You're not going to leave us, are you?"

"No. Sir, you will be careful on the stairs?" Miss Mather flung at Francisco. "He can pull quite unexpectedly." She glanced back over her shoulder. "Even when he isn't told to."

So, even agitated, she had observed his ruse to free her from Thorne's conversation. *Interesting.*

At the foot of the stairs, they led him down a passage between the busy kitchen and the empty servants' hall to a door. Miss Mather reached onto a high shelf for the key and unlocked the door.

"We'll take him now, sir," Arabella said, casting him a dazzling smile. "Thank you for your help! Without you, there would have been carnage!" Taking the leash from him, she led the dog into the dark garden, Susan at her heels.

Miss Mather showed no inclination to follow them.

"Will he trouble you again?" Francisco asked.

"Oh, probably," Miss Mather said bitterly.

"Perhaps," he suggested, picking his words with care, "you

would like to tell me your problem with him?"

She turned her head to stare at him. "When you are a friend of his? No."

"Not a friend," he murmured. "An acquaintance."

Her lips twisted. "One whom it is wise not to upset. They believe he will be Prime Minister one day, God help the country."

"You really *don't* have a high opinion of him."

"No, I don't."

"And yet he runs errands on behalf of your mother."

She leaned against the door frame, as though needing its support. "That is a different matter entirely."

"How do you know him?" Francisco asked curiously.

"He is our neighbor." She paused, glancing at him with a frown that seemed both surprised and appalled. He had a well-cultivated gift for drawing information from those who didn't want to give it. But with an oddly helpless shrug, as though recognizing it made no difference, she added. "In the country. Suffolk. Where my family still lives." She drew in a breath. "He has recently become engaged to my sister. My employment no longer suits any of them."

Francisco's head reeled, though with what, he didn't quite know. "Except you?" he managed.

"The Doves are kind. And I like the independence of my position."

He regarded her. "There are not many people who believe in the *independence* of a governess. I suspect you have the family well-trained."

"Except Pup," she said with a welcome hint of humor.

"Oh, I don't know. He growled at Thorne and was more than happy to herd you all away at my command."

A smile flickered across those soft, tempting lips. Then she met his gaze. "What is your interest in Thorne? And while I am about it, why pretend to be Spanish?"

He raised his eyebrows. "It was a masquerade."

"I believe we were unmasked by the time we met in Barclay

Square."

"But I wanted you to recognize me," he said reasonably.

She allowed him that one but continued to hold his gaze. He was happy to let her. "Why in the world did you steal the ring?"

He shrugged. "I told you at the time. I was looking for something I did not find."

"And you haven't told me what your interest is in Sir Anthony Thorne," she accused.

"When I find out, I might tell you."

A spark of humorous frustration gleamed in her eyes, but before she could respond, a wet nose nudged his hand.

Susan said, "He lifted his leg, but more to please us than anything else. I don't think he needed out at all. We could have saved everyone a lot of trouble by ignoring him."

"But then I would not have met you," Francisco said gallantly. "Allow me to take him back upstairs for you."

The girls and the governess exchanged glances.

"Perhaps just past the first floor," Miss Mather allowed. "I don't feel strong enough for another crisis."

The girls giggled and returned the leash to Francisco.

"How do you know Dominic?" Susan asked as they trooped back inside. Behind them, Miss Mather locked the door and returned the key to its shelf.

"We have a mutual friend," Francisco replied. Then, realizing more was expected, he expanded. "I was glad to see him again after being abroad for some time."

"In Spain?" Miss Mather asked sweetly.

"Mostly." He met her gaze, smiling. "How did you guess?"

"It must have been something about the accent."

He laughed and was sure he saw an answering glint in her eyes before she led the way up the staircase, past the baize door to the floor above.

"Must be supper time," Arabella observed. "The servants have a rest for a few minutes." She pointed to a wedged open door. "If you go through there, the supper room is at the other end of the hall, directly opposite the drawing room."

With odd reluctance, Francisco handed Miss Mather the lead. The dog looked up at him and wagged its tail.

"He likes you," Susan said.

Francisco ruffled the dog's huge head. "How do you manage him?"

"He's not usually this bad anymore," Arabella said. "He's pretty well trained now, just subject to odd bouts of mischief, especially at the worst possible times."

Susan nodded. "It's easier when Adrian's home, too, because he's quite strong now. Adrian's our brother, and he'll be home from school next week."

"Thank you for your help, sir," Miss Mather said firmly, bringing an end to these confidences.

Francisco bowed. "Thank you for the entertainment. I shall hope we meet again very soon." He was almost surprised to realize he meant it. Particularly to Miss Mather, who allowed him the merest nod before she herded her charges on up the staircase.

Francisco sauntered through the doorway and along the passage. Supper was indeed being served, and those guests not in the supper room had spilled across the hall and back into the other rooms with their plates of dainty edibles.

Emma Carntree appeared to be sharing a plate with Rollo Darblay, who was clearly flirting with her. Sir Anthony Thorne was on the other side of the room, seated around a small table with Catherine, Miss Darblay, and the sulky young man, who was eyeing Thorne with dislike.

Finding himself beside Dominic Gorse, Francisco inquired, "Is Thorne a close friend of the family?"

"I'd be surprised. If you mean the Doves. He's around my father a lot, talking politics. I'm too frivolous to be interesting to him."

"You don't like him?"

Lord Dominic shrugged. "Barely know the fellow. Rather full of himself, I'd have thought. Too full to be wasting time on debutantes."

Watching, Francisco rather thought the politician's attention was more on the argumentative young man. "Who's the other fellow?"

"Holles? Just down from university. We don't move in the same circles." Gorse frowned. "Though now I think of it, he's danced twice with Catherine."

"Is that bad?"

"Not necessarily. I think he's his father's only heir. Oh, damnation, I sound like my sister-in-law. Game of cards, Francis? Between you and me, this isn't my usual sort of party."

"I don't imagine it is. Or Darblay's?"

Gorse cast a glance toward Darblay and Emma. "Interesting."

"Do you think so? She seems to treat him more like an amusing puppy. I can't imagine he would suffer that for long."

To Francisco's surprise, Thorne followed them into the other room. "Ah, the knight errant," he greeted Francis with a light clap on the shoulder. "Is your quest complete?"

"If you mean the beast returned to captivity, then yes."

"Beast?" Gorse repeated. "You've met Pup?"

"I encountered him on the stairs, hotly pursued by a pair of very young ladies and their governess. He appeared to have left some carnage in his wake. It was the screams that attracted my attention."

Gorse grinned. "He is a walking—or at least galloping—catastrophe. But there isn't a spiteful bone in his body."

"The general opinion seems to be that he was looking for Lady Dominic."

"Probably. And you, too, encountered the family pet?" Gorse asked Thorne.

"He was recaptured by the time I appeared on the scene," Thorne replied. "But I had the honor of meeting your young sisters-in-law. And Miss Mather. Perhaps you would know, my lord, if she is a satisfactory governess?"

Gorse blinked.

"I have a particular reason for asking," Thorne assured him, "which I will be happy to relate to you and Mrs. Dove."

"I believe she is very highly thought of," Lord Dominic said stiffly. "She is quite part of the family, and my wife considers her a friend."

Thorne gave a small bow. "That is what I wished to know. I ask because I bear a letter to her from her mother, who has charged me with bringing her back to the family home."

"Why on earth would she do that?" Dominic asked, not quite amused.

"Because I am a friend of the family, who has known her most of her life. And because," Thorne added modestly, "I am betrothed to her sister. You must see that Miss Mather's position is no longer suitable."

"From what I saw," Francisco observed, helping himself to a glass of wine, which he offered first to Dominic, "the position seems to suit her very well."

The flash of irritation in Thorne's eyes was interesting, the flat threat behind it more intriguing still. "You," Thorne said mildly, "are not family."

"Neither are you," Francisco pointed out. He smiled. "Yet."

Lord Dominic frowned with impatience. "Look, this is between the lady herself, her mother, and Mrs. Dove. It's nothing to do with either of us. Fetch the cards, Francis. Thorne, play or go away."

SIR ANTHONY THORNE did not leave the Dove residence with Emma Carntree, but he still entered her house at the same time, thanks to her carriage taking him up just around the corner.

"That," Emma said with a shudder, shedding her evening cloak into the hands of her butler, "was one of the most excruciatingly insipid evenings I have ever spent. Giggling debutantes and ogling youths… Why on earth did you want to go?"

"I told you. My betrothed is connected to the family."

Emma sailed upstairs, leaving him to follow. "And that involves me how?"

"You are my eyes and ears," Thorne drawled. "As always."

She did not answer until he followed her into her boudoir, where she stripped off her gloves and threw them onto a chair. "You'll excuse me from saying the task is mind-numbingly dull at the best of times. Tonight was worse. I seem to remember you promising me excitement."

"You went to a masked ball at Maida Gardens," Thorne said lightly, "and received a secret message from a very dangerous young man. Was that not exciting?"

"Not when followed by weeks of tedium." She threw herself onto the sofa with undisguised discontent.

Thorne joined her. "Not even one week. What ails you, my sweet? You know I could not pay you a great deal of attention when the Doves are connected—"

"To your betrothed, yes, I know. I never expect or insist on your public attentions, Tony, but I do expect not to be *bored* quite so regularly."

"Then you had better tell me what you learned."

"Absolutely nothing," Emma snapped.

"Darblay would not talk politics?"

"Darblay talks of agriculture between bouts of outrageous flirtation."

"At least the flirtation would not fatigue you."

"It wouldn't have if he wasn't merely passing the time before he could leave. He was only there to escort his sister. Although he is a cousin of the Doves, I believe, if only through his sister's marriage to the Earl of Wenning."

"And the Holles boy?"

"Barely looked at me, but he was prosing on to anyone who would listen. Definitely a radical."

"What of Gorse?"

"Not a political animal."

"Pity. I would like him to disgrace his father."

"He's already done that, hasn't he? Neither of them seems the worse for it."

"And this Francis fellow?"

Emma shrugged impatiently.

"What is that supposed to mean?" Thorne asked, his attention sharpening.

"It means he barely spoke to me, which is a pity since he was one of the few adult males."

"Unkind to the likes of Darblay and Granton, I would have thought," Thorne said. "Tell me about Francis."

"I don't know anything about Francis," she said impatiently. "He will talk politics occasionally, but only on an intellectual level. He is not involved and seems to have no strong views."

He took her hand when she would have risen. "You would not keep things from me, would you? For the sake of past…affections?"

She stayed seated but did not look at him. "Why would I do that?"

"Perhaps because he is the one who got away, the only one who left you before you were ready to dismiss him. Perhaps you even love him."

"It is not love," she said flatly. She flung up her free hand with a hint of irritation, then turned her head, almost glaring at him. "But yes, there is something. If you must know, I have never met anyone so self-contained out of the bedchamber and so wildly passionate in it. But I don't understand your interest in him."

"I didn't have any until tonight," Thorne said. "And my interest is merely personal. I'm *almost* sure he deliberately came between me and my betrothed's sister."

"Do you have to marry her, too?" Emma asked with annoying sweetness.

"I am concerned by what she has descended into," he retorted. "In her youth, she was quite a beauty. I do not care for it to be generally known that my wife's sister is a faded, dowdy governess at the beck and call of penniless people hanging onto the fringes of the ton by some distant connection to a nobleman rarely in the country."

Emma studied him and then laughed. "Who cares about your wife's sister? Especially when she is not yet even your wife?"

"Marion wants her sister living with us as her companion."

Emma shrugged. "Sensible. Especially as you will be busy most of the time."

"Exactly. But imagine Matilda stays where she is. And when we host dinners and parties, my wife invites her sister, the governess?"

"I see your problem." Emma tapped one finger against her lips. "Well, you can't kidnap her. Bring the mother and sister here to command her."

Thorne sighed. It was sound advice, of course. The trouble was, he didn't want Marion anywhere near London until after they were married. And until the coming trouble was over.

CHAPTER EIGHT

MATTY THOUGHT THAT Catherine would sleep later the following morning, after the nervous tensions—mostly Mrs. Dove's—involved in hosting their own party. But in fact, as they prepared to take Pup for his early morning walk, Catherine ran downstairs to join them, much brighter and more cheerful than her bleary-eyed sisters.

They set off for Hyde Park with Pup on his best behavior. Apart from sudden halts to sniff, he walked to heel all the way to the park, where he snatched up the first stick he could find and wagged his tail hopefully. Off the main path, Matty unclipped his leash and let him loose.

While the younger girls chased the dog and threw his sticks for him to bring back, Catherine chattered to Matty about last night's party.

"Did you dance with Mr. Granton?" Matty asked.

"Once, I think," Catherine said absently. "I liked that it was a smaller party. It is impossible to really talk to someone for longer than a moment when there are hundreds of people present. So, you only ever know people in a superficial way."

"I suppose that is true."

"I think I would like to take up some charitable work," Catherine said unexpectedly. "It's so easy to be caught up in one's own problems, which are really nothing compared with having no food or shelter or watching one's children actually *starve.*"

Matty blinked. "That is very true. What sort of work did you have in mind?"

"I'm not sure yet. Perhaps teaching people to read would be a good idea? So that they can get better work? Or any work, really." Catherine frowned. "I have a lot to learn."

Matty regarded her in some surprise. Until now, Catherine's interests had been intellectual rather than practical. She didn't notice Matty's scrutiny, but her face cleared, and a definite hitch in her breath had Matty following the girl's gaze to a young man who was walking toward them. He looked perfectly ordinary until he smiled.

Ah...

Catherine was blushing but wreathed in smiles.

The young man bowed very properly. "Miss Dove. What a pleasure to meet you."

Catherine curtseyed demurely. "Good morning, Mr. Holles. Matty, this is Mr. Holles, one of our guests yesterday evening. Mr. Holles, Miss Mather, my sisters' governess."

While Matty and Mr. Holles exchanged grave bows and curtseys, the younger girls came bounding up with Pup at their heels. To give Mr. Holles his due, he did not flee or even cringe before the massive dog. He might have been wary, but he offered the dog a sniff of his hand, and once Pup had sniffed and flattened his ears, he even patted the great head.

Pup wagged his tail and licked Mr. Holles's wrist.

Catherine beamed. "He likes you."

"Pup likes most people," Matty pointed out. "It is more remarkable that Mr. Holles appears to like Pup. Sir, these are Miss Dove's sisters, my charges, Miss Arabella and Miss Susan Dove."

"You can throw his stick if you like," Susan said generously, offering the slobber-laden branch to Mr. Holles. "I expect you throw farther than we can."

No one could have blamed him for refusing, but without the smallest grimace, he grasped the stick and hurled it into the distance. Pup shot off after it while all the girls regarded Mr. Holles with considerable respect. Which, when he noticed, made his lips twitch.

Not without a sense of humor, then. "Will you join us, Mr. Holles?" Matty invited, thus winning a dazzling smile of approval from Catherine. Matty began to feel old. For no reason, Mr. Francis entered her head, quick laughter filling his dark, otherwise secretive eyes. Worse, she almost touched her lips in remembrance of his shocking behavior at Maida. *Her* shocking behavior, for she hadn't exactly thrown him off.

And somehow, without mask or Spanish accent, he was even more mysterious. Deliberately distracting herself from the inexplicable, visceral excitement he caused, she set about drawing out young Mr. Holles. He seemed vaguely surprised by the friendliness and liveliness of the younger girls but replied to them with good humor. He cheerfully threw sticks for Pup and did not seem to stand on his dignity like other gentlemen of his age.

And then, just when Matty was congratulating herself for not thinking of Mr. Francis at all for at least ten minutes, a horseman appeared at the end of the path. Although the sun was in her eyes, hiding his features, her heart gave a funny little lurch, as if it already recognized him.

Pup instantly abandoned his pursuit of the latest stick and bounded joyfully toward the horseman instead. The horse gave a skittish swerve across the path.

"Pup, *sit!*" Matty yelled, it a voice worthier, she suspected, of a military parade ground than a public park, and almost to her surprise, the dog skidded to a halt and sat.

"Oh, well done, Miss Matty," Arabella said, impressed.

The horseman moved on toward Pup, who was dementedly wagging his tail but still sitting right in the middle of the path. Catherine and Mr. Holles hurried forward to drag him out of the way.

The rider swept off his hat. "Miss Dove, a pleasure to see you again. And your pony, of course."

Of course, it really was Francis.

Catherine laughed and curtseyed before hauling the dog by the collar. Pup happily sniffed the horseman's boot.

"Holles, sir," their escort said with a slightly jerky bow. "We met last night."

"So we did. How do you do?" He bent from the waist in a flourishing bow that encompassed everyone who had hurried forward to intervene.

Matty clipped Pup's leash back on.

"Miss Mather, no wonder you bring order to your schoolroom."

"Not noticeably," she said tartly. "And there is no need to call attention to my unladylike roaring. It probably saved you being thrown."

"Almost certainly," said Mr. Francis, although his horse was perfectly still in Pup's company. Matty had the lowering feeling that its owner had it under far too much control to allow it any ill behavior at all, though he went along with the fiction. "Believe me, my comment was not criticism but gratitude."

"He's a beautiful animal," Holles remarked, petting the horse's neck.

"I brought him from Spain. But he's a country horse, not yet used to town traffic. May I join the party?"

"By all means," Matty replied. "Although we are about to turn for home. It's almost time for lessons."

Arabella and Susan groaned, and Francis laughed, dismounting with easy grace.

As they turned in the direction of the gate, the girls ran ahead with the dog. Catherine walked more sedately on the arm of Mr. Holles while Matty found herself beside Mr. Francis and his horse.

Awareness blossomed, confusing her thoughts, paralyzing her tongue. Mr. Francis, on the other hand, appeared perfectly comfortable.

"A friendship of long-standing?" he asked casually, nodding

toward the couple in front, whose heads were bent toward each other in close conversation.

"Oh, at least a few hours," Matty managed. She caught his startled glance and added hastily, "I believe they have attended several of the same parties in the last couple of weeks, but they seem to have become friends at last evening's event. Why do you ask?"

"Making conversation."

"I never took you for a gossip."

He smiled. "What did you take me for? Apart from an occasional thief, a knight errant, and master of monstrous hounds?"

"You appear to have covered the salient points of your own character."

"Is that all you see?"

"There is more?"

Somehow, he caught and held her gaze. "You know there is. Humor me."

Dear God, it was a mistake to look into those dark eyes. Behind their light teasing expression was a profound, quick intelligence, a promise of fun, excitement, and even wonder. But he wasn't laughing at her. In fact, she guessed that he was, at his core, a deeply serious man. Yet even beyond that unexpected gravity were layers she could not fathom, was afraid to fathom, for the depths she sensed were uncompromising, relentless, violent, and yet *cold*. And she was reminded with a jolt of her realization at Maida.

"You are dangerous," she blurted. And then was appalled and fiercely glad she had found the courage to say it.

His eyebrows flew up. Though the shutters had come down on his eyes, he did not appear angry or offended, "Astute," he observed. "And I suppose I did ask."

"It was not the answer you wanted?"

"No, but it will do. In the absence of friendship, I can at least offer protection."

It was her turn to be startled. "*Protection?*" she repeated, staring. "From what?"

"From whatever or whoever cuts up your peace."

Too late, she realized the other connotation of protection, that of a man keeping a mistress, and dismissed it as ridiculous. *Whoever cuts up your peace.* Her eyes widened. "Thorne? You think I need protection from *him*?"

"If you do, I doubt you are the only one," he said obscurely. "I believe him to be rather more ruthless than he might appear. In any case, you may send for me here."

She did not even see or feel his hand, but abruptly a card jabbed into her palm, and her fingers closed instinctively around it.

"Don't stare at me," he murmured. "People will talk. Especially if I take advantage and kiss you."

Heat flared into her face, and she tore her gaze free of his at last. "I don't believe I require that kind of protection." She meant it to sound angry, though, in truth, it sounded more dazed, with an edge of humor—where had that come from? "What exactly would you do if I was rash enough to send for you?"

"I expect I would turn up and look—er… dangerous. It's usually enough. And since we approach the gates, I shall bid you good morning."

Before she could reply, he tipped his hat, bestowed a dazzling smile that did very peculiar things to her insides, and swung into the saddle. He was already trotting away by the time she managed a bemused, "Good day."

INEVITABLY, MATTY WAS summoned from the schoolroom that afternoon to attend Mrs. Dove in the drawing room. She knew who she would find there with her employer, so she was not surprised when Sir Anthony Thorne rose from the chair opposite Mrs. Dove.

Matty curtsied. "Ma'am. Sir."

"Come in, Miss Mather," Mrs. Dove said with a trace of anxiety in her voice. "And sit down. You'll join us in a cup of tea."

Matty knew then that the game was over. Thorne had persuaded Mrs. Dove to dismiss her. "Thank you," she said tonelessly and took the place beside her employer on the sofa. She did not look at Thorne as she accepted her cup of tea, but she was vaguely aware of him reseating himself.

"Sir Anthony has given me a letter from your mother," Mrs. Dove said. "She wants you to go home."

"I know," Matty admitted. "But I am of age, and I would rather keep my employment."

"And you could not write to your mama and tell her so?" Thorne interjected. Matty knew why. He was pointing out her flaws so that Mrs. Dove would be glad to get rid of her.

"I did, though I admit I could have done it quicker."

"I expect you were wrestling with your conscience and the various expectations we all have of you," Mrs. Dove said surprisingly.

Matty blinked, a thread of warmth seeping into her cold veins. Was Mrs. Dove going to help her stay? "I was. And I found the wording difficult. But the letter should be with my mother by now. She knows my views."

"And are hers worth nothing to you?" Thorne asked at once. "Is your sister's happiness worth nothing to you?"

"Of course," Matty snapped. "I hope it is worth at least as much to you."

His eyes narrowed. "Meaning?" he asked gently.

"Meaning my sister's happiness is not dependent on whether or not I fulfill my obligations to Mrs. Dove."

"Your sister will be Lady Thorne, holding an important position in the political, as well as social, life of our country. It is not fitting that her only sister remain a mere governess in a stranger's household."

"When I could be an unpaid companion in yours?" Matty

shot back.

He actually smiled, and she realized her misstep. "Oh, if you want coin for being with your family, I daresay we might agree to a little extra pin money."

Matty flushed but stuck to her point. "It *is* about coin, at least partly, and I would rather earn it than be the recipient of charity."

"*My* charity," he said with a gleam of understanding that made her want to hit him.

"My sister's charity," she retorted and was glad to see a hint of color stain his cheeks. Oh yes, she understood him perfectly. He wanted Marion's inheritance, and he wanted nothing to interfere with his ever-increasing importance. She turned to her employer. "Mrs. Dove, my choice is to remain with you until your family no longer needs me."

"You are putting the lady in an impossible position, Matilda," Thorne said. "How can she, in conscience, continue to employ you when she knows it is against the wishes of your family?"

You blackguard…!

"Oh dear, this is not easy for any of us," Mrs. Dove said, glancing from one to the other like a trapped deer. "Least of all for my girls, being without a governess, and my son due home from school any day now…"

Was that a command in her vague, nervous eyes? *Being without a governess…*

"At the very least, ma'am, we owe each other a month's notice," Matty said, catching on.

"Or salary in lieu, surely," Thorne said smoothly.

Matty spared him a short stare. "Paying my salary in lieu hardly provides Mrs. Dove with a new governess. And she cannot wish to pay for two of us at once. But the matter is not for you to decide, even if you were already married to my sister." *Which I hope to God you never are.* She rose to her feet. "I believe we have all been kept from our duty long enough."

Mrs. Dove rose with her, forcing Thorne to stand, too. For a moment, Matty thought he would ask for time alone with her, but to her surprise, Mrs. Dove held out her hand to Sir Anthony with a polite smile.

"Thank you for bringing Mrs. Mather's letter to me. So kind."

Thorne hesitated for the merest instant, but in truth, there was nothing for him to do or say with any civility, except take his leave, which he did with perfect grace.

"I'm sorry," Matty said as the door closed behind him. "I never meant you to be caught in the middle of a family squabble. You know I will go now if you prefer it. And I will do everything I can to find you a suitable replacement."

"Oh, there's no need for that," Mrs. Dove said, patting her hand distractedly. "Family quarrels have a way of sorting themselves out, and in the meantime, we have bought ourselves a month's grace. Selfishly, I hope you will stay, for, frankly, I don't know where we would be without you."

CHAPTER NINE

FRANCISCO HAD TO keep reminding himself that the governess was not the main focus of his investigation. Yet, at the same time, he did not want to use her to obtain information, even though it would justify seeking her out, and he wasn't even sure why he wanted to do that. A few amusing conversations—and a rather delicious kiss, he reminded himself—did not make her important to his life or the task in hand.

And yet he worried about her. Thorne was about to marry her sister for reasons Francisco could not quite fathom. Thorne was not the sort of man to waste a marriage alliance on a love match, but what good the Mathers were to him was still a mystery. If Matilda was a governess, then her sister was hardly likely to be the heiress he was rumored to be courting.

What concerned Francisco more, although it was none of his business, was that the marriage would give Thorne too much control over Matilda. If she wanted to stay with the Doves, she should be allowed to do so.

But is that really the best thing for her? wondered an annoying voice in his head. *Is she not worth more than a dependent position in the household of a family already struggling with genteel poverty?* He wanted to see her dancing and laughing, uninhibited by her own or other people's cares…

But women really only ever chose between one form of dependence and another. Miss Mather had chosen dependence on her employer, but Francisco knew Thorne would not let that stand. He was a man who needed to move his pieces about the board, and she clearly knew that and was determined to thwart him. Francisco determined to help her, though his motives were hazy and, he assured himself, unimportant.

What *was* important was that he find the incomprehensible and shadowy connection between Thorne and the arranged unrest he was *supposed* to be thwarting.

And then he could resign.

In fact, he would have done so already had he not blundered the night he had intercepted the wrong ring and then sensed Thorne's involvement via Emma Carntree.

Perhaps it was time he had a closer look at the unrest itself. To that end, he decided to attend a couple of reformist meetings that were known to the authorities. At about five o'clock in the afternoon, in working man's garb, his hair in a tangle and his jaw unshaven, he slouched into an Aldgate hall that was more of a shack, and prepared to watch and listen.

In many ways, the speeches were predictable, and Francisco could not disagree with their aims. If there was a more militant note than usual, that was not surprising. Food and work shortages affected people that way.

What worried him more was the fiery young man who declared, "They can't keep it from us, not if we storm their bastions together. There are more of us, and they can't shoot us all."

"They can if they know when we're coming," an older man said derisively.

"But they *won't* know. Not until it's too late. My friends, we can do this with just a little planning. If we're prepared to drop everything and march when our brothers do, united and terrifying, we *can* make things right. Who's with me?"

March with our brothers. United and terrifying…

Francisco followed the men out again, absorbing their excitement, of hope. He exchanged a few serious words with several and eventually walked away with a gathering unease.

It seemed his instructor had been correct. There really was something more organized about this upsurge of unrest. Not least because he knew of at least two such meetings going on at the same time as this one. He hopped on the back of a cart trotting briskly westward and hopped off again near the river, not so far from Westminster and the seat of power. After a two-minute walk, he saw a group of men slouching out of another yard, talking together in low, intense voices about justice and protests and true change. Francisco had clearly missed that gathering, but he knew of another close by.

Francisco, making his way toward that next meeting, felt all his senses tingling at last.

Not that their coordinated efforts would work, of course. The authorities would get word, even without Francisco to tell them. The troops would be out in force, the ringleaders arrested before their march got anywhere near Westminster or wherever they planned to threaten.

What intrigued Francisco was who was pulling the strings and why. At the old warehouse near the docks, he hoped at least to glimpse someone he recognized, some troublemaker or radical known to him, someone with the organizational ability and the connections to coordinate these movements.

This meeting, a larger event, was nearing its end by the time he sauntered into the back of the old warehouse and lounged against the wall. But there appeared to be the same theme of organized and timed marching. Scanning the speakers, he did recognize a well-known rabble-rouser and a serious reformer. And then, among the audience, in plainer, more ordinary clothes than usual, he saw a couple he recognized only too easily.

Young Mr. Holles and Miss Catherine Dove.

They sat close together on the end of a row, and with their heads turned toward the speaker, Francisco could see their faces in profile. Holles was frowning and nodding, his expression both eager and serious. Beside him, Catherine was wide-eyed, drinking it all in.

Francisco's breath stuttered. A swift quartering of the audience found no trace of Hope Darblay or, thank God, Miss Mather. He did not want her to be the connection between unrest and Thorne, and he most certainly didn't want to examine the reasons behind that.

In purely gentlemanly terms, though, what the devil was Holles about, bringing a gently bred girl to a place like this? It was as well this meeting, like the last, appeared to be discreet and organized. There were no signs of paid agitators or folk hell-bent on destruction. Providing Holles had transport to get them home, he supposed neither of them were in much immediate danger.

That was before the door beside him opened again, and a female stalked in. A few heads turned toward her, though most stayed riveted to the final speaker. She paused only briefly, her gaze scouring the audience before she started past Francisco, making a beeline for Holles and Catherine Dove.

From sheer instinct, Francisco caught her arm and dragged her back. Her haughty glare should have annihilated him.

Except that alarm bells were ringing in his brain. Was she really the brave, worried governess whisking her one-time pupil out of perceived danger—again? Or could *she* be the connection to Thorne? If so, he couldn't understand how or why. He just knew he didn't like her being here for any number of reasons. And he certainly could not trust her just because she intrigued him, because he wanted her.

Dispassionately, he watched recognition dawn on her face. A twitch of a frown at the unlikely possibility, a slow widening of the eyes as she realized the truth, a mingling of shock and bewilderment before she tore her arm and her gaze free and glanced toward Catherine. Her mouth opened, but whatever she had to say, he could not allow it here.

He took back her arm, jerking her close to him. "Not here," he breathed in her ear and dragged her back to the door. The fellow minding it cast them a look of amused contempt, clearly gathering, as Francisco meant him to, that an angry wife had come for her husband.

Outside, she shook him off, glaring at him as he strode across the yard, away from the building. He knew she would follow, at least at a certain distance, and she did, even catching his arm and hauling him to a halt.

"Quietly, for God's sake," he murmured. "If you don't want to be accused of spying or worse. What are you doing here?"

She stared at him as though he were stupid. "Looking for Catherine, of course. More to the point, what are *you* doing here, like…that." She waved her hand at his disreputable costume. "Thieving again?"

She really did not know him. She was nothing to him, so it should not have hurt.

He refused to let it. "Slim pickings, I would imagine, but it's a thought. How did you get here?"

"By hackney, of course. The same way *she* did. What is going on in there? Why is she here?"

"That is a very good question. Almost as good as the other one—how did you know Catherine and Holles were here?"

She blinked. "*Holles* is here? Holles *brought* her here? Dear God, what was he thinking?" She swept one agitated hand up to her shabby hat and tugged once, dragging it askew. "Is it better or worse that she didn't come alone?"

"You tell me."

She didn't pay any attention to that, clearly following her own train of thought. "At least I'm here as a chaperone for going home." Her frown deepened. "Is it a political meeting? Some kind of workers' combination? No, the former if Holles took her, he—"

"How did you know where to come?"

"What?" Her gaze refocused on him, taking in his implacable tone along with his words. "The crossing boy heard what he told the driver."

"He?"

"Presumably Holles," she said impatiently. "I couldn't see

who was with her, and the boy didn't know. I didn't wait for a description."

"So, you got your own hackney?"

She stared at him. "Why are you interrogating me? You have no reason and less right. If you were a gentleman, you would have taken her straight out of that place instead of slouching there, uncaring, like a—a…"

"A what?" he asked pleasantly.

Her gaze lashed him. "I don't know. No words spring to mind."

The door of the building was flung open, and people began to spill out.

"Do they know you're here?" she asked unexpectedly.

"No. But then, I'm not." He pushed up his disreputable cap, almost like a salute. "If I'm not much mistaken, Holles will have his hackney waiting close by, so you had better seize them as soon as they emerge. And in two hours, you and I shall meet in Barclay Square gardens."

He strode off before she could speak. He had gauged the mood and tenor of the meeting. She was in no danger here, and neither was Catherine. And yet still, he watched from the shadows until he saw the three of them emerge from the yard, Miss Mather rigid with disapproval, Catherine trotting anxiously by her side, and Holles earnestly explaining. He even followed them along the road to the corner and watched them climb into the waiting hackney. Only then did he slouch away and begin to run.

MATTY HAD NO intention of going to Barclay Square gardens alone and in the dark, and certainly not at the command of a man whose very appearance was a lie. A man with the insolence to interrogate her, to tell her off for trying to look after her former pupil. Seething, Matty told herself she would have nothing more to do with him in whatever guise.

Besides which, she had lessons to prepare for tomorrow and a serious talk to have with Catherine on the impropriety of her expedition in Holles's company.

"Well, Mama would not have taken me, would she?" Catherine said reasonably when Matty broached the subject in the hackney going home.

"No, she would not," Matty agreed. "Can you really not see the reason for that?"

Holles spoke up. "I should not have suggested it. And you are right. By society's standards, I should not have taken her anywhere unchaperoned. But these matters that Miss Catherine is trying to understand are so important that they eclipse the triviality of mere convention."

"For you, perhaps," Matty interrupted. "A man. For a young, unmarried lady not yet eighteen and only just out? You know perfectly well you were courting her ruin should word of this foolishness ever get out."

Holles had the grace to blush, though he didn't look like a man who had backed down.

"It isn't foolishness," Catherine said intensely. "I had never even thought of these matters, the suffering and endurance and sheer injustice of the things I heard about tonight for the first time. One thing I never thought of myself was *ignorant*. I cannot be sorry I went. Though I am sorry, I put you to this trouble. But if you had not come, the outcome would be the same. Archie would have brought me home, just like this, and Mama would have been none the wiser."

"And you are content with that?" Matty pounced. "To mislead and lie to your mother? To sneak about? Have we not had enough of that? I believed I had your promise."

Even in the fading light, Catherine whitened. She had nothing to say.

But again, Holles did, though with difficulty. "I wish such

sneaking was not necessary. But it seems to be the compromise we need to employ."

"No," Matty said, fixing him with what Francis would no doubt call her basilisk stare. "It is not. Perhaps I was at fault for not teaching her more about the conditions in which most people live. To be frank, I don't know the worst of it, myself. I applaud her search for knowledge, and yours, for what that is worth. But this risk to her name and her person, I will *not* condone. Charitable work, even daytime meetings, chaperoned, I will not challenge. But there will be no more escapades such as this. Am I clear?"

They regarded her with some consternation, then glanced at each other.

"Think," Matty pursued, leaning forward to make her point. "Here we are, almost home. Anyone could look into the carriage and see us. Anyone could see us alighting and walking up the steps to the front door. Now, imagine I am not here. They see you two unchaperoned in a closed carriage at dusk. They see Catherine handed down by you or fleeing from you as they might imagine and sneaking back into her own house. What would they think? Then where would her reputation stand? If you are ruined, Catherine, so are Arabella and Susan. Apart from anything else, what then is the worth of the expense your mother has gone to for your come out in society?"

"It wouldn't be like that," Catherine said weakly.

"Why, do you expect me to lie for you?"

"Of course not!"

"Miss Mather, please stop," Holles begged. "You are right. I should never have been so thoughtless and selfish. Ruining Miss Catherine will not help the plight of the poor and powerless. I will speak privately with Mrs. Dove and undertake never to repeat tonight's mistake."

"Mistake?" Catherine repeated, clearly appalled.

He reached out and caught her hand. "It was a mistake. But I hope we can still talk?"

"I see no way of stopping you," Matty said wryly. "As for Mrs. Dove, unless she asks me, I see no need of worrying her. But Catherine, I need your word that there will be no more such starts, or I will be *obliged* to worry her."

Catherine looked mulish, scowling at Matty as she hadn't done since childhood.

"There are other ways," Holles said gently. "This is for the best."

Catherine sighed. "I suppose you are right. But it is so *restricting* having to be a lady. I didn't know what Viola meant when she said much the same thing, but now I do. Very well, Miss Matty, I give you my word."

And not before time. The hackney pulled up and since Matty was present and Holles's escort therefore unexceptionable, he alighted and handed the ladies down.

"Make morning calls," Matty advised him, for in spite of everything, there was something rather appealing about the serious young man. "Take her driving in the park. Unless she is no more than a convert to your cause."

With that, she sailed up the steps, herding Catherine with her. They entered the house with Matty's key and were fortunate to find no servant in the hallway. Providing no one had seen her get into the hackney with Holles in the first place, Catherine had probably got away with her latest unwise start. In any case, she was not very recognizable in her old schoolroom dress and a bonnet that looked to have been borrowed from a servant.

Contrary to recent behavior, Catherine was not a stupid girl, so Matty satisfied herself with a short, pithy lecture on the dangers of straying into the wrong parts of town and the irreversible ills of a lost reputation. Beyond that, Matty was satisfied with the promises already given, and leaving Catherine to debate her narrow escape, she was forced to confront her own dilemma. And the danger to her own reputation.

Francis.

Chapter Ten

After all she had said to Catherine, Matty could barely believe she was risking her own safety and her own reputation by going alone into Barclay Square gardens to meet a man.

She was aware that at night, even here in the safer, wealthiest part of town, the pleasant, secluded areas where people walked and let their children play in daytime turned into something rather different at night. And she did not want to go. Aside from the personal danger, her pride rebelled against obeying the curt command issued by Francis.

Let him kick his heels in the garden and be robbed. I have no reason to pay any attention to his orders.

Except, of course, she did. She needed to know why he changed from thief to gentleman to radical worker. And more importantly, what was his interest in Catherine? Twice, he had been there when she had visited places she should not. None of this inclined her to trust him. She had recognized his danger from the outset and had no desire to put herself in his power.

In the end, she made her decision at the last possible moment, springing up from the chair in her bedchamber, where she had been trying to talk herself out of it. She swung her old cloak about her shoulders and drew the hood over her hair. She veered to the rickety little desk, snatched up the paper knife she kept there, and slipped it up her sleeve.

Five minutes later, she was in Barclay Square, her eyes darting about r. From one of the houses on the far side came muffled music, its first-floor windows blazing with candlelight. Most of the dwellings showed lights of some kind, though the square itself was quiet. Residents had presumably already gone to their evening's entertainment and were unlikely to return for some time. A muttering footman in livery was walking a small pug on a leash around the outside of the garden. Two arguing gentlemen walked out of the square into Bruton Street. A hackney rumbled slowly toward her as though the driver were looking for a particular house.

Dropping the paper knife into her hand, she clutched it beneath her cloak and crossed toward the nearest garden gate. Her heart hammered.

She paused at the gate, listening, but she could hear nothing more threatening than the rustling of leaves in the breeze. Drawing in her breath, she lifted the latch and pushed open the gate.

Only then did she realize the carriage sounds had stopped. She jerked her head around just as a horse snorted only feet away, making her jump.

The hackney had stopped right behind her, blocking her from the view of the nearest houses. The carriage door opened, and a man leaned into the light of the outside lamp.

Francis.

"Miss Mather," he said and stretched down his hand to her.

Dear God, this was worse than going into the garden. Alone with him in a closed carriage… And yet she sighed with relief that she would not need to enter the garden after all. She hesitated only a moment, then shoved the paper knife back up her sleeve, grasped his hand, and was all but hauled into the hackney. The door slammed behind her and, even before she had pulled free of his grip and sat on the bench opposite him, the carriage moved on.

The rumbling of the wheels on the cobbles was the only sound she could hear. He had changed from his working man's clothes into the evening dress of a gentleman. He had even shaved.

"I believe I was promised talk," Matty said.

"Exactly, so don't look so petrified. I'm not abducting you, just driving around the streets to give us a little more privacy and less alarming surroundings."

"You mean the gardens are not a superior choice at night?" she marveled and was almost surprised to have reduced him to a short silence.

"You know they were not, and I should not have suggested it."

"Then why did you? To make sure I would not come and—"

"To see if you would," he interrupted. "I ask your pardon and applaud your bravery if not your good sense."

"If you had been a few seconds later, I would be in there now."

"No, you wouldn't. I've been driving around the square for the last quarter-hour. I would always have intercepted you."

She thought he added, "I hope," under his breath. She wished she could see his expression, but there was no light inside the hackney, and he had sat back into the shadows.

"I am guilty," he added, "of a touch of temper."

"Concerning me? Allow me to point out that you have no right."

One large, elegant hand waved dismissively across the window. "Right has nothing to do with it. I do not want you involved in this."

"Involved in what? I was barely there. Catherine and Archie were mere observers. *You* appear to be the one involved."

She barely saw him move, but suddenly he sat beside her, too close for comfort, and took her hand. It jumped in his, but she would not give him the satisfaction of pulling free. She wished she had worn gloves.

"I *am* involved," he said softly, "though in what exactly, I am not sure. Do you ever communicate with Sir Anthony Thorne?"

Whatever she had expected, it was not that. "Not for seven years. At least."

"What do you do with your free time?"

She stared at him. "That is not your business."

"It is. Do you go among the poor? Take an interest in politics?"

"Sir, you have a very odd notion of a governess's free time."

"Educate me."

He still held her hand, not ungently, but in the sort of firm grip that she could not break without an obvious effort. His fingers trailed over her wrist, and she knew he must feel the pulse galloping there.

"Mrs. Dove is kind to me," she blurted. "I am not bombarded with unreasonable demands or expectations to mend or clean the children's clothes. I am treated almost like one of the family. Which means Viola and Catherine regard me as their friend. The younger children look on me almost as an older sister or an aunt. My supposed free time is *absorbed* by them and by that ridiculous animal they named a pup."

Whatever response she had expected to her minor tirade, it was not the flashing smile suddenly on his face. His fingers moved on her wrist in an apparently absent-minded caress.

"That is what I thought," he murmured. "And yet you and Miss Catherine Dove keep turning up where I wish you didn't."

Her eyes were used to the dark now, to the occasional pale shafts of light from the street, so she met and held his gaze. "Why do you care?"

His fingers stilled. Then his thumb circled her palm. "I wish I knew."

Her whole hand tingled, so sensitized that each distracted caress sent thrills streaming up her arm to her heart, to places farther below that were hardly connected. And yet she found she no longer desired to avoid his touch. Had she ever?

"Who are you?" she demanded in a sudden, harsh attempt to break his spell.

"Were we not introduced?"

"I can't believe that any more than I can believe in the thief or the working man who attends political meetings." Finally, she tugged at her hand, but his fingers tightened, and she gave up. "*What* are you, sir? An English gentleman? A Spanish rogue? Who are you tricking?"

A rut in the road bumped her against his shoulder, but still, she refused to release his gaze. To be fair, he made no effort to avoid hers. He held her hand now in both of his while he played with her fingers. They felt like a gentleman's hands, smooth, though never soft. Strong, capable hands. Everything about him was strong and capable. She had known that from the moment he had held her in his arms at Maida.

"*Who am I tricking?*" he repeated thoughtfully. "That is harder to answer than you might think. Everyone, I suppose."

She frowned, annoyed at the evasion. "Is your name even Francis?"

"Sort of."

Irritated, she gave a mighty tug of her hand that freed it with more undignified force than she had intended. She reeled backward, righting herself with difficulty, and placed her hand back in her lap.

Francis merely picked it up again and held it between both of his. "My name is Francisco de Salgado y Goya. I was born in Spain, the son of a nobleman who opposed the French alliance. After my family was killed, Wellington himself sent me to England to be educated here. I have interests in Spain and elsewhere in Europe, but my loyalty seems to be mostly to your country. For whom I have done many things that make me proud and a few that don't. Something is wrong about this latest flurry of political meetings, and I need to find out what."

She peered into his face. "You are some kind of…agent of the British government?"

"Some kind," he agreed.

She did her best to take that in, wondering if she believed him or if it was yet another smokescreen, another false identity to veil the others. "What has that to do with Maida Gardens? With Catherine and me and Rollo Darblay's ring?"

He sighed. "With you and Catherine and the ring, nothing, I suspect. With Maida, a passing moment that may or may not be repeated. I made a mistake at Maida because I was tired and grumpy and distracted and followed the first path I saw. When I went back and met you, I was trying to rectify that path—if it was not already too late. I believe it was. But then, I found this connection to Thorne, and Catherine and you both appeared at this meeting. I am not a great believer in coincidence, and so I was suspicious."

"Of what?" she demanded.

He was silent, though his fingers idly stroked the side of her hand.

She said, "You don't want to tell me, do you?"

"I would much rather kiss you."

Heat flooded her, not just from memory but from sudden, shocking yearning. "To distract me," she said flatly.

"Not entirely." Unexpectedly, he dragged her hand up to his lips and kissed her knuckles. Then, opening her stunned fingers, he dropped another lingering kiss in her palm. "It is *you* who distract *me*. Someone is organizing these meetings, experimenting with getting lots of them to happen at one time, not just in London, but all over the country."

"With what aim?" she asked breathlessly as he curled her fingers back over her palm as though holding the kiss in place.

He sighed. "Practice, it seems. So that something more important can be coordinated? Some massive rising, perhaps, to force the government into concessions."

She gazed at her hand, at his long, seductive fingers wrapped around it, and swallowed. "But no one wants that kind of rising. No one would risk revolution."

"Except the desperate. They are not my concern. I want to find those pulling the strings and doing the coordinating."

"But surely no one who could *would*?" she protested. "Opposition leaders are as afraid of revolution as anyone else."

"That is what confuses me," he admitted. "I have no evidence, but my instinct is pointing me to Anthony Thorne."

"He does not believe in revolution," she said with contempt. "Or even reform, except a few minor concessions as a last resort to make the people grateful."

"Then you see the problem with my theory. But I believe he is clever, covert, and dishonest. And if I were you, I would not let my sister marry him."

Her breath caught. "You shift with bewildering speed between the general and the personal. If I have my way, my sister will *not* marry him, but I am very unlikely to have any say at all. Why would Sir Anthony foment unrest when he spends his parliamentary life quashing it?"

He stilled, gazing down at her hand which lay now on his thigh. The impropriety should have appalled her. Instead, she marveled at his warmth, at the hard muscle beneath her fingertips. It made her feel…odd.

"How well do you know Sir Anthony?"

"Well enough to avoid him."

"You don't trust him."

"I do not."

"You grew up in the same neighborhood…Why precisely don't you trust him?"

"God, where do I start? Even as an adolescent, he always considered himself so immeasurably above the rest of us. And yet he was charming. When he married, he ran through his wife's fortune in short order, getting into parliament, buying the London house, entertaining the right people. By the time she died, his estate had begun to show signs of neglect again. He needs his treasury refilled, and my sister just happened to inherit money from our great-aunt, who always had a soft spot for her.

And suddenly, he wants to marry her when he never so much as looked at her before. An *imbecile* could read his motives, but not Marion."

She forced her mouth to stop talking and swallowed. "That is not what you want to know, is it? It is certainly not what I should have said."

He regarded her thoughtfully. "I think, in your own way, you are as much a keeper of secrets as I. It is possible, you know, that your sister does not care about his motives. Perhaps she just wants to be Lady Thorne, because she loves him anyway, or because she wants the position he could give her."

"As wife to a prime minister, one day?"

"Well, your family clearly understands enough of that to know it will be unsuitable to leave you as governess to the Doves while your sister rises with the great man. Would you consider being governess to your sister's children instead?"

"Unpaid and dependent?" she retorted. "No."

"What are you not telling me?" he asked quietly.

"You wish to be bored rigid by my entire life story? I am not *that* poor a companion."

A smile flickered across his face in a ripple of light from a passing carriage. "You are a delightful companion. I even like your prickles and your gimlet stare."

"Basilisk stare," she corrected.

"Not so very basilisk. I never tire of looking at you."

"Why do you say these things?" she asked, hoping he could not hear the sudden wistfulness she tried to hide in irritability. "I cannot be flattered into doing whatever it is you wish of me."

Even in the dark, she could see something change in his eyes. By some trick of the passing light, he looked almost...fierce. And then his lashes, long and thick, came down.

"If I wish you to do something, I will simply ask. Compliments are not related."

"Then ask so that I can say no and be on my way." Even as the sharp words spilled out of her mouth, she was conscious of no desire to leave him. On the contrary, she felt curiously…alive. She liked him. She liked his strong, idly stroking fingers and his large, unsafe presence by her side.

"Very well. Thorne will call again, pester you to do as he wishes, and leave the Doves."

"We have agreed nothing can be done for a month since if I do leave, I owe Mrs. Dove notice."

"Is he the kind of man to wait a month on the word of two socially inferior women?"

"Mrs. Dove is not socially inferior. She is a cousin of the Earl of Wenning, who married beneath her. Lord Wenning is not nobody," she added thoughtfully. "And I believe they have returned to England."

His fingers relaxed on hers with something like relief. "Mrs. Dove is on your side? And can count on Wenning's support?"

"She does not want me to go. For the rest, I cannot say."

He nodded. "It is some protection for you, if necessary. In the meantime, Thorne does not strike me as the kind of patient man who will wait out your notice if it impedes his plans. Would you consider letting him try and persuade you? Listen to his arguments—and to his conversation?"

Her fingers, which he had flattened across his lower thigh, curled into a fist. Of course he was using her. Of course. She had always been aware of his flattery, so why did this feel like a bucket of cold water emptied over her from a great height?

"You want me to *spy* on him, *tattle* on him to you?" She jerked her hand away and clasped it with the other in her own lap.

"If you wish to use such childish terms," he said evenly. "To be frank, I would rather he had nothing to do with this, so if you can prove that, or at least show me how unlikely it is, I shall be grateful."

She stared out of the window. The carriage was ambling along the side of Hyde Park. It might have been the country except for the dim lights all around it. She wondered if a fog was coming down. Like the fog on her brain. "And I am to trust you. Believe you are who you say you are, without proof."

The silence stretched so long, she almost imagined he had quietly left the carriage by the opposite door. Almost. But she *knew* he was still there because every inch of her was aware of him.

"Perhaps you are acquainted with Mr. Ludovic Dunne," he said.

She blinked and turned back to face him. "No. Though I know who he is. He was responsible, I believe, for the truth of Lord Dominic's innocence coming out."

"If you take the children and their pony to the Green Park tomorrow, perhaps around eleven of the clock, I will try and arrange for Mr. Dunne to be there."

She frowned. "Why?"

"To vouch for me. We studied law together, a long time ago." Reaching up, he knocked on the carriage roof. The horses changed direction, veering across the road into South Street.

It crossed her mind that he was actually *hurt* by her lack of trust and yet amused by his own feeling. But no, that, too, had to be imagination. She could not hurt him if she tried. While she…

Oh, no, this is too confusing. I need to go home, away from him… Because she had finally realized something else, too.

"You held my hand to measure my pulse," she accused.

"It can help in the detection of lies." He took her breath away by smiling, the rare, dazzling smile that for no reason seemed to obliterate all offense and anger. "You should be pleased. You may not yet trust me, but at least I trust you."

Because her pulse raced whenever he touched her? Before he touched her? Pride would not allow her to leave him with that idea.

"It's as well I am immune to masculine fawning," she said with contempt.

A breath of laughter seemed to take him by surprise. "I take issue with *fawning*. For the rest, Miss Mather, you are entirely mistaken." He leaned closer, and she had to suppress a gasp as his hand cupped her cheek. Butterfly light, his fingertips trailed across her lips and down her throat. They paused at the pulse that galloped at the base of her neck. She could not breathe.

"M-mistaken?" she managed.

"You are not immune at all. And neither am I. So never tempt me, Miss Matty. Never challenge me. Or we will both lose."

Before she could properly comprehend his words, let alone speak, his mouth covered hers in a short, hard kiss that caused everything in her to leap. She could not hide her gasp, but his lips had already left hers, and he sat back into his shadowed corner, not touching her anywhere at all.

She should have felt safe, not bereft.

"The carriage will stop as far from direct light as possible," he murmured. "I will not hand you down for obvious reasons. I'm sure you can find your own excuses if you need them for being out of the house."

Even as he spoke, the hackney pulled up between the Doves' house and the next. Francis did not move, though when he spoke, she heard the smile in his voice. "Until tomorrow. Don't be late."

Bewildered and shocked, for once, she had nothing to say. She merely rose, opened the door of the hackney, and stepped down. She closed the door without looking back and marched somewhat blindly toward the Doves' front door.

Chapter Eleven

Even as he had written the note to Dunne last night, even as he strode around to the house the following morning, Francis knew he should not have involved Miss Mather in this business. Not that he imagined she would be in any actual danger from Thorne, even if the man was up to something; he would not invite scandal so close to his family. But somehow, that didn't make Francis feel better.

Which, of course, was why he had asked her. Because if he hadn't made use of her when she was so well-placed, he would have to have asked himself why he hadn't. There was no reason *not* to use her as he had used hundreds of people before. He was not the man to let a little thing like physical attraction get in the way of business.

He didn't like that about himself either. But he was damned if he'd change at this stage. Matilda Mather was not the sort of woman one seduced into obedience, and he had no intention of trying. But that she interested him on so many levels, *that* bothered him. And *that* was why he had asked her: to prove to himself she was no different from anyone else he encountered in the course of his work.

Only she was.

And he didn't like it. In fact, he had no idea what to do about it except ignore it. Mostly. Apart from his foolish exultation when he discovered she was not physically indifferent to him. Her reaction to his proximity, her rapidly changing pulse, had told him that. It never changed when she answered his questions, only when he touched her, caressed her. And when he had kissed her.

He shouldn't have done that either, but as he had warned her, he was not the man to refuse a challenge. A sweet challenge and a sweeter kiss, one he had had to force himself to end. In truth, he should not be tormenting himself by gaining her trust and her help. He should find some other tool to whom he was indifferent. Emma Carntree, for example, who had once made his own pulses race and was involved in an adulterous affair with Thorne. And yet her reaction to Francisco's return provided possibilities. He might be able to seduce her from Thorne.

For a moment, striding into Barclay Square where the Dunnes lived while in London, he forced himself to contemplate the seduction of his own former mistress. And found the whole business distasteful.

The haughty governess seemed to have turned his whole world upside down. Damn her.

He was shown into a graceful salon where Dunne and Rebecca were entertaining two babies and Lady Dominic Gorse.

"Ah, the unlikely host of today's Venetian breakfast," Dunne welcomed. "I don't suppose you thought to bring any food?"

"I thought I was the host of today's walk in the park. I don't recall any kind of breakfast being mentioned."

"Well, I'm not sure one has children at Venetian breakfasts," Rebecca Dunne said. "Let us call it, instead, an impromptu, private al fresco. Viola has a carriage packed with food and blankets."

"Then I hope it doesn't rain," Francisco said, seeing that his discreet meeting to convince Miss Mather of his credentials had got out of hand.

"So do I," Lady Dominic said, scooping up one of the infants. "I'll go and fetch the girls and meet you all in the park. Mr. Francis, might I have your escort to my carriage?"

Francisco could hardly refuse, though he eyed the child warily as he bowed them out of the room.

Her ladyship wasted no time. They were not even on the stairs before she demanded, "What is your business with Miss Mather?"

Francisco regarded her thoughtfully. "That is between Miss Mather and me. But I mean her no harm if that is what you are asking."

"You had better not," Lady Dominic warned. She stopped halfway down the stairs, forcing him to halt, too, and glared up at him. "I count Miss Mather a dear friend, and if you are prying into her affairs—"

"I'm not," Francisco interrupted. "Nor can I imagine why you might think so."

At least she had the grace to lower her voice, although there was no obvious sign of lurking servants. "I know what you do," she said darkly and then frowned. "Or at least, I guess some of it. I think you are the shadier side of Mr. Dunne, and if I had known your focus was on Matty, I would never have taken you to my mother's party."

Francisco regarded her thoughtfully. For some reason, he was pleased by her protectiveness, proof that Miss Mather had friends looking out for her. "You are very defensive of your old governess."

"She was never my governess," Viola said unexpectedly. "I was beyond the schoolroom by the time she came to us. But it did not stop her teaching me, from making possible…" She caught her breath and closed her mouth. Her gaze refocused on him. "Dominic and Ludovic both believe you are a good man. Miss Mather is a good woman, and I would do anything for her. My sisters and my little brother adore her. My mother relies on her. And I…" Her rather lovely eyes grew defiant. "I would do anything for the woman who taught me to read at the age of nineteen years old."

Whatever he had expected, it was not that, so he held his

tongue.

Viola's lips twisted. "She was the only one who recognized my condition, that my mind somehow transposes certain letters and makes reading not impossible but difficult. Without her, I would… Well, that doesn't matter. I tell you this only so that you understand. I will go to any lengths to prevent harm befalling her."

Francisco brushed an imaginary hair from his coat. "Why, there I believe we are in agreement, ma'am." And that, if only she knew it, was the strangest fact of all.

MATTY DIDN'T KNOW whether she felt more panicked or relieved when Viola appeared just as they were about to leave for the park.

"I brought provisions," Viola said briskly.

"For…?" Matty asked.

"Your al fresco party."

"Hurray!" the girls cried.

"I didn't know we were having one," Matty said.

"We are. Mr. and Mrs. Dunne will bring their children, and I am bringing mine. Dominic may even appear later on."

Matty swallowed. "We were just going for a quick walk in the park. I can't keep the girls from lessons too long."

"You were always good at the nature lessons," Viola said wryly. "I'll just explain to Mama while you all pile into the carriage."

"We won't all fit in the carriage," Viola objected.

"And there's Pup," Susan added.

Most people would have banished Pup at this stage, Matty supposed, but she and the Doves made do. Susan, much to her delight, was sent to sit with the coachman. Everyone else squashed into the carriage, where Arabella sat with her feet up on the bench, her knees bent under her chin, to make space for Pup on the floor. Even so, he sat largely on Matty's feet.

"Did you mention provisions?" Catherine asked.

"Strapped to the back of the carriage," Viola replied. "Rebecca Dunne will bring more."

It was not a long drive to the park, but several times Matty found Viola's gaze on her and knew she would be asked some searching questions. Somehow, Viola had got wind of her supposedly casual meeting with Ludovic Dunne and turned the event into a party. Matty didn't know whether to laugh or pray for strength.

In the end, as they all spilled out of the carriage at the park gates, she settled for calling after the girls and Pup, "Do *not* let him off the leash!"

She and Viola carried the food hampers between them, watching the younger girls run with Pup, while Catherine held on to her hat and hurried after them. Although it had all come to be normal to Matty, she saw from the shocked expressions of a haughty middle-aged couple that it was not.

"Pup is an unruly chaperone," Viola remarked. "But the girls will be regarded as eccentrics, not hoydens."

"Well, it did you no harm."

"Only when I tried to pretend I wasn't. Matty, what does Mr. Francis want with you?"

Matty was ready for the question. "He seems to want me to help with something, but of course, I don't know him well enough to agree. He said Mr. Dunne would speak for him. I can trust Mr. Dunne, can I not?"

"Implicitly. But why does Francis want *your* help?"

Matty didn't answer that, merely asked a question of her own. "Do you know him well? Does Lord Dominic?"

Viola shook her head. "Dominic says he is a gentleman, though of the more adventurous kind. He has land in England and Spain, but drifts in and out of society, for which he does not appear to give two hoots. Two years ago, scandal linked him to

Emma Carntree, though she seems more attached to Anthony Thorne these days."

"Does she?" Matty said flatly. She wondered if Marion knew, if Marion cared. Mostly, she recognized that if the likes of Emma Carntree appealed to Francis, Matty could not. A dazzling, brittle, adulterous social butterfly had nothing in common with a dowdy and dull governess with a sharp tongue, a basilisk stare, and a reputation to preserve at all costs. Somehow, it was small comfort that he trusted her enough to use her in his schemes.

And then, breaking through the trees on her left, she saw Francis himself, and her heart gave a funny little leap. He wore correct morning attire, buff pantaloons that hugged his muscular legs, and a well-fitting coat that emphasized the breadth of his shoulders. Every inch of him was the perfect English gentleman, handsome and fit, but that wasn't what truly took her breath away.

It was the laughter in his face. She could even make out the crinkles around his eyes as he grinned down at the small boy who pursued him. She had never seen him so relaxed, so intent on mere…fun. Then he glanced across and saw her. His smile didn't exactly die, but it grew distracted, and she didn't know whether to be glad or sorry.

The child whacked him on the hip and bolted, yelling, "Tag!"

Mr. Francis set off in pursuit. The chortling boy ran up to a couple approaching along the path. Matty had never encountered anyone quite so elegant as the lady. Surely, she would give the boy a set down and spoil his fun if he grabbed at her skirts. Perhaps she would even tell Francis off, too, which Matty definitely wanted to see.

But the lady only smiled tolerantly as the boy skidded behind her, grabbing her skirts in passing to pull himself on to the gentleman's coattails. The gentleman was tall and striking, his eyebrows dramatically dark, his hair a silver grey that at first made him look older. But as they grew closer to him, Matty saw that he could not have been much more than thirty years.

"Den!" the boy cried gleefully. "Ludo is Den!"

"Curses," Francis exclaimed, twirling an imaginary mustache. "Foiled once more."

"The child is Rebecca Dunne's son by her previous marriage," Viola murmured. "She and Mr. Dunne have another of their own, but she has been left with her nurse for the day."

At first, Matty thought Francis had not seen them and wondered if he would be embarrassed to be discovered in the indignity of "tag." But he turned straight from the Dunnes' boy and bowed with perfect savoir faire, and she realized she had never seen him embarrassed by anything, not his disguises, his bad behavior, or his good. She had never encountered anyone quite so *comfortable* with himself. Not satisfied or smug like Thorne but accepting. Was that his attraction? Because he accepted her, too?

There was no time for these confused reflections, for Viola was introducing her to Mr. and Mrs. Dunne and their son Tom, who executed a perfect bow for a small boy, along with a delightful grin. Then, spotting the dog at last, his eyes widened.

"He's huge!" he marveled. "May I pat him? Does he bite?"

"Only his dinner," Susan said. "Pup, sit."

Tom's jaw dropped. "He's a *puppy*?"

"Not anymore," Susan assured him as the dog sat on her foot, "but the name stuck."

Pup wagged his tail as Tom approached, dragging Mr. Dunne with him by the coat. The dog sniffed Dunne's hand and wagged his tail harder on receiving a head pat. When Tom followed with a tentative pat, Pup slurped at his hand and then his face.

Tom bounded back, laughing.

"He likes you," Matty assured him.

In no time, Pup was on his back, legs in the air to have his tummy tickled. Tom, laughing, released his stepfather's coat, and Arabella demonstrated how to make the dog's leg twitch with joy.

Even Mrs. Dunne stopped looking anxious.

Francis caught Matty's eye and gave what looked like a wink before he addressed Mr. Dunne. "I'll stay with Tom. Pup and I are old friends."

"Are you indeed?" Viola murmured.

Matty found Mr. Dunne's gaze upon her. He gestured with one inviting hand, and Matty moved with him away from the others.

"I understand I am to vouch for Francis," he said mildly.

"If your conscience will allow it."

"My conscience will allow me to tell you anything I know."

"Does he truly work for the government?"

"Yes, I believe so."

She stared at him. "You believe so? Don't you know?"

"Not with absolute certainty. But I have found he knows information that could only have come from government sources. I have never known him to lie to me. I would trust him with my life, and more than that, with the lives of my wife and children."

She nodded slowly. "You are friends."

"We studied law together. And we occasionally help each other in our…professions."

"Then you would advise me to trust him?"

He met her gaze. "If you have done nothing wrong, then yes. He is ruthless, Miss Mather, but he is not cruel."

"And is he honorable?" she blurted.

"Deeply." His lips twisted slightly. "Though it is his own honor, not necessarily yours or mine."

She regarded him with some frustration. "Forgive me, Mr. Dunne, but you are not a great deal of help."

"Perhaps if you were clearer about what it is you want to know…"

Why does he kiss me? "He says he wants my help," she said hastily. "I suppose I want to know if I should give it."

An odd expression passed across the solicitor's face. "He has never asked me for help—it is usually the other way about. But if he did ask, I would give it unconditionally. He would not *endanger* you."

She had never thought he would. Not the kind of danger Mr. Dunne meant, at any rate.

His cool, grey eyes were oddly piercing, assessing. "Speak to my wife," he said abruptly and fell back. Matty could only blink as Mrs. Dunne stepped smoothly into his place.

Rebecca Dunne was one of those women who seemed to have been born not only beautiful but supremely elegant in all she did. That in rank she was a mere solicitor's wife did nothing for Matty's sense of intimidation. Not that she would ever acknowledge that to a soul, but it did incline her to look at this odd meeting through Mrs. Dunne's eyes.

"You must find me very odd and very presumptuous," Matty said. "Demanding your husband vouch for his friend."

"I don't find it odd at all," Mrs. Dunne said. "To a sensible woman, Francisco is a difficult man to trust."

One confusing fact surged to the front of Matty's mind, that Francis trusted the Dunnes. "I have seen him as so many different people," Matty blurted. "I don't know which is real."

"If any," Mrs. Dunne said with the flicker of a smile. "To be honest, I suspect Francisco has the same trouble. He needs an anchor in life. So far, I believe that anchor to be his innate integrity. But that is a lonely life."

It was a day of discoveries. "You worry for him."

"I do." Mrs. Dunne turned her elegant head and held Matty's gaze. "He has helped save my life, risked his all for Ludovic, and given me sound advice aimed at my own happiness, even though it must increase his own sense of isolation. But I don't believe anyone can tell you to trust him. In your heart, you already do or don't, and nothing Ludovic or I can say will change that."

While Matty no doubt gawped, Mrs. Dunne searched her face, a smile tugging the corners of her mouth.

"I see."

Matty blinked. "What do you see?"

But the tete-a-tete was apparently over. "That breakfast is served." She waved a hand toward a blanket spread out under ever-increasing plates of food and Matty's charges. Lord Dominic had appeared from nowhere and was helping Arabella tie Pup securely to a nearby tree.

In something of a daze, Matty approached the blanket and knelt. She fixed a faint smile on her face, barely aware that the children were behaving with lively politeness and were looking after little Tom.

Why had she insisted on this? Because Rebecca Dunne was right. She did already trust Francis—Francisco de Salgado y Goya—though she had no clear idea why. Moreover, she most assuredly did *not* trust Sir Anthony Thorne, and with very good reason. In fact, she considered him a threat to her family in general and her sister in particular, and she knew suddenly she had always meant to help Francis.

He sat by her side, large, conspicuous, contentedly munching while exchanging occasional quips with the adults and banter with the children. They all liked him.

Matty liked him.

But she no longer knew how to join in with a group like this, save to keep her eye on the children, her charges, and their massive pet. For all but the Doves, she had become an observer of life, not a participant. Was that why she resisted Francis? Because he kept forcing her to participate?

And what the *devil* was all her hard-won independence for if she did not join in the business of life? Did not revel in the fun of this company, in the curious, intoxicating acquaintance of a man as overwhelming as Francis?

She frowned at the dainty pastry halfway to her mouth. Perhaps she was a tool in Francis's mission. But he had seen her as more than that, more than the governess.

Slowly, she turned her head and found his turned toward her. Her heart skipped a beat, and not just because it tended to whenever she looked at him. Long ago, Thorne had destroyed her ability to trust her own instincts. But she was trusting them now to recognize that Francis was a good man. Beyond that, what else was possible?

"If you're not going to eat that pastry," Francis said, "we could instead let the poor hound stretch his legs and take his mind off all this food he can't have."

She could keep her dignity and instruct the girls to go instead. Or she could take the chance and participate.

"It would be a kindness," she said, setting the pastry back on her plate.

"A few minutes without the whining might be nice," agreed Viola, who sat nearest the dog. "Thanks, Matty."

As Matty rose, she found Francis's large, slender hand stretched down to help her. It would have been rude to refuse it. And a shame to miss the sensation of his strong, ungloved fingers closing around hers, drawing her lightly to her feet.

It was not a crime to enjoy the respectful touch of a man or the sight of him strolling past her toward the tree that anchored Pup. She could allow the intense awareness of him walking by her side, tall, masculine… and dangerous, though not to her.

To her heart, perhaps.

Oh, no, just live in the present, Matty Mather. Stop trying to think ahead…

"Well?" he said lightly when they walked in silence for almost a minute. "Has Ludovic induced you to trust me? Or has Rebecca?"

"No," she said honestly, and since she glanced at him as she spoke, she caught an unguarded glimpse of his eyes before his black lashes swept down. Had she *hurt* him? She drew in a quick breath and spoke in a rush before her courage failed her. "But something Mrs. Dunne said made me realize I already do trust you. I have just grown unused to…believing in myself. I will help you with Anthony Thorne or with anything else I can."

His eyebrows flew up. A flash of surprise lit his dark eyes, and then they softened, just as he let Pup draw him off the path.

"That's a very handsome offer. I confess you have surprised me."

Pup was snuffling around, following the trail of whatever had led him in this direction in the first place. He halted for a proper, very delicate, and thorough sniff among some gnarled tree roots.

Francis said, "I am touched."

She glanced warily up from the dog, expecting mockery or at least amusement. She found neither, only his warm, steady gaze that somehow made it difficult to breathe.

"You touch me in many ways, you know. All the time."

"I d-do?"

As though seeing the sudden heat under her skin, he touched her cheek with the backs of two fingers. "You do."

"Why?"

At that, a smile did spring into his eyes, and his fingers moved, cupping her cheek. "I don't know. You are rather wonderful. Behind those prickles and dull, governess clothes, you are all light and color. I like that. I like it very much."

His face swooped nearer, causing her stomach to dive, and his mouth took hers. A gentle, tasting kiss that deprived her of what breath she had left and turned her bones to liquid.

Without meaning to, she slid her fingers into his hair and kissed him back. *Trust…trust.*

"I was almost engaged to Anthony Thorne," she blurted against his lips. "Until he found a richer lady."

He drew back a little, a faint frown tugging at his brow as he gazed down at her. What he would have said, she never discovered, for Pup, with impeccable timing, lunged suddenly back toward the path, dragging the surprised Francis with him.

Matty drew in a shuddering breath and followed. By the time she reached the path, Francis had the dog under control once more and was waiting for her, smiling as though nothing had happened. As though she had said nothing.

I've ruined it, she thought miserably as they walked back toward the others. *He'll think I'm doing this for revenge. Not for him…*

Chapter Twelve

By the time she returned to the house with her charges, Matty's mind and emotions were still churning. She wondered what it was she was afraid of having ruined. And yet the anxiety was almost drowned in excitement because she was going to help Francis. She was, hopefully, going to prevent Thorne from ruining her sister's life and her own. And over all, the memory of that kiss. Of all three kisses.

Preoccupied and dazed, she was unprepared for the commotion that struck as soon as she opened the front door. Pup began to bark and bounded free immediately, dragging the leash from Catherine's hand to gallop up the stairs from where a young man's laughing voice could be heard.

"Adrian!" squeaked Susan.

"Pup!" exclaimed the male voice above in accents of pure delight, while Matty's pupils shot off in the dog's wake without permission, yelling their brother's name. Even Catherine shrugged, smiled, and hurried after them.

Matty followed with more composure. She could never find in her heart to scold them for their excesses of joy in such reunions, and she was not about to start now. On the other hand, she knew she should at least muffle the racket since she had no idea if Mrs. Dove was entertaining callers.

As it turned out, she was, for as Matty crossed the first-floor landing to head toward the bumping and laughing from the schoolroom area, the drawing room door opened, and Mrs. Dove stood there with her cap very slightly askew and a harassed look in her eyes.

"Thank God," she uttered, closing the door behind her. "I mean, there you are Miss Mather, just in time." She lowered her voice to a conspiratorial murmur. "Adrian is home! And your mother is here. Help!"

MATTY FROWNED AT her in consternation. "My mother is *here*? In London?" she whispered.

"Here, in my drawing room!" Mrs. Dove hissed. "Along with your sister."

Matty forced herself to breathe. "I'm sorry, ma'am. Have…have you agreed to anything with them?"

"Of course not," Mrs. Dove said, clearly affronted. "Well, except what we already agreed with Sir Anthony." She jerked her head toward the door in unmistakable command and walked back inside.

Matty followed her more slowly, though the smile she fixed on her lips suddenly felt genuine as her mother rose from the sofa, arms outstretched. "Matilda!"

"Mama," Matty said, going to her and returning the embrace. "What in the world are you doing here?"

"We've come for the Season," Marion said as Matty turned to her. Marion's embrace was briefer and cooler. Dressed in a smart new Pomona morning gown, she looked healthy and…more hectic than happy, though she turned her best smile on her sister as she pulled back. "Or at least for what remains of the Season! Anthony will introduce us to everyone who matters."

"He called here just the other day," Matty said. "He never mentioned that you were coming. But then, you did not write to me either. Where are you staying?"

"Grillon's Hotel, until Anthony can find us a suitable house."

"Well, I can call on you there this evening if you like. I have duties to attend here."

"I wouldn't worry for today," Mrs. Dove said. "Adrian is home, as you can probably hear, and you will get no lessons done for the rest of the day. Spend the time with your family."

"Thank you, ma'am."

"Perhaps you would like to change your dress," her mother said pointedly, "and walk round to Grillon's with us now?"

"My wardrobe is not extensive, Mama," Matty said dryly. "Unless you wish me to wear an evening gown at midday, we must make do. But if I embarrass you, I could meet you in the park at dawn instead, and no one need realize we are related."

Her mother scowled. "Don't be ridiculous, Matilda. But then, this stubbornness of yours—"

"Perhaps we could discuss it on the way?" Matilda suggested. "Mrs. Dove, thank you for looking after my family and for the afternoon. I shall be back before dinner time."

Her mother and sister both bridled at that, though they could hardly begin a quarrel under Mrs. Dove's gracious smile.

Instead, the quarrel began on the walk to Grillon's.

Mama sniffed. "I cannot believe you are all but a servant to that poor little dab of a woman who would probably be completely overlooked at our country assemblies."

"No, I don't think she would be," Matty said calmly.

Her mother glared. "You are just being awkward."

"Not in the slightest. Mrs. Dove may be a trifle vague, but she is every inch a lady and would always be recognized as such."

"Actually, Matty has a point," Marion pointed out before their mother could join the battle. "Is Mrs. Dove not related to a nobleman?"

"She is the Earl of Wenning's cousin."

"Do they visit?" Mama asked with a hint of sharpness.

"I believe the Wennings have been abroad for a couple of years, but her ladyship was kind to Viola, who is now Lady Dominic Gorse. The countess's sister, Miss Darblay, is Catherine's great friend."

"Is she Viscount Darblay's daughter?" Marion asked.

"She is."

Mama sniffed. "At least she is well connected, but it makes no real difference."

"It makes no difference to any of us," Matty said calmly, "because, as I said in my letter, I have every intention of staying on with Mrs. Dove. But you need not worry that anyone of the ton will connect your name with mine."

Mama scowled. "Apart from the Darblay girl and Lady Dominic and presumably their families!"

"I very much doubt they sit around discussing friends' governesses with their families," Matty said. "But I can easily persuade Viola and Hope to secrecy should they ever meet you. Along with Catherine, of course."

"That would not cast us in a good light," Mama snapped.

Matty let them ponder that until they reached the hotel, but she didn't fool herself it would change anything. The real quarrel was about to begin.

SIR ANTHONY THORNE was conscious of such excitement in his veins that it was getting harder to conceal. He had set a date when all hell was to break loose all over the country, and he had a great deal to do in order to be assured it would happen, that all his people were in place.

Of course, at the quiet times, at night, he needed an outlet for his excessive energies, which was why he had allowed Emma Carntree to stay in his house. Normally, he came to her when her husband was absent.

In the name of discretion, his valet only ever knocked on the bedchamber door to signal the arrival of morning tea. When the knock came, Emma still slumbered in a tangle of sheets, a beam of unkind daylight playing over her profile. The lines around her eyes, the relaxed sag around her mouth and jaw, were very evident, and she looked every one of her two-and-thirty years. Or perhaps just the last decadent dozen.

But there was no denying her usefulness. He would probably find a way to keep her on when he had won, when he was married.

He rose, donned his robe, and walked into his private sitting room where his valet had left the tea, along with the newspapers and morning post. With a yawn, he poured himself a cup of tea, added a luxurious amount of sugar, and rifled the heap of letters.

He paused at one bearing the seal of the Earl of Wenning and eagerly opened it. A card fell out. Not, alas, a private note of support from his lordship, to whom he had sent out some feelers via mutual friends, but an invitation to her ladyship's ball next week.

Well, he had never moved in the earl's circles before, so this was certainly a step forward. And there would surely be opportunities for private discussion. A week was little enough notice for such an event, but Thorne did not doubt that the polite world would move heaven and earth to be there. The couple's turbulent relationship had provided gossip for years, after all.

In addition to which, Lady Wenning was everything that was charming and fashionable, and her husband bore a great deal of weight with diplomatic and government circles. If Lord Wenning's support was not quite necessary to Thorne, it would certainly be very welcome in the aftermath.

An overlooked hand-delivered epistle fell off the table into his lap. Intrigued, he picked it up and broke the seal. An unpleasant spike of mixed unease and irritation pierced his smugness. It was from his betrothed, which should have been pleasant, only she had written it from Grillon's Hotel in London.

Damnation, I told her not to come…

But she had, to retrieve Matilda from her servitude, she said gaily, and so they might as well enjoy some of the pleasures of the Season while they were here.

Thorne groaned aloud just as Emma appeared, yawning, wearing one of his nightshirts. It was endearingly huge on her. Less endearing was her demand to know what had him groaning at this time of the morning.

"My betrothed," he said bitterly, tossing the brief epistle on the desk. "I don't have *time* to dance attendance on her, extract invitations for her, and squire her about town."

"Well, my dear," Emma drawled, a touch of amused spite in her eyes, "if you cannot control your own wife, it doesn't bode well for the rest of your plans, does it?"

He regarded her with dislike. "Or yours. You and I won't be seeing much of each other until I can get rid of her."

"Cheer up. With luck, she can take the governess with her."

He rose abruptly. "I need to go out."

"Where?"

"Grillon's," he snapped.

In fact, it was hours later before he was shown into Mrs. Mather's sitting room and greeted by the sight of his betrothed side-by-side on the sofa with her sister. Their heads were together as though in earnest discussion, which made him fleetingly uneasy. But then Marion saw him, and her whole face lit up. She sprang up to meet him, both hands extended, and he allowed himself to kiss them in an apparent excess of devotion.

"Marion, my dear, what a charming surprise! Mrs. Mather, your servant. I wish you had apprised me of your coming. I could have found you a house rather than this—" He waved one disparaging hand around the perfectly appointed sitting room. "As it is, I thought we had agreed you would stay in the country until the wedding."

"Ladies are allowed to change their minds," Mrs. Mather said, smiling broadly.

Although…was that a hint of warning behind the smile? A declaration of at least occasional disobedience? He supposed he had thrice-blasted Matilda to thank for that. Though, perhaps, if they could persuade her to leave her employer, he might make do with the complication of their presence. He might have to.

"Indeed they are." He released his betrothed's hands to allow her to resume her seat and pulled up another chair to join them. He smiled at Matilda, who had clearly been pried from her employment, although she still looked so frumpish that he wanted to shudder. To his surprise, she gave a small smile in return. "You must be delighted to be reunited with your family."

"Of course," she replied.

"I gather you and the excellent Mrs. Dove have parted ways after all?"

Matilda's brows flew up. "On the contrary. She kindly allowed me the afternoon free."

"Matty was ever stubborn," Mrs. Mather said with a sigh. "Although, to be sure, the Dove woman is at least ladylike and well connected."

"To Lord Wenning, to be precise," Thorne said. "A man of some influence and a highly desirable ally."

"You don't wish to be embarrassed by your own connection to his cousin's governess," Matilda said with a sympathy he did not trust for a moment, although she looked serious enough. "But, as I have been telling Mama and Marion, it need not trouble you. Lord and Lady Wenning are unaware of my existence, and that is unlikely to change."

"Perhaps," Marion said impatiently, "but it would be much more comfortable if you could simply come with me to parties and balls and the theatre. Oh, Anthony, you will be able to see that we receive invitations to the *best* parties, won't you?"

"I daresay," he replied. He supposed he could make the best of it. Perhaps it was even a good thing that his betrothed should be here to witness his triumph. He just had so little time to dance attendance on her right now, and he certainly didn't want them picking up rumors of his entanglement with Emma.

"And for Matilda?" Mrs. Mather asked.

"Sadly, not while she is the governess," Thorne said gently.

"You are quite right," Matilda agreed, much to his surprise.

"It would not be appropriate, and I am expected to look after the younger Doves while their mother is out with Catherine."

"Then leave them!" Marion exclaimed. "And enjoy yourself for once."

"You mean attend you in my one evening gown?" Matty asked politely.

"We can buy new gowns."

"Marion," she said patiently, "then you would draw me to the attention of people who might conceivably recognize me for what I am. Catherine's friends and even some of Viola's would know me."

"But you have just told us," Thorne intervened, "of their vaunted discretion. Besides which, being a governess is a respected profession for an impecunious lady."

"Which is one reason I prefer to keep it."

"It would not be suitable once Marion and I are married."

"On the contrary, it suits me very well," Matilda snapped before taking a deep breath and trying for a more conciliatory tone, which was interesting in itself. "Though I will think about what you have said. I have no wish to quarrel with my family."

To Thorne, it felt like an important obstacle had been cleared. As the inevitable tea was brought in and served, he wondered fleetingly why it had become so important to him to win this trivial fight with Matilda.

Because he did not like to be defied. Because she had once adored him. Because his marital home would be just a little brighter with her in it—wearing a new set of clothes, obviously. And because she possessed the intelligence and political awareness that Marion lacked. She would be the true hostess of his political dinners. In fact, he was conscious of the vague regret that it was not she who had inherited the family money. And then he would simply have rekindled their old romance and married her.

After all, she *had* once loved him. Secretly, she probably still did.

CHAPTER THIRTEEN

FRANCISCO, ONCE MORE attired as a non-descript working man, had spent most of the day following Thorne. He had emerged briskly from his own somewhat dilapidated townhouse some fifteen minutes after a hackney had whisked Emma Carntree away. Intriguingly, the man had spent some time at Horse Guards and then made several calls around Piccadilly and St. James. From one of those calls, he had emerged in the company of a senior army officer.

Why the interest in the military? Francisco wondered as he followed his quarry on to Grillon's Hotel. Was he hoping to ensure no bloodshed at the coordinated marches? That only made sense if Thorne was indeed behind the protests. More likely, from what Francisco knew of the man's politics, was that he wanted to ensure the complete suppression of unrest. If there truly was a connection between Thorne and the radicals, Francisco had yet to discover it. A visit to Maida Gardens by Thorne's mistress, wearing a red posy, and Thorne's vague interest in everyone's politics were really not enough to condemn a man as an agitator. Or even an agent provocateur...which was an interesting line of reasoning.

At Grillon's, by flirting with a maid, he learned that Thorne was calling on a Mrs. Mather, newly arrived in London.

Poor Matty, he thought, with genuine regret, because they

must have come to drag her home. His stomach was rumbling by the time Thorne emerged from the hotel with a dowdy lady, whom he offered his arm.

Francisco found himself scowling when Matty took his arm. Even though he had no reason to be annoyed. He had *asked* her to converse with Thorne, and they did seem to be pretty deep in conversation. How could she possibly have been engaged to such a smug, slippery fellow? Old affections, even betrayed ones, could linger on. The thought hurt him somehow. He hoped it didn't hurt her.

Fortunately for Francisco's ridiculous possessiveness—which felt alarmingly like jealousy—after a few moments, the hotel porter summoned a hackney, into which Thorne politely handed her and closed the door.

Francisco's relief was out of proportion. He actually took a step after the hackney before, reluctantly, turning the other way and following Thorne as far as Westminster, where he entered the hallowed halls of the Parliament. Francisco hung around, deep in thought for more than an hour, before he gave up and went back to Covent Garden to wash, shave, and change.

He intended to spend the evening around the clubs, hoping to run across Thorne and observe who he spoke to, overhear, if possible, what they said. Yet, somehow, he talked himself into first going to the mews behind the Doves' house and bribing the lone stable lad he found there to take a message via the kitchen to Miss Mather. Then he ambled up and down the lane, feeling rather too much like an adolescent awaiting his first assignation. It was only this morning he had kissed her in the park, and yet his mind was already far too full of her, of the feel of her soft lips beneath his, erupting into passion.

There was something about Matilda Mather, and he suspected it was as dangerous as she called him.

She slipped out of the gate into the lane with her serviceable cloak flung around her shoulders, the hood covering her hair. She glanced to the right and left before hurrying toward him. A frown of worry creased her brow.

"What is it?" she demanded before he could speak. "What is wrong?"

He drew her hand through his arm and strolled back the way he had come. "Nothing, unless you know more than I. I only wondered what came of your encounter at Grillon's."

Her frown deepened. "Not many things pass you by, do they?"

"Not when I'm paying attention. Your mother and sister are here, presumably, to renew their supplications in person?"

"That, and Marion wants a Season before she marries. I can't help thinking that is an excellent idea, for she might just meet someone she likes better than Thorne."

"She might, but fortune-hunters come in all guises."

"You are a cynic," she remarked, casting him a look of curiosity that he wasn't sure he liked.

"I have been about the world a bit. Did Thorne let fall anything significant to you or your sister?"

"Not really. Though he seemed quite excited by the return of Lord Wenning. Thorne wants his support, both in the Lords and among his foreign office contacts. And Marion wants to go the ball at Wenning House next week. He has promised to try and get her a card, though I'm not sure cadging extra invitations for country bumpkins is the best way to endear oneself to the nobility."

"Your family are country bumpkins?" he said, amused. "I find that hard to believe."

She shrugged. "Country gentry, then, without a hint of town polish."

"Is that how you see yourself?" he asked curiously.

"No, I see myself as the governess. It's how other people perceive us that is the issue. I cannot but think Thorne will hurt Marion in the end. I don't want other people doing it, too."

"So what would you have her do? Hide in the country or spread her wings?"

"Are you making fun of my own partially clipped wings, Mr. Francis?"

"Not at all. I'm wondering how many people actually *see* the governess."

"Very few," she replied tartly. "Had I not been wearing a red tulip at Maida to attract your attention, *you* would have walked past me and still would, after several meetings."

"And kisses," Francis reminded her, just to make her blush. "Don't forget the kisses. And I beg to differ. But then, despite my jaunting about the world, I am a country man at heart."

"Are you?" she asked doubtfully. Her color had risen, but curiosity seemed to have overcome embarrassment.

"Indeed. When I first encountered your enterprising young friends at Maida, I was looking forward to retiring to the country. I have leased a charming little place in Kent."

"You would retire to Kent rather than Spain?"

From habit, he smiled and drew his gaze free. "There is nothing for me in Spain."

"I heard you had land there."

"Did you, by God?"

"Isn't it true?"

"Yes, as it happens, but I have no intention of ever living there."

"Why not?"

"Bad memories. Miss Matty, should you ever wish to change professions, interrogation would suit you very nicely."

"I believe I have learned from a master."

He held both hands to his heart. "You overwhelm me." Then he covered her hand on his arm. "What else would you like to know?"

"Why I have been summoned here."

He considered, for in truth, there was no real reason for "summoning" her at all. "Two reasons. First, to ask you if Thorne has any connection to the army. Was he ever a soldier?"

"No, I don't believe so. Though according to Mama, he was

very proud of dining with the Duke of Wellington last year. And your other reason?"

"To arrange to meet here at this time every day."

At least he had the satisfaction of having surprised her, though her expression was quickly veiled. "My reputation would not survive it."

"Yes it would. The lane is quiet, and with your hood up, no one will know you."

She hesitated, her gaze on the ground at her feet. "Is it necessary?"

"No," he admitted, "probably not, but I'm hoping it will be fun."

She snatched her hand from his arm. "Then you are doomed to disappointment," she muttered and fled through the gate back into the house.

It would not have sounded encouraging to most men, but Francisco was smiling as he sauntered on to the other end of the lane and turned his feet in the direction of St. James.

⁂

AS MATTY RAN up to her bedchamber to be rid of her cloak and pat her breeze-blown hair, her heart still beat a wild tattoo. She had no idea what was happening between her and Francis—Francisco—though she suspected it was idle amusement on his part and folly on hers. And yet something glowed within her because he did not mind that she had been informally engaged to Thorne. If anything had changed, it was that he seemed to trust her more.

She paused before the glass, pressed one hand over her heart to calm it, and just for an instant, let herself smile—a quick fugitive smile that lit her eyes with sheer excitement. Her life was suddenly much more complicated, even difficult, but somehow Francisco had raised it to fun.

Perhaps she should not even believe in his flirtation except as a means to obtain her help, but she had the impression he was as taken by surprise as she. *Is it so hard to believe?* she asked her reflection with its fading smile. *If he sees me? After all, men flirted with me before.*

Before Thorne. Before she had become a governess. Her first posts had not been easy or pleasant, but she had endured them. Not the first time, she wondered what Francisco had endured, the extent of the memories that kept him from living in the country of his birth. Where he had once told her his parents had been killed. She had almost felt his pain when he mentioned it, even hidden by flippant words and veiled eyes. There was so much she wanted to know about him.

She hurried from the room, trying to thrust Francisco from her mind so that she could join the family celebration of Adrian's return.

WITH MATTY'S HINT about Wénning, Francisco made White's his first port of call, and sure enough, there in the coffee room, he glimpsed the Earl of Wenning himself, with a group of friends who included none other than the scandalous young Duke of Dearham. The latter seemed to be receiving the ribald congratulations of his friends for his recent unexpected marriage to a distant cousin few of them had met.

"The matchmaking mamas are desolate," Lord Calton assured him. "You foiled all their plans *out of season*!"

"Yes, I did, didn't I?" the duke said amiably.

"So, what have you done with the poor lady?" someone asked. "Have you left her buried in the country so that you can continue your wicked ways?"

"My dear fellow, I am utterly reformed, I assure you."

"He probably is," Calton agreed. "I've met the lady, and *I* would reform for her."

"Good God," the Earl of Wenning said lazily. "When do we meet this lady with such unique power?"

"At your lady wife's ball, of course," the duke replied. "It's the one event we can fit in, for we are en route to the continent on a delayed wedding journey. Not sure I can make it last two years like yours, Wenning."

"I was working for most of that. Besides, mine had been postponed for longer than yours. We deserved a little extra." Wenning's heavy-lidded eyes glanced up as Francisco strolled past, moved on, and then whisked back, widening.

Francisco bowed. "My lord. Gentlemen."

Not all of the earl's companions were known to him, and he didn't really want Wenning introducing him by his own name when he was always Francis in England now. Instead, since the room was quiet, he found a seat on his own, ordered a brandy, and picked up a newspaper. Over the paper, he could keep an eye on the door and watch for Thorne.

But after only a few moments, Wenning sauntered up to him, smiling, hand outstretched.

Francisco rose and took the hand. "Francis. At your service."

"Glad I didn't put my foot in it. Good to see you here. How are you?"

They had met in Constantinople when Wenning had given him unexpected aid in a nasty moment. Francisco had returned the favor when the earl and countess were traveling. There was more to Wenning than met the eye, and Francisco rather liked him. He liked his beautiful, indomitable countess, too, cheerfully traveling, as she had been with a small child in her arms and in the early stages of another pregnancy.

There had been an understanding, a closeness between the couple that did not rely on physical proximity or flowery phrases. Francisco had secretly envied them that closeness, and as he recalled it now, his mind conjured the image of Matty Mather, her fine eyes dancing while her eminently kissable mouth remained serious.

"Well," Francis replied. "As I see, are you. How is her ladyship?"

"Thriving. It is an adjustment to be home. I expect for you, too?"

"Oh, I have been back several times since I last saw you."

"Then you never did retire? From the post you do not have."

"Not quite. Tell me, Wenning, are you acquainted with Sir Anthony Thorne?"

"Yes, slightly. I hear he has become everyone's man of the moment."

"I hear he is eager to renew his acquaintance with you. Or at least make the acquaintance."

"I don't involve myself in politics, only with policy."

"If you would do me a favor, which, of course, you are not obliged to do, you could listen to him."

"I always listen. You'll come to Grace's ball?"

"Am I respectable enough?"

"My dear fellow, you are a member of White's." Wenning grinned and passed on toward the dining room in the wake of his friends.

Shortly after that, Thorne arrived in company with a fellow member of parliament and a young baron whose name Francisco couldn't recall. They were soon in company with a large group of impressively important men, including Dominic Gorse's father—the Marquess of Sedgemoor—and two senior army officers.

Francisco, having seen enough, strolled off to keep his dinner engagement with the Dunnes in Barclay Square.

⁂

"GUESS WHO I met tonight?" the Earl of Wenning said to his wife as he lay down beside her and blew out the last candle.

"Johnny Dearham, Calton, probably my brother Rollo, if White's hasn't blackballed him for debt—"

"Francisco de Salgado."

She turned into his embrace. "Really? I would have thought London a little dull for him! How is he?"

"Investigating. Did you, by chance, invite Sir Anthony Thorne to the ball?"

"Of course," she replied with a hint of self-mockery. "He is said to be the upcoming man, the rising star of the party."

"I wonder who it is who keeps saying that?"

"Himself, probably. Hope says he is entirely self-confident. He is also, according to her, engaged to marry the sister of the Doves' governess."

"I thought a man like him would look higher for a bride."

"Apparently, the sister inherited a fortune."

"Ah."

"And the governess, whom I don't believe I've ever met, seems to be quite out of the ordinary. She got Hope and Catherine out of considerable trouble at some risk to her own reputation."

Wenning sighed into her responsive ear. "I gather Hope is proving to be as much a magnet for trouble as you were."

"Thank you for the *were*."

"My pleasure," he murmured, delicately nibbling her lobe. "Thorne asked me if you would consider inviting his betrothed and her mother to your ball."

"Hope asked me to invite the governess as well."

"Will she not feel out of place?"

His wife's arms slid around him. "I have no idea. One can only ask, though I confess I am curious. Perhaps I shall call on the Doves tomorrow. Shall I invite Francisco?"

"Invite Mr. Francis."

She drew back an inch as though peering at him in the darkness. "Why is he using a different name?"

Wenning shifted, looming over her. "Do you know, I find right now that I don't care?" He closed his mouth over hers, and neither of them cared about anything but each other until the morning.

WITH ONE THING and another, Matty felt she had been neglecting the education of her charges. So, she worked them hard the following morning, sending Adrian out with Pup and then refusing to let the boy distract his sisters.

It all went swimmingly until just before midday, when Adrian stuck his head around the schoolroom door. "Lady Wenning is with Mama and Catherine, and apparently, she's asked to meet you two, as well. Miss Matty's to bring you," he added with a cheeky grin.

"Oh dear," Susan said nervously. "Is she *very* stuffy?"

"Lord, no. And she likes Pup."

"Oh well, she can't be that bad," Arabella said. "And Viola likes her."

Matty rose calmly. "Just be sure she likes you. Best behavior, please. No running and remember how to curtsey."

Adrian spread imaginary skirts, dipped his knees, and fluttered his eyelashes behind a make-believe fan, causing the girls to giggle all the way along the passage and downstairs to the drawing room. Under Matty's watchful eyes—and to the accompaniment of Pup's thumping tail as he welcomed them from his post lying on their visitor's feet—the girls sobered long enough to curtsey.

"My daughters, Arabella and Susan," Mrs. Dove said proudly. "Girls, your cousin Lady Wenning."

There was no starch to her ladyship. She rose, smiling, and offered a hand to each girl. "I can't think why we haven't met before, although I suppose it's my fault for being abroad for years! I'm very glad to meet you now. Hope and Viola have told me so much about you! And Pup, of course."

"He's taken a shine to you, my lady," Arabella said shyly.

"Call me Cousin Grace, or I shall feel old."

The girls looked awed, and her ladyship turned her smile upon Matty.

"Miss Mather," Mrs. Dove said, hastily, "the girls' governess and friend to us all. Her ladyship, the Countess of Wenning."

Matty curtseyed. "Your ladyship."

The countess offered her hand to Matty, too. "Miss Mather. I understand you have been a particular friend to my sister, too. I thank you for it."

Since Mrs. Dove was looking intrigued and Catherine alarmed, Matty had no idea how to answer. Fortunately, Lady Wenning turned and picked up her reticule from the chair she had risen from. As she straightened, Matty saw that she was pregnant, a condition hidden again almost at once by the full cut of her gown.

"I have already spoken to my cousin," Lady Wenning said, extracting a card and holding it out to Matty. "She is happy to spare you from your duties, especially since you may come with her or with your own family."

Matty took the card and blinked at it. Her name was written on it in a flowing hand, inviting her to a ball at Wenning House.

"Oh no, my lady, it would be most unsuitable," she blurted, then collected herself enough to add, "Though I thank you deeply for thinking of me. I shall remember your kindness."

"Well, you must decide," Lady Wenning said lightly, "though I hope you will come. Cousin Jane, I must be off. But I hope you will call soon. Bring all the children—even Pup!—and they can meet their new cousin. We're off to the country soon after the ball and are likely to stay there for some months." She beamed. "What a delight to meet you all! Goodbye for the present!"

The family all trooped out to see her off, Adrian hanging on to Pup's collar. When Mrs. Dove returned, Matty was still standing where they had left her, the countess's card still held in her nerveless fingers.

"Will you go?" her employer asked.

"Of course, I cannot," Matty said, forcing a smile. "Though I appreciate her kindness in asking."

"Then return it by accepting," Mrs. Dove advised. "Your mother and sister are invited, too. And we all have cause to know you are a lady."

Matty let out a breath. "It is a life I have left behind and do not miss." She smiled faintly. "Indeed, such a party would always have been above my touch, ma'am. Now, where did those girls vanish to?"

Although she had no intention of attending the countess's ball, as the day went on, she found herself thinking several times about the invitation. Was Lady Wenning truly so grateful for her help in retrieving the ring for Hope? It was interesting that Hope had even told her when she would not tell her brother, who owned the ring. Or did the invitation stem from more general gratitude because Matty kept an eye on the adventurous debutantes, both Hope and Catherine?

But there were surely simpler ways to show such gratitude. Had her mother somehow got to the countess and asked her to invite Matty, too?

No, her mother would never overstep in such a way.

But Thorne would.

CHAPTER FOURTEEN

IT WAS ALMOST the first thing she told Francisco late that afternoon when he had pulled her into an unused carriage house in the mews.

Jerked almost off her feet against his hard chest, she said crossly, "You'd be well-served if I screamed or boxed your ears. Lady Wenning has invited me to her ball, and I think Thorne is behind it."

Francisco didn't even blink. "You think he wants to renew his advances?"

"Of course not. I think he wants to make my position with Mrs. Dove untenable. Either she will be annoyed by the governess getting above herself and dismiss me, or I will be so overwhelmed by the joys of polite society that I will resign my post at once and cling to Marion."

"And yet," Francisco said thoughtfully, "one would have thought he had bigger fish to fry than a stubborn almost sister-in-law."

As though distracted, he had not released her. He still held her by one wrist, his other hand at her back, almost in waltz position, although much closer than was proper. Yet the casual nature of his hold made her hesitate to escape. She didn't want to make a fuss about it, betray her own increasing awareness when he didn't seem to notice she was basically in his arms. He wasn't even looking at her but gazing over her head.

"I suspect my mother's arrival imbued his plan with some urgency," she said as calmly as she could. "What are his bigger fish?"

"I'm not sure," he said. "But he is gathering about himself a large variety of powerful men, of his own party and the opposition. And then there are the generals and militia commanders. And everyone thinks very highly of him."

Idly, his thumb brushed back and forth across her wrist, causing secret little thrills to spread across her skin. His gaze came slowly down to hers.

"Still looking for my lies and betrayal, Mr. Francis?" she said, rather proud of her steady voice.

A warm, if rueful smile touched his eyes. "No. Truth be known, I'm looking for clues that you like this closeness as much as I."

"I can't imagine why you would suspect such a thing."

"You are still here," he pointed out, lifting her hand and placing it on his shoulder.

And now, somehow, it was impossible to retreat. "Only because I am supremely indifferent to—"

"Liar," he said softly. His hand swept down her back, drawing her against the full length of his body.

His heat spread through her like wildfire. She wanted to run. She wanted to lay her head on his shoulder and just…*feel*. Instead, with some vague idea of bringing one of them to their senses, she thrust her hand over his shoulder and clutched the soft, waving hair at the back of his neck. The word, "Enough!" hovered on her lips, to be commanded in her best governess voice of disapproval.

But an audible sigh of pleasure escaped his lips. His head eased back into her touch with such obvious pleasure that her scold died along with her resistance, drowned in a sudden flood of wonder and desire. She moved her fingers through his hair, caressing his nape, and his hand crept sensuously up her back to cup the back of her head, her cheek.

"Your touch is sweet," he whispered. "So very sweet."

She had never seen such heat in anyone's eyes. It melted her bones, even before she became aware of the hard ridge growing against her abdomen. How could she feel so weak and yet so excited at the same time? She could not even halt the exploration of her fingers in his hair, stroking his nape, dipping beneath his cravat.

His hungry gaze dropped to her lips. Butterflies plunged through her stomach, and her hand at his neck tugged his head lower. A smile flickered on his lips before they found hers and sealed.

Gasping into his mouth, she flung her other arm around his back and clutched his coat as though to stop herself from falling. She gloried in the plunder of his lips and then his tongue. After the first delicious shock, she even returned the kiss. Unable to be still, she gave a tiny wriggle against him, loving the sensation of his hard chest against her breasts. He moved, too, then, sliding a knee between her legs while the amazing kiss deepened yet further.

She was lost in him, in the intensity of her arousal and the pleasure of his kiss, of his entire, caressing body.

His hands cupped her face, slowly loosening the kiss. "Matilda Mather," he whispered against her lips, "you will destroy me."

His words made no sense, but at least they brought back reality with an unpleasant little jolt. She drew back a bare inch—it was all she could manage. "What an odd thing to say when it is I who would suffer most if we were seen."

Her voice sounded odd, a little husky, and not quite steady.

He rested his forehead against hers. "We are not seen."

"But I will be missed," she said, still making no effort to remove herself.

Slowly, very slowly, his arms fell away, and he stepped back. She felt curiously forlorn.

"Perhaps it is as well," he said lightly, "before I forget myself further."

And that is to be it? A confused weight of half-formed thoughts seemed to land on her, crushing her. A feeling that there was so much more to be said, by her and by him, a sudden fear that she was reading too much into a situation that meant nothing. That he had to be merely persuading her, though to what she had no idea, using her because she was simply not the sort of woman men fell in love with. Certainly not men like *him*.

But that had been such a stunning, powerful kiss… *To me.*

There seemed to be nothing to do but turn and walk out. She could not look at him because she had given so much of herself, *too* much of herself away.

With an attempt at briskness, she nodded and spun away, but she had only taken two steps before he spoke.

"Matty?"

She paused.

"I think you should accept Lady Wenning's invitation."

She frowned as she glanced back over her shoulder. "To keep watch on Thorne?"

His lips quirked. "To dance with me."

For no good reason, a breath of laughter escaped her, and she strode out of the carriage house with a suddenly light heart.

It was not just her heart. Over the next few days, her whole being felt light and tingly and sweetly excited. And yet, she had to acknowledge that she should not allow herself to be carried away. It seemed, almost in spite of herself, that she trusted Francisco de Salgado. But she did not know him.

The day after their encounter in the carriage house was Good Friday, so Mrs. Dove granted the children freedom from lessons and gave Matty leave to visit her family if she wished. Meanwhile, all the Doves, including Pup, went to spend the day with Viola.

Matty gave in to the inevitable and walked round to Grillon's

Hotel, where she was pounced on with great glee by her mother and sister.

"We've received an invitation to Lady Wenning's ball!" Mama said triumphantly.

"Thanks to Sir Anthony," Marion reminded her. "And Matty, you are included! There is definitely an s on the end of Mather." She grabbed a card from the mantelpiece and thrust it under Matty's nose. "See? Mrs. Mather and Misses Mather*s*."

Matty did not say she had already received her own invitation. She had not yet decided what to do about it, her flat refusal weakened, stupidly, by Francisco's last words to her: *"To dance with me."*

"Even if it is not a slip of the pen," Matty said, "I still could not go. I have nothing remotely suitable to wear. If I embellish my evening gown at all, it will fall to pieces."

"You must have a new ballgown, of course," Marion said. "There is a most generous quarterly allowance from my inheritance, more than enough for our purposes."

"Marion, it will be a waste of your money," Matty said flatly. "Even if I went to this ball, there will be no others."

"There will be once I am Lady Thorne."

"But I will still be Miss Mather, the governess."

Mama scowled, and Marion flounced onto the sofa. "Honestly, Matty, why are you so wretchedly stubborn? You cannot *like* being a governess!"

"Actually, I do like it," Matty said. "Though it's true, I haven't always. Marion, you have chosen your future life, though you know I don't approve of your choice. I must choose mine also, despite *your* disapproval. Please, now, can that be the end of it?"

"No," Mama said, "because yours makes no sense, and *I* do not agree."

"Well, if we are going to quarrel, I would be better returning to the Doves and preparing my lessons for next week."

For a moment, they both regarded her with some consternation, knowing she meant every word, though not understanding why.

"Don't be petulant," Mama said without heat. "Have a cup of tea, and then we shall go shopping. You might see a gown you like, and even if you do come to the Wennings' ball, it does not commit you to others."

This was, Matty reflected as she accepted a cup of tea from her mother, the same tactic she and Mrs. Dove had used on Sir Anthony Thorne by invoking her required month's notice.

SHE RETURNED TO the Doves' residence in plenty of time to meet Francisco in the mews. As she threw her old cloak around her and hurried across the small back garden to the gate, she wondered how he would react when she told him she seemed to have agreed to the ball. Would his eyes light up in the way that made her heart skitter? Would he think she was going merely because he had persuaded her? This was loweringly close to the truth, though she would never admit it.

In fact, she would be in control of this encounter. There would be no skulking in carriage houses, no improper closeness, let alone kisses. She could not think when he kissed her, when her whole body was on fire with barely understood desires. So they would walk sedately in the mews and *talk*. About Thorne and Francisco's investigation and what could be achieved at the ball, of course, although she was very conscious of the longing to discuss personal things, too, to discover his life, his loves and hates, and everything that made him Francisco.

Her heart drumming with uncomfortable and yet pleasurable anticipation, she closed the gate behind her and walked up the mews lane. She walked to the end of the lane without seeing another soul, then turned and walked back the way she had come.

Someone was lounging near one of the occupied stables—a

youth in a cap and the clothes of a stable lad. At first, she thought it was Francisco in yet another disguise, and laughter bubbled up in delight. But no, even Francisco could not shrink by several inches or take as much as ten years off his appearance. This was definitely a boy, though he straightened from the fence and removed his cap as he approached.

"Miss M?" he asked cheerfully.

"Why?"

The boy blinked. "Mr. Francis asked me to pass on a message. Here you go." He slapped a folded scrap of paper into her surprised hand, grinned, and shambled off down the lane, hands in pockets.

Matty closed her mouth on an inevitable sigh of disappointment, although the note seemed to burn her palm. Perhaps it proposed another assignation…

Surreptitiously, she glanced up and down the lane to make sure no one had observed, then hid the note beneath her cloak and returned to the house. She thought she might scream if the children had come home in the interim and were desperate to talk to her. But all was still quiet, and she made it to her chamber without being waylaid by anyone.

Closing the door, she shrugged off her cloak and threw herself onto the bed, unfolding the note.

Sorry. Called away for a few days. Save a waltz for me. F.

She blinked it at, unreasonably furious. How dare he…?

How dare he what? Do the work he is obliged to? Disappoint someone who has no claim on him?

Or assume she would go to the ball just because he had suggested it? Which, she realized with a scowl, she would.

FRANCISCO HAD SPENT a great deal of his life traveling. In comparison with many journeys over difficult terrain, in wartime, or through lawless country—or all three—a private post-chaise to

Manchester was not a great undertaking.

A few words of intelligence from his instructor had sent him north, his emotions almost resentful as he contemplated his missed moments with Matty Mather. And yet the journey passed without much recourse to his book. The realization that he missed her was a novelty. He hoped she missed him, and not just because it would make her easier to manipulate. In fact, he felt vaguely ashamed of his previous passages with women where this had been his prime motivation.

Emma Carntree, oddly, had been the last to affect him so, which was one reason he had been so unforgivably distracted at Maida the night he had stolen the wrong ring. He allowed himself to recall all of Emma's considerable charms and found himself utterly unmoved. He began to understand that she had not inspired his desire to retire from his frequently unsavory work. It had really been the other way around. He had come upon her just when his need for a different kind of life had begun to nag at him. And he had wondered.

He supposed that growing need had been Ludovic Dunne's fault. His old friend was the only other person he knew so dedicated to justice. They had been like sole crusaders on their separate paths, beacons of light in the murky depths of society. Ludovic had largely pursued the law at home for his own and others' justice. Francisco's chosen path had frequently taken him outside the law, both here and abroad, for the higher purpose of *right*. Or so he had always assured himself. But right and his chosen country were not always the same thing. And that had begun to bother him, even before Ludovic had entangled himself in the affairs of Rebecca Cornish and her son and ended by marrying the woman.

Francisco liked Rebecca. She was brave and loyal and fun. He was glad that Ludo had found happiness and a sense of peace with a wife who understood and loved him. She welcomed Francisco to their home and tolerated the all-night drinking sessions that set the world to right whenever he appeared.

And yet, he had more than once thought of avoiding them altogether. For Ludo's contentment emphasized what was missing in his own life. Something he could never have. Ludo had always needed a Rebecca, he saw now. Francisco had chosen a lonelier path where some faithless, shallow Emma was all he truly deserved, for he had done terrible things for his country, things no decent woman, let alone a gentle lady, should know about, never mind tolerate.

Certainly not Matty Mather.

He should never have touched her, not after that first encounter at Maida. But she drew him. Even in her dull clothes, with her basilisk stare that could turn so sweetly to one of confused passion. She was not indifferent to him. She could love him.

Only she couldn't. She could love what he showed her of himself—if he were lucky. *But if she knew…* The face beneath the waves that disturbed his dreams too often rose into his mind, along with other victims, with his own family.

No, he could not be honest with her and keep her. Nor could he be dishonest and pretend he was something he was not. Not to her.

What he should do was leave her alone. He didn't need her in order to pursue the truth about Thorne, whatever excuses he had been making to himself. Yet the thought of hurting her, of abusing her already bruised confidence, made his stomach roil. He had flirted his way into a situation he could do nothing to right.

And yet his dreams, as he bounced and shuddered along the Great North Road from posting inn to posting inn, were of her, dressed in bright colors, welcoming him home in the sunshine. Of peaceful evenings together before a pleasant fire, children playing in the garden and up and down the stairs. Noise and laughter and peace.

And Matty, lying naked among a froth of pillows, her arms reaching for him in urgent passion.

That, God help him, was the life he wanted. He hoped to God she didn't want it, too, or they would both be doomed to suffering.

⁂

THE EVENING OF his arrival in the city of Manchester found him in a tavern favored by working men and a few of the middling sort. He stood by the counter for a while, gazing around the patrons and listening to the surrounding conversations.

There were a lot of grumbles over food prices, bosses, family members who couldn't find work, mixed in with the usual taproom conversations about sport, family, women. But he heard very little of a political nature, which was not promising considering the information he had been given.

At last, ordering another pint of ale from the tavernkeeper's wife, he said to her, "When she heard I was coming here, my sister-in-law said to look out for her cousin in this tavern. You don't happen to know Bert Brown, do you?"

"And if I do?"

"Is he here this evening?" Francisco asked patiently.

Unsmiling, she searched his face, looked him up and down, and met his gaze with open ferocity. "You cause him any grief, you'll be run out of here so fast you won't walk for a week. And I don't care if you own a dozen mills or work for the magistrate."

Francisco smiled. "Neither. I gather you like him."

"I do," she said fiercely. "We all do, so remember it. He's a good man."

"So I have heard, and he has nothing to fear from me."

"He'd better not," she grumbled. "Table by the window. By himself."

A young, respectably dressed working man sat by the window, writing busily in the poor light. Francisco had noticed him before because he looked too serious and busy for a tavern on a

Saturday night. Occasionally people greeted him or clapped him on the shoulder, making him look up and smile before returning to his writing. An educated man, then.

Francisco picked up his ale and strolled across the floor to the window. "May I sit here?" he inquired.

Brown glanced up and waved amiably enough at the vacant stool.

Francisco sat, took a pull of the ale, and said, "Mr. Brown, I believe,"

"That's me." He didn't look up this time.

"Pardon my curiosity, but what on earth can you be writing so busily?"

"Letters. You sound like a man who can write for himself."

"You're writing letters for other people?" Francisco asked, intrigued, for he did not seem to be copying from anything. "How do you know what to say?"

"They tell me at the beginning of the evening and take their letters away at the end."

"Don't you ever get mixed up?"

"No." He didn't stop writing, even for a moment.

"You are a man of many talents," Francisco marveled. "And I admire your dedication, but I'm afraid I need a moment of your time."

"For what?" The pen dipped in the ink bottle and scratched across the page.

"You organized political meetings, specifically timed ones. You began the organization of a protest march and then stepped aside."

The pen hovered in the first sign of uncertainty Francisco had seen, then signed a name. He sanded the letter, then folded it before glancing up at Francisco. "I did. There was nothing illegal in any of it."

"So why did you give up?"

Brown inscribed a direction on the folded paper and added it to a small pile at his elbow. He pulled another sheet of paper in front of him. "Who are you? And why do you want to know?"

"My name is Francis. I am…investigating a spate of carefully timed and coordinated meetings that have taken place all over the country. Yours included. But so far as I know, you are the only organizer to step aside. I'd like to know why you did that."

Brown sat back, for the first time giving him his full, formidable attention. "Why? You want information, so you can be ready to kill and imprison people who only want a fair shot at life for their families?"

Something in his tone caught Francisco unaware. "That is why you stepped down. You feared for them. Why?"

The man continued to meet his gaze in silence.

Francisco leaned forward. "Brown, I don't want these people to die. I don't want anyone to die. If coordinated marches would win a little more justice in the world, I'd cheer you on. But it won't, will it? You worked that out. How? What's going on?"

Brown took a deep breath. "I don't know. But something is wrong. I never liked being *told* when to hold meetings, let alone when to march. Marching together is a strong idea, but it depends so much on who is behind it and why."

"Do you know who is behind it?" Francisco almost had to sit on his hands to prevent him from seizing Brown by the shoulders.

"I can guess."

"How?"

Brown twirled the pen in its stand between strong, capable fingers. "At one meeting, I saw a man who was out of place. A gentleman. Not even a wealthy mill owner like the ten-a-penny rich men you get around here. A *real* gentleman." Brown regarded him. "A bit like you."

"I doubt it, though I thank you for the compliment. I think. What was this gentleman doing at your meeting? I know a few gentlemen of radical inclinations myself."

"He wasn't. He listened and looked pleased amidst his minders, and then he left again. There was no trouble. No one was followed, arrested, or threatened. I never saw him again, but I had this feeling it was he who was pulling the strings, all over Manchester and beyond. What I don't know is why."

"How do you know," Francisco asked slowly, "that he wasn't a radical, as devoted to your cause as you?"

"Because I recognized him from a sketch in a newspaper. He's a reactionary to the core."

Francisco's heart beat harder. "And his name?"

Brown held his gaze without flinching. He looked almost—defiant. As though he fully expected not to be believed. "Thorne. Sir Anthony Thorne."

CHAPTER FIFTEEN

"I SHALL BE the envy of every gentleman," Sir Anthony said, smiling when he called at Grillon's to escort the Mather ladies to Wenning House. "Not one, but three such beautiful ladies on my arms!"

"Three might prove a trifle undignified," Matty murmured. "I shall walk behind as befits the governess."

"Why do you always sound as if being the governess actually makes you superior?" Marion demanded. Nerves made her short-tempered.

Sir Antony handed each of the ladies into his carriage, and Matty realized there was no turning back. She *was* going to the ball. Until this afternoon, she had half-hoped the gown ordered before Easter would not be ready in time, but when she had arrived at Grillon's—Mrs. Dove having almost pushed her out the door—she had found not only the ball gown but a pretty new evening gown she had idly admired on the same shopping expedition.

"Marion," she had said shakily, "you are killing me with kindness." Wearing her down to accept the inevitable. When Matty had not even given up hope that her sister would never marry Thorne.

"It's the least we can do," Marion had said. "For years, we could not have survived without your salary, little as it was. Now, things are different." She had glanced at the door to be sure her mother was not in hearing distance and lowered her voice. "You do not truly mind, do you, Matty, that I am marrying Anthony?"

The anxiety in her voice had been genuine, and Matty had sat on the bed, choosing her words carefully. "I am not jealous if that's what you mean. And I shall certainly not hold it against you."

Relief had relaxed the set of Marion's shoulders as she sat beside Matty and took her hands.

Matty had gazed at their interlinked fingers and then looked up into Marion's eyes. "Sir Anthony let me down, Marion. I do not want him to do the same to you."

"He won't," Marion had said brightly, jumping to her feet once more. "We are all older and wiser."

And certainly, this evening, Thorne appeared to be every inch the doting husband-to-be, solicitous and charming as he helped them down from the coach and into the splendid house, leaving them at the cloakroom to change outdoor shoes for dancing slippers, and then conducting them through throngs of other milling guests to the ballroom, where more heaving crowds of silken, perfumed, and bejeweled people awaited them.

Lord and Lady Wenning, one of the most beautiful couples Matty had ever seen, welcomed them just inside the door with gracious goodwill and bade them enjoy the evening.

Was Francisco here? Impossible to tell with so many guests thronging one of the biggest grand balls of the Season. Sir Anthony, however, seemed to know just about everyone they passed and paused to introduce them. Eventually, he managed to find a chair for Mama among the dowagers, even introduced her to the lady next to her. And then the orchestra struck up the opening waltz, and everyone swept back to leave the dance floor clear. Lady Wenning was led out onto the floor by a very handsome, fair young man.

"The Duke of Dearham," Sir Anthony murmured to Marion. "And Wenning is dancing with the new duchess. Marion, will you honor me with the waltz?"

Marion was delighted to. Matty watched the floor fill, was happy to catch a glimpse of Catherine dancing with Mr. Holles and Hope Darblay with another young man she did not recognize. She could not see Francisco among the dancers, so began to peer about the crowd. Mrs. Dove waved to her from several yards away. Viola broke through a sea of people to greet her and be introduced to Mama.

"Viola, allow me to introduce my mother, Mrs. Mather. Mama, this is Lady Dominic Gorse."

Viola smiled warmly and offered her hand. "Delighted to make your acquaintance at last, Mrs. Mather. Your daughter has been a wonderful friend to me."

Mama blinked in surprise. "You are very gracious, my lady."

Matty was pleased. She had never seen Viola in society before, but she knew she had struggled in the days before her marriage. Confidence—won primarily with the love of her husband—had made her gracious, friendly, and easy to talk to. As if she had finally let her true nature shine.

Matty was still thinking about that when the waltz ended, and Viola moved away. Marion and Sir Anthony returned, the former looking charmingly rosy from their dance.

"Matilda, may I have the pleasure?"

Matty blinked at Thorne's hand held out to her. She was no debutante, expected and even obliged to dance. If she said no now, she could not be so rude as to accept other offers—if there were any. If Francisco was even here.

Sir Anthony smiled, almost like the boy he had once been. "Please."

"Thank you." She took his hand and walked with him onto the floor to join a set for the country dance.

It was so long since she had danced that she feared she would forget the steps and embarrass herself and everyone else. But in moments, it seemed dancing was as simple as walking, and the steps and figures came back to her without thought. And Thorne was a pleasant partner. He may have been a slightly stiff dancer, but he was dignified, looked as if he was enjoying himself, and made conversation.

It was all very friendly, reminding Matty of how long she had known him and how unlikely any of Francisco's suspicions were to be true. Not that he had revealed exactly what these suspicions were, but she could not but doubt them.

When the dance had ended with his bow and her curtsey, she took his arm and said quietly, "Tell me the truth, Sir Anthony. Why are you so eager for me to leave my post and live with Marion and you?"

He looked down at her, and she could almost see him composing a gallant and respectful reply that would tell her nothing. And then his lips closed again and curved in a rueful smile. "Why, guilt, Matilda. I behaved ill toward you and would make what recompense I can."

He could not have said anything to surprise her more. "You have nothing to feel guilty about. You were quite right that we should not have suited."

It was his turn to betray surprise, and she suspected he was not quite pleased by her response.

"Evening, Thorne," drawled a male voice. "Is this your beautiful betrothed that you have boasted of? You must introduce us."

The man confronting them was tall and handsome and vaguely dissolute in appearance. The archetypal jaded aristocrat. Sir Anthony, it seemed, had a wide variety of friends, and he did not look at all displeased to be interrupted by this one.

"Alas, not my betrothed, but my betrothed's sister. Matilda, allow me to present his lordship, the Earl of Calton. Calton, Miss Matilda Mather."

Since Lord Calton held out his hand in clear expectation, Matty gave him hers and, when he bowed over it, found his smile unexpectedly engaging. A charmer looking for fresh prey.

"Enchanted," he murmured, managing to look as if he actually was. "I do trust you are free to bestow the coming waltz upon my unworthy self?"

"I am free to do so," Matty replied. "I haven't yet decided if I should."

The earl's eyes danced.

Sir Anthony laughed. "Oh, he is perfectly safe, Matilda, at least in the ballroom."

"Then I would be churlish to refuse."

"Perhaps a glass of wine or lemonade while we wait?" Calton offered, drawing her hand through his arm.

"Thank you," Matty murmured and was expertly escorted through the throng to be presented with a glass of sparkling champagne.

"So how come we have not before, Miss Mather? Are you new to London?"

"No, but I do not go out much in society." She sipped her champagne. *I am only a governess.* What would he say if she spoke those words aloud? Laugh, she rather suspected, but he would still dance with her. He would never be so rude as to withdraw his invitation, though he might abandon her rather sharply afterward.

"Why not?" he asked, his glass already half-empty. "Ah, too late. It's waltz time. Johnny, guard those with your life. We shall return."

The command was issued to no less a person than His Grace of Dearham, who only acknowledged it with an amused glance and a quirk of the lips as he continued his own conversation. Matty had no time to observe more as she was led onto the dance floor and swept into the arms of the earl.

"You are a bluestocking," he guessed. "Your heart given to scholarly pursuits, except for one ball a year. I fully expect you to abandon a glass slipper as you flee at midnight."

"What nonsense you talk." She was smiling as, over his shoulder, she finally beheld Francisco, and her heart skipped a beat.

He looked so handsome, so peculiarly steadfast and alone by

the tall French windows, his evening dress emphasizing the raven hair and sun-bronzed skin. Her heart flooded with emotion, with sheer happiness because he was here.

Calton said softly. "It is a lucky man who inspires that expression in your eyes."

Dragged back to her partner, she said carelessly, "I don't know what you mean."

He turned her in the dance, perhaps to see who had caught her attention, but as she spun, Matty saw a woman appear at Francisco's side, claiming his attention. Emma Carntree.

Pointless, silly jealousy. She kept her gaze on Calton's face and smiled. "I expect you have a reputation as a flirt to keep up," she said kindly.

Calton blinked. For an instant, he looked as if he didn't know whether to be insulted or alarmed, and then he laughed. "Miss Mather, I like you! But please don't annihilate my reputation to anyone else."

"Is it your means of hiding from matchmaking mamas and predatory debutantes?"

"Something like that," he admitted. "But what of you, ma'am? Why are you not already married?"

She could no longer see Francisco or Lady Carntree. "A lack of inclination. On my part and anyone else's."

"I'm not sure I believe that."

"I'm sure you would agree, my lord, that there is more to life than marriage."

His smile appeared once more. Dispassionately, she thought it must slay many a heart, though there was an element of honesty about it that she rather liked.

"I would," he said, "but it is an unusual opinion in a young lady. You are brought up to consider nothing else."

"I am no longer young."

"Shall I fetch your walking stick?"

She smiled and caught sight of Francisco, propping up one of the pillars, in amiable conversation with Archie Holles. It was a relief to see Lady Carntree nowhere nearby.

When the waltz ended, Lord Calton showed no immediate desire to abandon his eccentric and somewhat distracted partner, as she had more than half expected. Instead, he placed her hand on his arm and said, "Now, let us see if Dearham has kept his word and guarded our champagne from rampaging footman."

"You are very sure of yourself, commanding dukes to undertake your trivial business."

"Oh, Dearham and I are old and disrespectful friends. Are you acquainted with him?"

"I am not."

"He is the world's most approachable duke and probably the most amusing." He leaned closer. "And I learned all I know about flirting from observing him."

She cast him a look of mock disparagement. "I'm not sure I believe that."

By then, they had returned to the table where their glasses still stood in exactly the same place. The Duke of Dearham still lounged there, although the crowd around him had changed. By his side was a lovely young lady who smiled at Calton with genuine friendliness.

"Kitty, my heart, you look ravishing," he said, his free hand on his heart. "Allow me to present to you, Miss Matilda Mather. Ma'am, Her Grace, the Duchess of Dearham."

The young lady smiled and offered her hand when Matty curtseyed. It was a naturally friendly gesture and yet Matty was sure she glimpsed a hint of uncertainty behind the eyes. It reminded her a little of Viola on her best behavior two years ago, before Lord Dominic.

"Are you acquainted with my husband?" the duchess asked, reaching for the duke's arm. Rather to Matty's surprise, the duke turned immediately to his wife, and so Matty was introduced to him, also.

Goodness, and I'm only the governess…

"Miss Mather," said Hope Darblay's voice beside her. "A

pleasure to see you here."

Matty smiled and moved to make space for her. "And you, of course."

"Good evening, Hope," the duke said cheerfully. "Allow me to present you to my wife. Miss Darblay is Rollo's sister. Is the reprobate your escort this evening?"

"Yes, he is around somewhere, probably in the card room."

"Your Grace promised me the next dance," Calton reminded the duchess, who immediately turned her smile from Hope to him and took his arm.

Hope's expression was so subtle and so swiftly gone that Matty almost missed it. The reason for her unexpected arrival on the scene strolled away with the duchess without even noticing her. Unrequited love was painful.

But Hope's smile was back in place, and one of the young men on the fringes of the group asked Hope to dance, after which the duke, much to Matty's amazement, offered her his hand.

As she danced, she wondered what on earth her family would make of her dancing with the dashing duke, whom she discovered to be an entertaining partner. Less flirtatious than Calton, he had open, likable manners and a sense of never taking himself too seriously. He was also witty and made her laugh, and after one such incident, she was delighted to see Francisco watching her from the card room door, although his gaze shifted almost immediately.

When will he *ask me to dance?*

FRANCISCO, HAVING RETURNED to London only that morning, dog-tired, was not at his best. He had arrived late to the Wennings' ball and saw Matty immediately.

He observed her in glimpses, glorious colorful glimpses between the other dancers, waltzing in the arms of the libertine Earl of Calton. Something in his chest tightened, for though he rather liked his lordship, Matty was not the sophisticated woman Calton no doubt imagined. He was certainly very focused on her, and she, damn her, was laughing up at him with all the force of a sunburst after rain.

Her hair had been styled in a softer, looser manner than normal, with some sparkling jewel highlighting the gorgeous auburn glints. The curve of her graceful neck and shoulder made him want to growl, while the deep blue of her shimmering gown complemented her figure, and her sheer beauty, to perfection. He had been right all along, and now he was not the only one to see it.

For an instant, her eyes widened as she caught sight of him, and then Calton had her attention once more. He had no name for the emotions pulling at him.

"I knew you couldn't stay away," drawled a feminine voice beside him.

"Emma," he said indifferently. "Apparently, neither could you."

"The whole world has come to see if our host and hostess are still on speaking terms. Disappointingly, they seem perfectly cordial."

"No scandal to entertain you, then?"

"I wouldn't say that. Thorne is making a perfect fool of himself, trotting after his betrothed like a devoted puppy. Where will his ambitions be when everyone is laughing at him?"

Francisco looked at her at last. "Where indeed. What ambitions are these?"

Emma grimaced and took his arm, urging her to walk with him around the perimeter of the dance floor. "Political ones, of course. And the money to carry them out. I don't suppose you'd like to wean the girl off him?"

He raised one amused eyebrow. "You want *me* to marry her?"

Emma laughed. "You could do worse, financially speaking, though I see you have set your sights on a different lady. Who is she?"

"Who?"

"The woman dancing with Calton?"

"I have no idea. Calton owes me a monkey."

"I believe he's good for it. Champagne?"

Obligingly, Francisco swiped a couple of glasses from a passing footman and gave one to her.

Her fingers brushed his. The expression in her eyes as she delicately placed her lips over the rim of her glass was all but indecent. "When are you coming to see me, Francis?"

"I'm seeing you now."

"You know exactly what I mean."

"Am I to play hide and seek with Thorne for your favors?"

"Thorne is beginning to bore me. Besides, he is otherwise engaged."

Francisco raised his glass to her. "So am I, Emma. So am I." With a slight bow, he stepped back and walked away.

His quarry now, at least until the next waltz, was young Archibald Holles of the radical tendencies.

He found the boy skulking against a pillar, watching Catherine Dove dance with a young man he didn't know.

"Holles," Francisco murmured.

Being well brought up, Holles straightened at once and bowed. "Sir."

"You and Miss Dove have become friends," Francis observed, shamelessly stealing Holles's place against the pilar but facing the other way so he could not see Matty dancing with a nobleman far better suited to be her husband than he.

Husband? Where the devil had that come from?

"Indeed," Holles said frostily.

"Don't freeze me out. I haven't come to scold or applaud you. Actually, I want to pick your brains about something else entirely."

"You do?" Holles looked both alarmed and impressed.

"I thought I saw you at a political meeting last week. Near the docks."

"I often attend such gatherings."

"I know, which is why I've come to you. There were several meetings that same night."

"Were there?"

"Yes, and I think you know that. You are an educated man, more than a cut above most of the people who attend these gatherings. Have you ever been asked to organize such meetings?"

Holles frowned, looking suddenly wary. "Why do you ask?"

Francisco lowered his voice, though there was no one near enough to hear. "Because I am worried."

Holles's lip curled. "For the established rich and powerful?"

"No, for the protesters," Francisco said bluntly. "If you know who is trying to coordinate this march next week, I wish you would tell me."

"So you can have them arrested?"

"If necessary," Francisco admitted. "No, don't flounce off, Holles, this is serious, and you could prevent a catastrophe."

Something of his tone must have penetrated the boy's pride, for he paused before he had quite flounced. "What do you mean?"

"Do you see here, in this room, the person organizing these protests? The man who asked you to lead one?"

Holles stared at him. "Of course not." He shuffled slightly, then admitted reluctantly, "I've never met any leaders beyond the speakers at each meeting. I don't know where or who the timings come from. But at the last one, I had a note shoved into my hand, and I met with one of the speakers, who asked me if I could easily raise a band of students and well-born youth for the march. Sir, what is this about? What is it to you?"

Francisco made a decision. Too much of this situation was already arranged in darkness. "I'm afraid," he said, "that you're being set up for slaughter. Not by ignorant-but-well-meaning enthusiasts for change, but by someone ruthlessly seeking personal power that will benefit no one else."

CHAPTER SIXTEEN

WHEN HER DANCE with His Grace of Dearham had ended, Matty felt she should at least try to rediscover her mother or Marion. She would rather have hunted down Francisco, but pride forbade it. Instead, she was making for her mother's position with the dowagers, where she also glimpsed Marion with a distinguished-looking escort, when a gentleman stood up almost in front of her.

He looked vaguely familiar—darkly and rather dramatically handsome—so she nodded in return to his amiable smile and, since he didn't move out of her way, prepared to go around him.

"We must have met since I know who you are, Miss Mather," he said. "Rollo Darblay."

She paused guiltily. "Of course! I'm so sorry, there's such a sea of faces tonight—"

"No need to apologize," said Hope Darblay's brother amiably. "Allow me to walk with you a few moments."

"Certainly," Matty replied. Darblay had a certain reputation, but since she had already danced with famed rakes Dearham and Calton, she saw Darblay as no greater threat.

"I owe you considerable thanks," Darblay said quietly. He gestured with his hand, drawing her attention to a familiar opal ring. "You don't need to say anything. I know you won't land Hope in the soup."

She glanced up at him warily, and he held her gaze. "She told you."

"Eventually. I just wish she had done so at the time! You understand my gratitude is not for the ring but for what you risked to help my sister and keep her safe."

Matty flushed uncomfortably. Darblay was clearly determined to say the words, though they were sincere for all that.

"I've said this to Hope and Catherine, and I'll say it to you, too. If she gets into any more scrapes, please come to me? I've been getting out of my own for years, so I have plenty of practice. And I've a lot less to lose."

"I don't anticipate further troubles of that nature," Matty said. "I believe they both got a fright."

Darblay looked grim for an instant, obviously possessing a clearer picture than Matty of the dangers stalking naive young girls at Maida Gardens, particularly with one of them in not terribly convincing male garb. Then he shrugged. "There was no harm done, thanks to you. I ask only that you don't take such risks again. I'm not an ogre, and I've no idea why my sister thought me one."

"I think it was more understanding of what they had done than fear of you that kept her silent. How is your father, sir? Hope tells me he is under the weather."

"Not too clever, but I daresay he'll bounce back. Evening, Francis."

And just like that, the moment was upon her.

He had come up on her other side, as though from nowhere, his mere presence flooding her with awareness, so that the words of sympathy she had meant to say to Darblay dried in her throat.

"Good evening," Francisco said. He had come to a halt, and somehow, Matty and Darblay did, too. "Sorry, Darblay, I've come to steal your companion for the supper waltz."

"Don't you think you might be too late?" Darblay challenged.

"No, it's a long-standing arrangement."

"And yet the lady says nothing."

They both looked at her, and for a moment, she almost bolted. If she had been sure her legs would obey her, she would have.

"The lady," she managed, "could not get a word in. Though I don't recall any mention of supper, I believe I did promise a waltz to Mr. Francis."

"Then I must bow out gracefully," Darblay said, inclining his head. "And Miss Mather?"

With her hand already being drawn through Francisco's arm, she glanced back at Darblay.

He smiled. "My thanks again."

"If only he knew," Matty murmured as she walked a little shakily at Francisco's side, "that it was you I had to save his sister from."

"Nothing is ever quite as it seems. Which is what makes life so interesting. Is everything well?"

"Thorne is here, being most attentive to my sister and to me. I could almost believe him to be a changed, much kinder person."

"Except?" Francisco prompted.

"Except before tonight, he had hardly been near my sister, with the excuse of being busy elsewhere."

"I suspect that's true. I understand he has disappointed another lady, too."

She looked at him somewhat sharply, wondering again how close he was to Lady Carntree. Only then she noticed the exhaustion in his eyes and the shadows beneath. "You are tired. Go home and sleep. We can talk tomorrow."

A smile flickered. "I don't want to sleep. Or even talk much. I want to dance with you."

The butterflies in her stomach leapt. It didn't matter how foolish she was. She wanted to dance with him, too. Wordlessly, she turned into his arms as if it was the most natural place to be. He held her for one still instant before the music began, and he stepped forward, turning her to the rhythm of the waltz.

He said, "You are even lovelier than I imagined."

"You have met me before," she said dryly.

"Not in colors. I dreamed of you in colors, but still, you take my breath away."

The words were so much what she wanted to hear from him that she could not afford to take him seriously. "What nonsense you talk. You must be very tired indeed."

"The ballgown does not make you beautiful."

"I know." And it shouldn't have hurt.

"You always were. But the gown, at last, is a fitting setting for you. I am glad to see you shine here."

"Have you been drinking?"

"No, though I would like to be. I would like to drink wine with you, Matty Mather, and talk about our lives and solve the problems of the world together."

"What would that achieve?" she asked harshly, for his words struck a chord, meeting her own desire to know him as he truly was.

His smile was twisted. "Another fantasy. Shall we just dance before my blathering mouth truly offends you?"

He held her gaze, and they danced until the tension seeped out of her. "I am not offended," she admitted. "I am just… I am not used to compliments, and I don't know why you say these things. I don't know… I don't know *you*."

"Therein lies my only hope. Does it hurt you to spend time with Thorne?"

"It hurts me that my sister will think I am working against her."

"Does she love him?"

Matty considered. "I think she would like to. She is flattered, as I once was, and enjoying her status of an engaged lady. But she is *miffed* when he does not call. She does not *miss* him." *As I miss you. Please, God, don't let me have said that aloud…*

He nodded thoughtfully, dancing her nimbly around a couple who had strayed too close. Though she had enjoyed her previous dances of the evening, this was what she had truly longed for. *Him*—his natural grace, the exciting hint of exuberance beneath his confident, controlled steps.

That un-nameable recognition she had felt during their waltz at Maida Gardens hit her once more, making her ache and yearn. And yet, at the same time, pure contentment seemed to rise up from her toes, intensifying into pure happiness so that for no reason except that she could not stop it, she smiled up at him.

And slowly, almost wonderingly, he smiled back.

EMMA, LADY CARNTREE, was not having an enjoyable evening. Despite knowing that Thorne would neglect her for his gullible betrothed, she had looked forward to the Wennings' ball, hoping at least to eclipse her hostess, who had once held such sway over the ton. And preferably laugh with her more sophisticated friends at the unpolished Mather girl making a fool of herself before the entire ballroom. That would punish Thorne nicely.

Her other ambition, only half-admitted, was, since her husband had retreated to the country in ill health, to entice Francis back to her. For though she liked Thorne's power in the world, it was her ex-lover's power in the bedchamber that she craved most, and not just to annoy Thorne. He had left her before she was ready to let him go. There was unfinished business between them, and no one had ever made love to her so adventurously, so intensely, so relentlessly satisfyingly. Bringing him to heel would be the perfect end to what she planned to be a delightful evening.

But it was not proving to be delightful at all. Lord and Lady Wenning had greeted her as gracious hosts, but the earl's eyes had not lingered on her, and the countess's had shown no chagrin, nor even much interest in the daring new gown she wore over dampened petticoats. Of course, Emma had maintained her little court of mostly youthful admirers, but as soon as she had left her post by the door, there had always been a larger crowd around Grace Wenning, even as she had rustled about her duties as hostess, introducing dance partners and doing the pretty by the dowagers and gouty old gentlemen.

Thorne himself, bent almost double over the insipid girl he intended to marry, had looked straight through her when she had ventured a smile of wicked pity. And so far, the wretched bride-to-be had not even supplied any amusement, let alone made a fool of herself.

Emma was already at a low point when she finally saw Francis arrive, looking outrageously handsome in immaculate evening dress, like a tamed pirate with his bronzed skin and wayward curls. As he sauntered across the room, closer to her, she saw that he looked tired and a little distracted. Well, she knew a few tricks to cheer him up.

He had paused in front of the French window to the terrace, a perfect position for a swift turn under the stars. So, she had joined him there. He didn't even notice until she spoke, for his gaze was on the dance floor—on an unknown woman in blue dancing with Lord Calton. But Emma could detect no threat in someone so understated and past the first flush of youth. He was, she presumed, merely gazing into space.

Or so she had thought until he had brushed her off like an importunate fly.

For a little, she revived her evening by flirting outrageously with Rollo Darblay, and she might well have forgotten her huff had she not, only a little later, seen Francis waltzing with that same lady in blue. And not only dancing. He had *never* looked at Emma with such an expression, never once smiled at her like…*that.*

A sharp spike of jealousy shot through her, consuming her. Everything was wrong, damnably, impossibly wrong, and she would not tolerate it.

Emma, waltzing at the time with a dull but devoted swain who was more or less speechless at his luck in landing her for the supper dance, all but dragged her partner off the floor in the wake of Francis and his partner.

Her plan was simple. To force an introduction to the woman who had won his wayward attention, eat supper in their company, and make the lady in blue fully aware of Francis's relationship with her. That this relationship had ended two years ago no longer weighed with her. She truly felt outraged, almost betrayed. Or so she convinced herself. Certainly a desire to lash out, to hurt, roiled in her stomach, curling and reaching like a snake ready to bite.

It was all a matter of timing. So, while she charmed her swain whose name she could not even recall and gaily instructed him as to which morsels to place on her plate, she watched Francis's progress. He seemed in no hurry and was making the unknown woman laugh, damn him.

She was also delighted to notice Sir Anthony Thorne not far behind her, attentively helping his betrothed to the delicacies of her choice. She smiled at the thought that he would see her sitting with Francis, for she had no objection to making Thorne a little jealous, too. And more to the point, she knew that, for some reason, he did not like Francis, was even suspicious of him. Thorne did not like people with any mystery behind them. He liked to know exactly who they and their antecedents were. And their politics, of course. Francis never spoke of either, and yet was accepted by the noblest and the highest of sticklers.

Francis and his lady had left the buffet tables and were walking across the dining room toward an empty table with four chairs. Perfect.

"Oh, we have more than enough to eat," she informed her partner, with one peremptory tug on his arm. "I must sit down." She sailed away from the food as though searching for just the right table, for she wished to come upon Francis face to face and exactly the right place. This required a burst of speed, which rather took her devoted swain by surprise, though he kept up gamely.

She contrived the encounter with almost perfect timing, arriving somewhat breathlessly at the still empty table for four, only a couple of seconds before Francis would have reached it.

He halted at the table in front, an expression of faint surprise on his face as he saw her. She smiled and set down her plate.

"Good evening once more, Francis." She gestured to the empty chairs while her partner obligingly held one for her to sit, which she did, smiling invitingly at her prey.

"Good evening," Francis said politely. He set his plate down on the table in front where, for the first time, Emma noticed Rebecca and Ludovic Dunne, whom she knew to be friends of his. Rebecca, once Lady Cornish, was beautiful and had once been considered delightfully scandalous. But her third husband, though a gentleman, was a mere *solicitor*, however feted. Surely Francis was not choosing…

Francis moved toward Emma, though he was not looking at her. Was he embarrassed? Afraid? He should be.

He turned his back on Emma and held the chair beside Dunne, who had risen to his feet.

The lady in blue, close up, was not insipid at all. Instead, she radiated quiet elegance and *character*. She was, in fact, quite beautiful. She inclined her head to Francis with a hint of humor and smiled at Dunne before swirling into the seat beside him.

As Francis took his place beside Rebecca Dunne, there was nothing for Emma to do but smile brightly at her swain and pick up her fork. He had not even acknowledged her invitation to sit with her, had not deigned the civility of introducing his supper partner. As though Emma were nothing to him and never had been.

That understanding that she could not be acknowledged in public as more than an acquaintance did not pierce her anger. Neither did the fact that the Dunnes were his particular friends, and there had clearly been an arrangement about supping with them. Emma felt slighted and furious.

"Who is the lady with Francis?" she asked her partner carelessly.

"Afraid I don't know either of them."

Seething, though no longer with any clear idea why, Emma got through supper, although, unable to bear it the bitter end, she excused herself to her swain and made her way to the ladies' cloakroom. It was blessedly quiet there, with only Lady Rampton present, along with her maid, who was stitching some torn flounce.

The two ladies exchanged distant smiles. Emma's late mama had been Lady Rampton's godmother, but though they had known each other forever, they had never got on. Lady Rampton, married to the Marquess of Sedgemoor's heir, was a high stickler and had never approved of Emma's frivolity. While Emma found the other woman Friday-faced and dull. However, she kept relations cordial, and had, in fact, introduced Anthony Thorne to both Lord Rampton and his politically influential father, the marquess.

Emma went to a looking glass, wondering whether to summon her maid, just for something to do. She tugged at a couple of ringlets and adjusted a hairpin before smoothing her skirts. The damp petticoats had dried in the heat of the ballroom.

The cloakroom door opened, and a lady in blue drifted behind Emma toward a privacy screen. A few spiteful ideas offered themselves to Emma, including knocking down the screen and exposing the wretched female. But there seemed little point with so few people here to appreciate it.

Instead, since Lady Rampton was leaving, Emma went with her, murmuring, "A moment's peace to set one up for the second act," she said humorously. "Shocking squeeze, is it not?"

"Shocking," Lady Rampton agreed.

"I don't suppose you know that lady in blue who came in after us? She is quite beautiful, though I am sure I have never laid eyes on her before."

"No, you wouldn't have," Lady Rampton said dryly. "If I ever knew her name, I've forgotten it, because of course, we have not been introduced. She is merely the governess to the Dove children, so what Grace Wenning is about inviting her here, I have no idea."

Emma blinked. "*Governess?*"

"Yes, astonishing, isn't it? I only know because my brother-in-law Dominic married into the family, and I don't mind telling you, Emma, they are not quite the thing. Eccentric, you know. We encountered them in the park one day." She shuddered delicately. "It was not the match I would have chosen for dear Dominic, but there, he had been through a great deal, and his father felt obliged to allow it."

Emma, conscious of a rare urge to hug the other woman, smiled brilliantly instead.

Did Francis know she was a mere governess? Was he just being kind to her? She was halfway to the ballroom before she made the obvious connection.

Sir Anthony Thorne.

Thorne's betrothed had an inconvenient sister who was a governess to the Doves. The wretched lady in blue was the sister of Marion Mather, soon to be Lady Thorne.

And considering how Thorne had treated Emma since the arrival of his wife-to-be in London, she had no compunction about encompassing his discomfort in her cunning little revenge plot.

CHAPTER SEVENTEEN

MATTY HAD NEVER imagined a ball could be like this. Or at least, not since she was seventeen years old and had actually attended one for the first time. In the country, she had always enjoyed the dancing, the meeting up with old friends, but the awkward flirtations and jealousies and the spiteful comments that resulted had put her off. As had the excessive formality and the rules of behavior governing a young lady in public. Even before Sir Anthony had picked her up and dropped her for another, balls had become a disappointment to her.

She had expected no better of this one. Worse, in fact, for as a mere governess, even one who had helped her hostess's sister out of a scrape, she knew she had no right to be here among the ton. She had come, pathetically, because Francisco had asked it of her, and she had been prepared to help him. But since he had asked her to dance, her world seemed to have changed. As if he no longer flirted with her, but...*courted* her.

The whole evening had turned breathless and wonderful. She had even enjoyed herself with the Dunnes, joining in their lively conversation and banter and beginning to know Francisco just a little better. And she liked him all the more. She liked his quick ripostes and his sardonic humor, his knowledge of the world that infused any more serious conversation.

Afterward, her trip to the cloakroom had been largely to calm herself, to ground herself back in reality. But her heart still beat for Francisco.

Returning to the ballroom, she heard the orchestra playing once more. It was time to find Marion and her mother, whom she had scarcely even glimpsed all evening, though inevitably her eyes sought and found Francisco first. He was walking with his host, the Earl of Wenning, though she could not tell if their conversation was lighthearted or serious. Wenning was a diplomat with government connections and a seat in the Lords.

She came across her mother almost by accident and sat down beside her. "Well, Mama? Are you glad we came?" She followed her parent's gaze to Marion in a lively country dance. "Marion is."

"I imagine you are, too," Mama said smugly. "An earl and a duke among your dance partners, I'm told. And the earl at least is not married. Who was the gentleman who took you into supper?"

"Mr. Francis," she said casually. "Where is Sir Anthony?"

"Dancing with Lady Wenning."

"Why, so he is."

"He is an important man," Mama said with another trace of self-congratulation.

"Do you know," Matty said casually, "that he is already living off his expectations of Marion's fortune?"

Two spots of color appeared on Mama's cheeks. "Don't be vulgar, Matilda."

"The vulgarity isn't mine."

"It is when you bring it up at such a time! You've never forgiven him, have you? You are jealous of your sister's good fortune."

"I have forgiven him, for we would never have suited."

Her mother sniffed derisively. They said no more on the subject since other people came and sat near them, and in due course, Marion returned with shining eyes, making Matty smile at her sheer enjoyment. And only minutes later, Lady Wenning appeared with a handsome widower, whom she introduced to them as, clearly, another prospective dance partner.

"Oh, and here is Mr. Francis, too," she added as Francisco appeared at her shoulder. "I suspect he needs no introduction. Don't forget, gentlemen, the next dance is a waltz!" She smiled and bustled off.

Feeling heat tinge her skin, Matty introduced Francis to her mother and sister. The widower, fortunately, shook Francis's hand and gave his own surname—Danvers—which Matty had already forgotten.

And then, without clearly recalling how, Matty found herself back in Francisco's arms, waltzing.

He held her just a shade too close. "When this is finished, Matty Mather, will you talk to me?"

"I'm talking to you now."

"Yes, but holding you in my arms, it seems I am quite incapable of thinking what is best for you, for us. When I'm free…"

"The whole world is not sitting on your shoulders, Francisco," she said gently. "You must decide what is best for *you*. And I will look after myself." She smiled. "And thus, your troubles are halved."

"No, they're not," he said on the ghost of a laugh and swept her around and backward, and somehow, they were on the terrace, dancing in the chill of the evening, the breeze stirring her hair and cooling her skin.

Inside, however, she was warm and, somehow, both contented and excited. His eyes were intent on hers as they danced more slowly to the end of the fortunately empty terrace—thank God for a chilly spring night!—and finally stood still.

"May I?" he asked huskily.

It was the only time he had asked permission. But God knew she had no desire to refuse him.

"Yes," she whispered and lifted her face to his.

This kiss was different, too, achingly tender, soft, and sweet, almost like a vow. And it might have stayed that way had she not panicked when she felt him draw back and wrapped her arms fiercely around him, opening her lips to command, to plead. And then, with a sound between a groan and a sigh, his tongue drove into her mouth, and he plundered, demanding her ever-deeper response.

She gasped, returning his kiss with all the emotion and arousal that had been building between them all evening. His hand cradled her nape, deliciously caressing, while his arm pressed her so close into his body, she could feel every inch of him. His free hand swept down her side, moving in to cup her breast, and she thought she would faint with pleasure.

She clung harder, trying to drag him closer, and then a voice sounded behind them. His mouth left hers, and he whisked her around the corner out of sight.

She stared up at him, still dazed. Almost idly, his fingers massaged her nape while he listened for any shocked laughter or ribald comment that would signal they had been seen.

None came. It seemed to be two military gentlemen enjoying a cigarillo together on the main terrace.

Francisco's gaze came back to hers, at once humorous and rueful. "Close," he whispered in her ear. He reached behind her, and she saw that he was trying the handle of another, single door to the ballroom. It gave beneath his fingers.

"You first," he whispered. "And we shall finish our dance with a little more propriety…" He kissed her mouth one last time, brief and hard, before releasing her.

Her hands trembled slightly as she straightened her gown and checked her hair, which was still miraculously in place. No doubt he had great experience at all but ravishing ladies at balls without any outward signs. He gave her a crooked smile, as though suspecting the direction of her thoughts, and opened the door for her. She slipped inside, looking quickly around to be sure no one was paying her any attention.

An instant later, Francisco's fingers twined in hers, drawing her behind a group of chattering dowagers, and then between two empty chairs, back onto the dance floor. A shiver of laughter shook her, reflected in his eyes as he laughed silently back.

Why had she ever thought his eyes cold or hard? They really were not at all, not when they looked at her. *I love you*, she thought in wonder. *I really, truly love you…*

IT HAD BEEN decided the day before that Matty should return with the Doves and their young cousin, who had been pressed into service as escort for the occasion. However, leaving her mother and sister in the capable care of Sir Anthony Thorne, it was not easy to find Mrs. Dove in the chaos of everyone's departure.

Eventually realizing that they were no longer in the ballroom, Matty made her way to the cloakroom to find her borrowed evening cloak and outdoor shoes, then on to the front hallway in a fresh crush of people. She had just reached the foot of the staircase when she was accosted by a lady who held her back.

"Why you are Miss Mather, are you not?"

Matty brought her distracted gaze to focus on Lady Carntree. "Yes, I am."

"I'm Emma Carntree."

"I recognize you," Matty admitted. "I have seen you at Mrs. Dove's house."

Emma's smile dawned, not malicious precisely, but very, very amused. "Where you are the governess."

"I am," Matty said, neither proud nor defiant.

"And you are a friend of Mr. Francis?"

Wary now, Matty allowed herself to be drawn aside from any listening ears, while the throng pressed forward to the front door, calling to each other, to their maids and footmen, and to their host and hostess.

"I am acquainted with Mr. Francis, yes. I'm afraid your ladyship must excuse me. Mrs. Dove is expecting me."

"One moment of your time will be of considerable benefit,

Miss Mather. I would guess we are probably of an age, but my experience of the fashionable world is infinitely greater. You might call me a veteran of the London Season, and I could not live with myself if I did not warn you of the danger."

"What danger?" Matty was growing impatient and kept her attention on the front door. She could not see the Doves or their cousin.

"Francis and other men of his ilk. They flirt, they fawn upon the ladies of the ton and interfere, you might say, with each other's domestic arrangements. Since they are gentlemen, of course, unmarried ladies should be safe from ravishment and seduction."

Matty jerked her gaze back to Emma's, a blistering retort rising to her lips, and was stayed by the other woman's smile.

"Only, you're not, are you?" Emma said gently. "A lady, I mean. You are only the governess, and I could see immediately that to Francis you are fair game. Good night, Miss Mather."

For a moment, Matty stared after her, angry at the woman's insolence as much as her traducing of Francisco's character. But she refused to let a jealous woman's spite spoil the magic of her evening and moved on with the crowd.

Finally making it to the front steps, she looked around for Mrs. Dove or her carriage.

"Whose carriage are you looking for, ma'am?" asked a footman in Wenning livery with great civility.

"Mrs. Dove's."

"Oh, here, Miss!" said another footman, beckoning to her from the street. He wasn't one of the Doves' servants, but Matty assumed he was Sir Anthony Thorne's and had recognized her.

She thanked the Wennings' man and hurried to the other, who led her to the right along the road to an open carriage door. He even handed her inside, then kicked up the steps and slammed the door before she had even sat down. The horses lurched into motion, hurling her onto the bench, and she saw that the carriage was empty.

"Wait, this is a mistake!" she called aloud. But the horses were going so fast she doubted the driver would have heard. Wishing she had a parasol, she knocked furiously on the carriage roof. "Stop this instant! Halt!"

Surely the driver would have to have been deaf not to hear the combination of yelling and banging, but the horses did not slow, merely swerved around a corner at breakneck speed, throwing her around on the bench.

Hauling herself up, she tried to pull down the window and found it stuck. Close to panic now, she realized they were on Piccadilly, heading eastward, away from where she needed to be. She commenced thundering on the roof again, for at the pace the carriage was going, she could not throw herself out the door without hurting herself badly, either in the fall or by coming under other carriages, other hooves. She could do nothing until the carriage either stopped or slowed down.

It seemed inclined to do neither, for all her thumping and shouting. And then, abruptly, it slowed amidst a lot of blowing and snorting from the horses. Matty gripped the handle, and since the carriage really was stopping, she waited until it did to throw open the door and leap down without bothering about the steps. She slammed the door behind her.

"What do you think you're doing, imbecile?" she shouted at the coachman, who glanced back at her from his box, muffled almost to the eyes.

He didn't answer. In fact, before she'd even finished speaking, he'd flicked the reins at the horses and had the temerity to drive off.

"Don't you dare!" Furiously, she hurried after him, but the carriage swung around the corner, and she stopped dead. She had no desire to get back into that carriage. Instead, she looked around her for another. Surely, they had not come so far that she could not walk home, but in full ball dress, she would really rather not…

She had no idea where she was. The street was wide enough,

although the buildings on either side were somewhat run down. She could see no name on it. A few closed shop fronts gave little away. Two colorful, if bizarrely dressed women across the street were staring at her.

A group of drunken men on her own side of the road began to move toward her, calling out to her. A shadow moved in the doorway nearest her. With a surge of much sharper fear, she clutched her evening cloak closer about herself and hurried toward the end of the street, pulling the cloak hood over her head as she went.

Just as she reached the corner, a man stepped around it and smiled toothlessly. "Hello, my pretty. Want to come with me?"

"No, thank you," she muttered, brushing past him, praying she would not end in a blind alley.

She found she *was* in an alley, dark and narrow, but at least it was short, and at the end of it, several lanterns showed her a place she recognized—the Theatre Royal at Covent Garden. She had been right. She wasn't so far from home. The trouble was, this was not a place to be alone at night. Even much earlier in the evening, after the opera. Now it was three o'clock in the morning, and all these people were still haunting the streets, and she could not fool herself it was for innocent fun.

She hurried across the square, trying to look as inconspicuous as possible. If she could make it as far as Oxford Street, would there still be hackneys available? At least it was quieter on this side of the square. No one seemed to be milling around the streets beyond, so she was less likely to be accosted.

With a moment to breathe, she allowed herself to wonder how she had got here, and more precisely, who was responsible. It could not have been an accident, even allowing for an insane driver. A liveried footman had called her by name and put her into the carriage, which had left her here. She could see no point, except to frighten her. And the Doves when she didn't appear. And her mother and Marion when the Doves inquired.

Word would get out that she was missing. It wouldn't matter

that she was entirely innocent. Even the Doves could not believe this ridiculous tale! Which meant that she was ruined unless she got home very, very quickly. And Francisco—what would he think of her now?

But who would do such—

Hard fingers grasped her arm, and she swung around in alarm to see a large stranger with pockmarked skin and long side whiskers. His breath stank. But before she could even begin to shake him off, a lantern was thrust into her face, almost blinding her. She flung up a hand to protect her eyes and saw a slow, avaricious grin form on his thick lips.

"Well, well, well, what have we here, gents? Not so very young, but skin like that don't need no paint. And I bet that dress buys a few bottles of gin!"

Of course, he wasn't alone. Two ruffians loomed on either side of him. Of her.

"Come on, love," one of them said cheerfully, hauling her with terrifying ease. "Come with us!"

CHAPTER EIGHTEEN

FRANCISCO HAD NEVER in his life hung around after a ball or any other function just on the chance that he might catch a glimpse of a woman who enchanted him. But then, no other woman ever *had* enchanted him, not like this. He had much to think about before tomorrow, and much to do just to have a hope of preventing disaster. And yet here he stood in the shadows of Wenning House like a besotted adolescent.

He had not gone near her since the waltz after supper. Just by dancing with her twice and taking her into supper, he must have alerted the tabbies to gossip possibilities. Thankfully, neither he nor Matty were well known to the ton, so she might avoid talk since he left her alone for the rest of the evening.

From his place in the shadows beside the Mount Street house, he had watched Sir Anthony Thorne await his carriage in the company of Mrs. Mather and Miss Marion Mather. Further along, nearer to him, Mrs. Dove and her daughter sat in their carriage, peering out of the window occasionally, presumably to look for Matty. Once, the young relative who was their escort got down and strode toward the steps of Wenning House, but Mrs. Dove summoned him back.

"Henry, don't go back in, we shall just lose you, too. The servants will send her to us."

Thorne handed his ladies into a carriage, which set off at a decorous pace, but still, he could see no sign of Matty. Unease had him taking two paces back toward the house—and then he saw her, hurrying beside a footman in the wrong direction.

Something was definitely wrong.

He walked faster. But the footman boosted her through an open carriage door and swung it shut. The carriage shot forward immediately, away from Francisco and at a spanking pace both unnecessary and unusual. His stomach twisted ferociously, but he could not catch the carriage, not on foot and with all these people holding him up.

He swung back toward the Doves' carriage and suddenly glimpsed Emma Carntree, one elegant foot on the step of her own carriage, a smile on her lips that he did not like. As if she sensed him, she shifted her gaze to him. Her smile broadened, and he *knew*.

She stepped inside, and her footman closed the door.

Fear threatened to paralyze him, as it had not since he was a boy, and nothing he could do could save the people he loved.

Not again. Dear God, not again, not her…

He would not allow it. Ruthlessly, he forced down the fear and the horrors of his memory and his imagination, and at last, his brain began to work. He strode up to the Doves' waiting carriage and tipped his hat.

The young relative opened the window. "Sir?"

"Ah, Mrs. Dove," Francisco said amiably, looking beyond the young man. "I bear a message from Mrs. Mather, who apologizes profusely for keeping you waiting. She insisted on taking both her daughters back to Grillon's."

"Drat the woman," Mrs. Dove said below her breath before adding more civilly, "Thank you, Mr. Francis."

Without waiting to hear any more, Francisco tipped his hat again and strode off in the direction of Bruton Street.

EMMA WAS RATHER pleased with herself. On the brief carriage ride home, she amused herself by imagining the governess's face when she found herself among the thieves and courtesans—to call them no worse—who haunted Covent Garden at night. She imagined Thorne's face when he realized his precious sister-to-be was ruined. And Francisco's when he realized his so innocent lady in blue was nothing but a whore.

And all accomplished with the briefest word to her favorite of Thorne's footmen. It was really quite brilliant.

Stepping down from her carriage, she was admitted to the house by the sleepy night porter, who bade her goodnight and began to lock the door behind her, preparatory to going to bed himself. Emma swept on toward the stairs but quite suddenly was hauled into the dark reception room to the left.

A hand was clapped over her mouth, and she was held motionless in a terrifyingly strong grip. The porter clumped along the hall toward the servants' stairs at the back of the house, humming tunelessly to himself as he went. His candlelight flickered briefly in the doorway, and Emma found herself staring into the hard, pitiless eyes of her one-time lover.

It's Francis. It's only Francis. But somehow, the knowledge did not comfort her. There had always been something only semi-tamed about him, and now he wasn't tame at all. Dragging her with him, he softly closed the door, locked it, and pocketed the key.

"I'm going to let you go now. But if you scream, if you even move, I'll snap your pretty neck before any of your servants have as much as wakened. Do you understand me?"

Dear God, even his voice was different. Cold, clipped, merciless. The blood chilled in her veins. She nodded desperately, and keeping hold of her, he slowly took his hand away from her mouth.

She gulped in air. "Francis," she said shakily. "There's no need for this. The servants still have orders to admit you anytime."

"Where did you send her?"

"What are you...?" Before the question was even out, he had spun her around so fast she was dizzy. Both hands closed around her throat, appallingly strong and immoveable.

"Don't, Emma. Don't even try. Where did you send her?"

"Oh, nowhere very far away. No one will hurt her, for God's sake. I only wanted to give her superior person a little fright. Go and fetch her for all I care."

"From where?" he repeated.

It was too soon, so she tried a smile.

His fingers tightened, actually choking her.

"Covent Garden," she gasped. "She'll only be left there, not harmed."

"*Not harmed?*" He flung her from him as though she was too loathsome to touch. Though released, she only cringed before the savage contempt in his face. "Do you expect me to believe you have really no idea what harm could befall an unprotected woman at this time of night? Would you like me to send *you* to fetch her?"

Every word felt like a lash, and she had no real idea why. "Francis..."

He didn't even pause in his stride as he unlocked and wrenched open the door. She stumbled after him, intent on retrieving her position with him, making him forgive her. But he pounded down the hall, unbolting the front door without any care now as to noise. An instant later, he was running down the steps and away, leaving the front door wide open for the chill wind.

DRAGGED DOWN AN alley she hadn't even seen, a filthy hand over her mouth, Matty had one moment of hope. A young woman with a shawl over her head slunk past them, pressed as far into the wall as she could get, head down.

Matty made a noise behind the suffocating, stinking hand, not quite a scream or even a wail, but it should have been enough to at least make the girl look up and see. She didn't. She kept her head down and hurried on, all but clinging to the wall. Not that the poor creature could have done anything against three grown men, but if she had been prepared to acknowledge the abduction, she might have brought help…might she?

Matty didn't know what awaited her as they dragged her through a door opening onto the alley. They shut the door behind them and bolted it.

She could die, which seemed so cruel when she had only just met and loved Francisco.

Francisco, Francisco…

More likely, the men would steal her gown and reticule and leave her to limp home in her underwear. Unless they took that, too, for it was new and fine and could probably be sold easily, too. Rape was another possibility. They could sell her on to a brothel from which she could never escape. Not because she wouldn't try but because she would have nowhere to go. No decent family, including her own, would want her after such a fate. For it was the way of the world to blame female victims.

She was shaking when they let her go, and she had to summon the pride to stand straight, to cast all her fearful thoughts aside, and concentrate on the current situation. If she could not get out of it, she could surely buy herself some time.

She was in an ill-lit room off the poky front hall, and her three captors stood between her and the closed door.

At first, all she could hear was the thundering of her own heart, her own rapid breathing. Then she realized there was noise above the ceiling, a few desultory voices like the humming of a bee in the distance. She doubted, however, that those above would be her friends. Her captors were clearly prepared to let her scream, secure in the knowledge that in this place, no one would come to her aid. So she didn't give them the satisfaction.

The lantern was set on the dirty table. A couple of tallow candles were lit, giving off their evil smell but at least showing Matty her surroundings: a bare room with two old, upholstered chairs leaking their stuffing.

Matty regarded her advancing captors and coughed as though it could dispel her own terror. At least it might serve to stop her voice from shaking.

"You have made a dire mistake in taking me in such a way," she informed them. "But if you stand aside now, I might be persuaded to say no more."

One of them, thinner and smaller than the others, grinned in clear admiration. "Lor', can't she talk? Got a posh one here, Gerry."

"You have no idea," Matty said grandly. "So, whatever you were planning when you laid your filthy hands upon me, think again."

She had their attention, if only because they were admiring her speech. They stood in a still row, between her and the door, all looking amused to a greater or lesser degree. The leader, he of the side-whiskers and the thick lips, gave her a mocking bow.

"Your highness! In our shoes, then, what would you do?"

She let herself appear to consider, though not too long in case they got bored and... "As I see it, you have two reasonable choices," she said determinedly. "The most sensible, as I've said, would be to simply stand aside and let me go. Such gentlemanly behavior would reap its own reward, in that I would not go to the authorities or even describe you to my extremely large brothers and their host of ferocious footmen."

"It's true it pains us to pass up such generosity," the thin man began in accents meant to imitate her own. "But—"

"My second suggestion would be ransom," she interrupted. "You would lose my goodwill, of course, but you could rake in a much larger fortune than the pittance yielded by selling my clothes. Or the pennies Madame Whoever upstairs would be prepared to pay for me."

"Got to allow, no one likes an unwilling whore," said the largest of them, scratching his head.

The others regarded him with scorn. "She'd be willing," the leader said. "By the time old Madge has finished with her, she'll be—"

"I gather you don't want to be rich?" Matty interrupted, trying to hide her desperation in her best governess voice. "This—" She waved a disparaging hand about the room. "…is the sum of your ambitions? Hasn't it entered your head that my family would pay dearly to have me returned safe and sound?"

Of course, it was already too late for that. She was already ruined, and all she could do was postpone any assault as long as she could.

"How much?" the big one asked. "Hundreds of guineas?"

"Easily," Matty replied grandly.

"She's got a point," the big man told his compatriots.

"Don't be a bigger ass than you were born," his leader snapped. "A guinea in the hand is worth more than the hundreds in your dreams!"

"Don't know that it is," the thin man said judiciously. "Ransom is risky but rewarding."

"What would you know about it?" the leader demanded with contempt.

"I've heard, and you'll be a fool if you don't listen, too!"

"Oh, for—"

Fight, Matty prayed. *Go on, fight among yourselves, and maybe you won't even notice me go…*

The trouble was, they still stood between her and the door, so she merely shuffled a few inches forward and to the side, waiting for any moment.

"Never mind the bloody ransom!" the leader, Gerry, uttered in frustration. "Just go and get Madge!"

Matty poised. If one left the room, it might give her more chance…

"Not until we've decided on our best course," the thin one

said stubbornly. "Madge will want her share, of course."

Gerry cast his eyes up to the peeling ceiling. "You want to hold a woman like her for ransom? The whole place will be swarming with the law in no time!"

"Same if we sell her to Madge," the big man pointed out.

"Yes, but then we have our money, and Madge pays any consequences. But do tell, how does your massive brain suggest we screw this imaginary ransom from her family? Pay a morning call, perhaps? Sure, the butler would be happy to offer us tea and crumpets. Or maybe we could get the reformers—or the vicar!—to write a note for us!"

The thin man, who had looked indignant at such sarcasm, ended by scratching his head in a crestfallen manner. From which Matty gathered that none of them could write.

"Madge can write," the thin man offered at last, though without much hope.

"Yes, but we'd never know what she'd written," Gerry pointed out.

Matty took a step nearer the door. "I could write your note."

"We'd never know what you wrote either!" Gerry exclaimed, though it was, Matty hoped, a step forward that he seemed to be regarding her in the same light as his mutinous companions.

"What reason would I have to thwart you? I want to go home."

"You could write where to find you."

"I don't *know* where to find me!" She swallowed. "Why don't you bring me writing materials now? The sooner you deliver the note, the sooner you'll get your money."

They all regarded her with varying degrees of hope and skepticism while Matty's insides twisted.

"We can do both," Gerry said cunningly. "Take off the cloak."

The order was to his underlings, but as the big man took a step nearer, she began to unfasten it herself. The big man merely swept it back, so he and his fellows could see the silk ball gown beneath.

"That'd fetch a fine packet," Gerry observed. "Get it off her, and then we'll talk ransom."

"My family will only pay my return *undamaged*," Matty said desperately, backing away again. "They'll never believe that if you take my clothes."

Gerry grinned as though lapping up her fear like gin. "You can tell them what story you like when you're free. We ain't going to argue. Now, boys," he added harshly, "if you p—"

A mighty crash drowned out his final word—a splintering of wood and an explosion of glass as something large catapulted through the window and the flimsy curtains and rolled across the floor toward her.

Matty had just grasped that it was a man when it lashed out with its feet, bringing the large man crashing to the floor, too. In almost the same movement, he sprang to his feet, spun, and swung his fist into the thin man's chin, knocking him into the pile of limbs that was the large man trying to stand.

Francisco.

The stunning realization drowned every other thought, hope, and fear.

He found me… And she would not let his rescue fail for the want of a little spirit on her part.

While Francisco faced Gerry, charging him with head lowered like a bull, Matty lunged to the table and snatched up the lantern. Francisco side-stepped Gerry and seized one arm, twisting it hard up his back. Gerry scrabbled over his shoulder with his free hand and kicked back with his heel. The blow missed his knee but scraped punishingly down his shin.

The other two had managed to disentangle themselves and were now advancing menacingly on Francisco. A blade glinted in the thin man's hand.

This was the point Matty had hoped for earlier, the moment she could walk out the door without anyone noticing. Now, it didn't even tempt her. She rushed at her abductors, swinging the lantern, and brought it down on the large man's head.

He staggered, swinging around to face the unexpected new danger. Even dazed, with blood beginning to ooze down the side of his head, his eyes were murderous. Matty raised the lantern again, this time in self-defense.

"Enough!" The single word cracked through the air like two pistol shots, causing everyone to glance at Francisco, though the large man raised one arm protectively over his head.

Francisco held Gerry in an armlock, a curved, wicked-looking dagger at his throat. The man breathed heavily, furiously in his grip, but did not make the mistake of moving.

"I'll slit his throat, and the fight will be more even," Francisco offered. "Or you can drop your weapons and wave goodbye pleasantly."

Matty understood without instruction. Her entire body might have been shaking, but she could still hurry to the door while Francisco followed her, dragging Gerry with him. The other two, still armed, followed, but very slowly.

Matty opened the door a crack and peeked through. The tiny, dark corridor, leading to stairs at one end and the front door at the other, was empty. There seemed to be no sound from upstairs now. Were they preparing to attack, or had they simply fallen asleep?

Matty threw the door wide and stepped out into the hall. "There's a bolt on the outside of the door," she murmured.

"Perfect," Francisco replied, moving in her wake. At the last moment, he thrust Gerry hard back into the room, and as the other two charged him, he slammed the door and bolted it.

This would have been my prison, she thought numbly. God knew for how long, subjected to what abuse…

Francisco's fingers curled around hers, drawing her to the front door. Behind her, she heard movement rustling on the stairs.

"Someone's coming," she whispered.

"I know." By the light of her shaky lantern, he turned the

large key, wrenched the door open. A thundering on the stairs followed them as they fled out of the building.

Francisco didn't hesitate. He ran to the left, hauling her with him, past the wrecked window to her prison, where her captors were trying to climb out, and down another dark alley.

"A late-night game of tag," he murmured, diving down another lane. "Who'd have thought it?"

In spite of everything, a choke of half-hysterical laughter fell from her lips, and he spared the time to grin at her as he hauled her through a backcourt and over a wall into another street. She could hear the distant pounding of feet, but it came to her at last that Francisco knew this territory as well as they did, and that he was leading them on a wild goose chase which they would have to give up or risk bringing the law down on themselves.

Eventually, Francisco led her into a wider street, skirting the square by the theatre and onto another. He took a key from his pocket and unlocked an unobtrusive door on their right. Pulling her inside, he closed and relocked the door, after which, by the light of the flickering lantern she still held, he led her up a clean, ornate staircase until, two floors up, he unlocked another door and drew her inside.

"Where are we?" she whispered.

"My rooms." He closed the door, turned, and took her in his arms. "You're safe, Matty. You're safe."

CHAPTER NINETEEN

SHE THOUGHT SHE would burst into tears. She didn't; although she gripped Francisco's shoulders so tightly, it must have hurt. Her whole body shook and, yet the comfort of his arms, of his body, seeped into her, warm and healing.

For some time, neither of them spoke. He stroked her hair, might even have kissed it, while her recent, sudden danger faded into the knowledge of safety. Of rescue by the man she had loved without reason. Now she had a reason, and somehow, that held in check the questions starting to clamor in her brain. It was too sweet just to wallow in him, in his strength and goodness and courage and skill and…

Perhaps she was crying after all, for wetness trickled down the side of her face. Only when another drop landed on her temple did she realize the tears were not hers.

She lifted her head, reaching up to cup his damp cheeks. "Francisco," she whispered, stunned. "Oh, Francisco, no one hurt me. They only frightened me so that I was never so glad to see anyone in my life. I could not believe it was you."

His arms tightened. "I thought I would be too late, that I'd never find you, never be able to save you." His voice was husky, uneven as she had never heard it. This, after hard-eyed intrigue, relentless investigation of the highest in the land, and daring rescue—to say nothing of delicious, knowing kisses—this, at last, was Francisco de Salgado in a moment of weakness, utterly vulnerable. And her whole being ached for him.

Reaching up, she kissed the salt tears on his cheek and slid her hand down to take his arm. "Can we make tea?"

"Coffee," he said, dashing his free arm across his eyes. "Sit through there. I'll bring it to you."

She hesitated, but only for an instant. He needed the moment, and perhaps she did, too. Although cold without his closeness, she walked into the room he had indicated. A glow from the fireplace attracted her to a dish full of spills, with which she set about lighting the nearest lamp and the many candles scattered about the room.

Apparently, he liked to be well lit. Perhaps he worked into the night.

His sitting room was homely rather than fashionable. A comfortable sofa stood before the fireplace and two well-used armchairs on either side. A low table sat between them. In the corner was a stout bureau and hard chair. The windows were hung with quality velvet curtains against the cold, and several paintings hung on the walls—no portraits but landscapes and an interior of what looked like a jolly inn.

Matty drew the guard back from the fire, poked it into life, and added a few more coals. Then she knelt beside it and waited for Francisco.

He was not long. He brought a tray with a coffee pot, cups and saucers, and sugar and cream.

Still kneeling on the floor, she poured two cups of strong, black coffee and watched him sit on one armchair and add sugar to his. She reached for the cream jug. "I need to go home. Mrs. Dove will have raised a massive hue and cry."

"I nipped that in the bud. She thinks you're with your mother."

Matty wasn't even surprised. "How did you know I'd been abducted?"

"I was close to the Doves' carriage when I saw you conducted to another. It bolted too fast to have been a friend's, and I saw at once who was responsible."

It was one of the things that had baffled her from the beginning. "Who?"

"Emma Carntree." He raised his cup and drank. "She is angry and spiteful."

"Because you rejected her?"

A smile flitted across his face and vanished. "Thank you for knowing I did. Yes, that, and, I think, she is wroth with Thorne for dancing too much attendance on your sister while ignoring her. Finally, she's paying the price for being the dashing mistress, and she doesn't like it. I'm sorry. What happened to you was my fault."

"No," she said simply. Then, laying down her cup after a long, welcome sip. "Is that what upset you so much?"

His gaze fell to his coffee. He was leaning forward in his chair, not relaxed at all. "Partly." She thought he would leave it there, but without further warning, he began to talk. "I have not loved anyone for a long time. Not since the French came to our home and shot my parents and my sister in front of me. I only escaped because a rifle misfired, and I could run. I did not save them, but I survived. I always survived. And then you… I was so afraid I would not save you either."

Horror and pity welled inside her, for his family and for what he had suffered. And yet leavening the emotion was a growing wonder because surely his words meant he loved *her*?

She shifted, leaning her arms on his knees until he looked at her, and the haunted blackness in his eyes warmed to something softer and more compelling.

"How old were you?" she asked matter-of-factly.

"Fifteen."

"And you are still making up for something no one could have stopped."

"Revenge is the word you are looking for. I have been taking it ever since."

"But the war is over."

"And it's no longer quite so important to endanger myself for the country that took me in. Hence my intention to retire." He stared into her eyes, frowning. "Matty, don't look at me like that. I'm no hero, no knight in shining armor. Because I managed to help you tonight does not wipe out the terrible things I have done."

"Do you want to tell me about them?"

A shudder shook him. "God, no."

"Things that *someone* had to do," she guessed. "Things, perhaps, only you *could* do. Like tonight." She dropped a kiss on his knee, and his hand cupped her head with something like wonder.

"You must remember it's largely my fault Emma went after you so maliciously in the first place."

"I haven't forgotten," she assured him. She folded her arms around one of his legs so that she could lay her cheek on his thigh. It jerked minutely beneath her and was still. "How did you find me?"

"I scared he wits out of Emma until she told me you'd be abandoned in Covent Garden. It could have been worse. It could have been Seven Dials only a little further on. I grabbed a hackney—the driver and horse were both tired and on their way home, but by a mixture of bribery and bullying, I made him hasten to Covent Garden, where I hung out of the carriage, demanding news of you from any passerby. A couple of young…ladies going home from the piazza admitted to seeing you alone, flustered, and in a huge hurry. Another girl told me she'd seen three men wrestling you into a building in this street."

The girl with the shawl? "How did you find the right one?"

"It was the only one with a light, and when I stuck my ear against the window, I could hear your voice. I could even see a tiny bit of the room through a chink in the curtains. The window and front door were both locked, but since the wood was rotting on the window frame, I decided to give them a fright and crash through. I wasn't sure it would be quite so easy, but even so, I dazed myself as much as them."

"No you didn't. You were wonderful, amazing. You were my knight in shining armor. You are." She propped her chin on his thigh and looked up into his face.

His breath caught. His eyes looked almost desperate. "You owe me nothing," he said urgently.

"Of course not. There are no debts where love is concerned."

Confusion joined his desperation and something that was not quite hope but a *fear* of hope. He seemed to have stopped breathing altogether.

"I love you," she said honestly. "I loved you before you saved me."

His eyes closed as though in torment. "Don't. Don't, Matty. You don't *know* me."

"It seems I know enough." She rose up on her knees, reaching up to his neck, and his eyes flew open once more.

The world stood still. Only her heart seemed to move in rapid, hopeful beats. And then he dropped his head until his mouth covered hers. Only then, with the sweetness of his kiss and her own rising happiness, did the tears squeeze from her eyes and trickle back into her hair, where his roving fingers felt them.

With a sound like pain, he gathered her into his lap, holding her against his chest. "Don't cry, darling, please don't cry."

"Only for happiness," she said shakily, laughing at the same time. "Oh, Francisco, please, will you kiss me?"

He did, with delightful thoroughness.

FRANCISCO WAS IN acute danger of casting all sense to the winds. He had been flung so rapidly from fear to determination, back to fear, and then into the blinding happiness of being loved by *her*, that the only thing to do seemed to be to lay her down by the fire and make wild, exquisite love to her.

In fact, he was half out of his chair before the screaming of the more sensitive part of his brain kicked him back into it again.

She had been abducted, terrified, and almost sold to a brothel. The last thing she needed was a man taking advantage of her. He allowed himself the bliss of kissing and stroking her because she seemed to like it so much, but somehow, for her, he managed to control the insistence of his arousal, to calm the flare of passion until she simply lay against him, looking so contented he thought his heart would break.

In a little, he reached over her and found their cooling coffee, which they drank together in the same chair. He poured them another, and with her still in his lap, she asked about his paintings, and they talked, incongruously, about art and the different countries portrayed, and then about anything and everything.

Outside, the watchman cried six o'clock. Only three hours had passed since her abduction.

"You need to go home and sleep," Francisco said. "I'll go and find you a hackney."

"I don't want to sleep. This feels like home. I thought you lived at Albany."

"I have rooms there, too. For the ton, largely. I have a servant there."

"But not here?"

"No." Desire thrummed through him still, like a pleasant backdrop to the pleasure of her company. "You can sleep here for a little if you like. I can't imagine anyone will look for you very early after the ball last night, but you will have to go home and change soon."

She sat up in his lap, her movement stirring his arousal. "How long do we have?"

"A couple of hours. Maybe three."

Her gaze dropped to his lips. "Do you want to sleep? You were tired, even at the ball."

"I was," he admitted. If he was tired now, his body didn't seem to know it.

"Will you sleep beside me?"

He took her hand and placed it over his galloping heart. "If I lie beside you, I will not sleep."

She had to be feeling the ridge of his erection beneath her hip, but it did not seem to frighten her. She raised their hands from his chest and pressed his palm over her heart instead. "I am selfish. I don't want you to sleep."

Her heart raced beneath his fingers. He lifted his gaze slowly from her breast to her lips and finally to her eyes. "Do you know what you're offering me?"

She nodded once.

She was wonderful. He hadn't even offered her marriage, though he fully intended to. Somehow, he thought, she knew that. Somehow, she knew him. And instead of being ashamed and appalled, he was awed.

He rose with her in his arms. "A taste," he whispered. "A taste of love."

Her lips clung to the side of his neck as he walked slowly with his precious armful to the bedchamber.

As he laid her on his bed, a rare surge of doubt washed over him. He had only ever made love to experienced women who understood the game and did not cling. But *this* was no game. *This* tied him into emotional knots because she loved him, because he would die rather than hurt her.

She gazed up at him from the pillows, her beautiful eyes glowing with desire and longing. And then his doubt seemed to infect her, too, for the glow dimmed.

"You don't love me," she whispered.

"Oh, my dear." He sank onto the bed, caressing her soft cheek with the backs of his fingers. They were not quite steady. "If I didn't love you, there would be no problem."

She smiled, and the glow was back, along with more than a hint of wonder and an understanding he had never expected. She pushed herself up from the pillows, laid her arms around his neck, and kissed his mouth as though she would never stop.

While they kissed, her busy hands untied his cravat and thrust his coat back off his shoulders. It came to him with a flood of amusement that she was seducing him, and by God, he liked it. So, he smiled against her lips and set out to show her just how much.

Unfastening her elegant ball gown and unlacing her stays, he dragged his mouth free of hers to kiss her throat and shoulders and nudge the gown further down her breasts until they were tantalizingly, almost completely exposed. Then he returned to her trembling mouth and dealt with the ties of her chemise. From there, it was a simple matter to haul her across his lap and whisk the garments from her body.

Dear God, but she was lovely, naked and rosy with desire for him. He devoured her with his eyes and his hands and lips, delighting in her bold caresses beneath his shirt, over his back and shoulders. Only when her teeth nipped his shoulder in frustration did he lay her back on the pillows, between the sheets, and tear off the rest of his own clothes. They landed on the floor, on top of her abused ballgown, and then he was back on the bed, skin to skin with her, his mouth fastened to hers.

She welcomed him eagerly, with stroking hands and blissful sighs that intensified into gasps and moans and something very like a sob. He recognized her need with fierce triumph, but he would not rush these moments. He worshipped her entire body with his mouth, murmuring endearments and delights until she was squirming beneath him for more.

Only then did he slide into her body, speaking in a roughened, uneven voice. "Will you marry me, Matty Mather?"

The words served a double purpose, distracting her from possible physical discomfort, and, he was relieved to see, filling her with joy.

"Yes. Oh, yes!" She clung to him, rocking instinctively with him. And somehow hanging on to the shreds of care and consideration, he taught her the pleasure of love, and received it.

THERE WAS A sweet, delicious decadence in lying naked in her lover's arms as the sun came up behind the curtains. The wonder of physical bliss overlaid the joy of loving him and being loved. This beautiful, amazing man with the *clever* body would be her husband. Then they could sprawl in bed all day if they wished. She wondered, vaguely, how often they might do this and smiled into his chest.

He was lazily stroking the tangled hair against her shoulder. "Would you like to live in Kent? At least to begin with. I rent a pleasant little property there, though I doubt Dunne will sell it to me. It marches with his stepson's property."

"We could live there for now and decide in the future."

"A lady after my own heart."

A thought seemed to strike her, for she lifted her head from his chest to look at him. "Are you rich, Francisco?"

He smiled. "A fine time to ask that. This is why I love you. I am comfortable."

"Will you show me your lands in Spain, too?"

For a moment, she thought he would throw up all those barriers again. He didn't, though he looked faintly surprised about it. "Yes. We can include it in our wedding journey if you like." He kissed her nose. "With you, I think it might even lay a few ghosts. When will you marry me?"

"Whenever you like," she said honestly. Then, "Oh dear, Mrs. Dove!"

"Well, you've already *sort of* given notice to keep Thorne off your back. So, three weeks for the banns to be read will see you free."

"And I should do something about finding a replacement who will be good for the girls…"

The smile was dying on his lips.

"Did I say something wrong?" she asked quickly, and to her

relief, he hugged her closer.

"No. No, but I too have a task to finish before we can marry."

"Thorne."

"Thorne. But I don't want to think of him now. There will be time enough later. This is our stolen time, Matty Mather, yours and mine."

She parted her lips, and he rolled her beneath him for a long, full-body caress.

But outside was complete daylight, the world was bustling, and it was time to go home. She had to care about her reputation for Marion's sake, at least.

"I should go," she said reluctantly.

He eased away from her and swung his long, muscular legs over the side of the bed. "Make yourself comfortable. I'll go out and fetch us some breakfast. And a hackney."

Although she didn't want either of them to move, she found a new, intimate pleasure in watching him stride naked across the room to the washbowl and perform his ablutions. He pulled on an old pair of breeches and a coat fashionable society would never be allowed to see, cast her a quick grin, and left her.

In the silence following the click of the closing apartment door, she drew a breath and thought with awe of everything that had happened in less than twelve hours. A shaky yet excited laugh fell from her lips. This was a new world because Francisco loved her, because she would marry him and be…happy.

She left the bed and set about washing and dressing. Miraculously, her ballgown had mostly survived its adventures, although the unpleasantly dirty hems might give the best of laundresses a difficult task. She could not manage most of the fastenings by herself, but discovering her cloak in the hall, she swung it around her shoulders for both warmth and modesty. Then, using Francisco's brushes, she untangled her hair. Finding all the discarded pins was a difficult task, but by the time Francisco returned, she had managed to put up her hair in its usual, simple style.

"I brought breakfast," he said, bustling into the kitchen, where she was eyeing his stove with misgiving. He kissed the top of her head. "And coffee. We have ten minutes until the hackney will be here."

A twinge of panic disturbed her contentment, but she sat at the table with him, buttering bread and drinking coffee while she contemplated the parting with a thousand doubts. Something must have shown in her face, for he reached out and covered her hand on the table.

"It isn't over," he said softly. "We've only begun."

She twisted her hand around to squeeze his fingers. "I know. I am content."

"I will spend my life trying to keep you so." He lifted their joined hands to his lips and kissed her knuckles. "I think we both need today to sleep and recover the power of thought. Tomorrow, I will set things in motion."

"Thorne."

He smiled. "Among other things. Come, the hackney will be waiting."

She rose, trying to find her brisk, no-nonsense-governess state of mind. It was a struggle, for she felt suddenly all at sea. Until, in the hallway, he took her in his arms and kissed her thoroughly.

"Until tomorrow," he whispered against her lips, then drew the wide hood of her cloak up over her hair and opened the door.

Grasping the cloak around her to hide her unsuitable evening attire, she walked down the empty staircase with him and out into the bustling daylight of life. A carriage waited right at the door. Francisco handed her into it and closed the door. She heard his voice murmuring to the driver and the clink of coins changing hands, and then the carriage moved off.

Francisco raised his hand to her. She touched her fingers to the window, and then she could no longer see him.

CHAPTER TWENTY

NOBODY IN THE Dove residence appeared to think anything of Matty arriving that morning in the ballgown she had worn last night. The children had gone off to the cellar to play one of their imaginative games—something of a tradition when Adrian came home—and neither Mrs. Dove nor Catherine had yet emerged from their bedchambers.

Only as she changed into her usual morning dress did tiredness begin to catch up with Matty. She wanted nothing more than to crawl into bed and dream sweet dreams of Francisco. But a sense of duty caused her to press on and send for the girls, along with a cup of strong coffee.

Somehow, she managed until midday without quite falling asleep at her desk. A brisk walk with Pup and the children enlivened her briefly, and she was able to set the girls' lessons for the afternoon. After which, she thought she was safe to close her eyes just for a few moments…

"Miss Matty, you need your bed!" exclaimed Catherine's voice with some amusement. "Clearly, you are not used to such dissipation."

Matty jerked her head off the desk. "What dissipation?" she demanded aggressively and hastened to wipe the unladylike drool from her mouth with a handkerchief.

"Last night's ball," Catherine replied, laughing. "Were you

dreaming?"

Matty smiled guiltily. "Yes, I rather think I was."

"Well, you are in luck, it's teatime, and lessons are over for the day."

"Do you know, I think I might forego tea and just stay quietly in my room."

"Shall I send a tray up to you?"

"Oh, no, I shall wait for dinner."

As it turned out, she slept right through dinner and through the night to wake at dawn with a smile on her face and happiness in her heart. Today, she would see Francisco again.

SHE WAS ALSO able to think more clearly with the cobwebs of exhaustion swept from her mind. Despite a tendency to lapse into sweet, blushing daydreams of Francisco, she also thought about the ordeal of her abduction and about her sister and Sir Anthony Thorne. And in particular, what he, the ultimate reactionary, could possibly have to do with rabble-rousing.

As a result, when she accompanied the children on a midday walk with the dog, she decided to return via Grillon's and left Adrian in charge of Pup.

She found her mother and Marion in their sitting room, surrounded by flowers, entertaining a morning caller, whom she quickly recognized as Danvers, the widower who had danced with Marion at the ball. Of Thorne, there was no sign.

"Ah, there you are, Matilda!" her mother greeted her. "We were about to come in search of you."

"You mustn't do that, Mama. I have duties," Matty said hastily, kissing her mother's cheek. "I can't stay long." She offered her hand to Danvers, who bowed over it with perfect politeness and betrayed no surprise to find her so dowdily dressed.

"His lordship brought me these delightful flowers," Marion

said, pointing out a particularly colorful vase on the mantelpiece.

"How beautiful," Matty murmured. So Danvers was *Lord* Danvers, not a mere esquire. Well, that trumped Thorne's baronetcy, which had to be a good thing.

"Oh, and these came for you here, from a mysterious admirer," Marion said with an arch smile. "Look, the card is only initialed! Who could F.S. be?"

Francisco de Salgado. She could not help blushing with warm pleasure. He had sent her yellow roses. Her longing to see him was like an ache. Perhaps this evening, before dinner, in the mews as before…

"And how is Sir Anthony?" Matty inquired to distract the too-perceptive observation of her family.

"I scarcely know," Marion said with a discontented frown. "I have not seen him since the night of the ball."

"He is a busy man," Mama pointed out.

Lord Danvers looked unhappy and just a shade impatient. "I have promised this afternoon to my daughters. We are going to the park to feed the ducks. But if such entertainment distracts you, we would be happy if you joined us."

Marion smiled a gentle, appreciative smile.

"Sir Anthony may call," Mama pointed out.

"Then it will be his turn to be disappointed," Marion said. "Mama and I would be happy to join you. Matty?"

"Alas, I have my duties," Matty said, bestowing a smile of approval on Lord Danvers. She must make a point of inquiring about him, but at least Thorne appeared to have a rival, if only out of pique.

MATTY ARRIVED BACK at the Doves' house somewhat breathless to discover her pupils in the drawing room with their mother. They regarded her from the sofa with triumphant grins.

"I am so sorry," she began to Mrs. Dove. "I called on my mother—"

"Yes, yes, very proper," Mrs. Dove interrupted, drifting toward the door. "I had better change. I suppose *you* will do, Catherine. Miss Mather, would you see the children are suitably dressed..."

"Suitably dressed for what?" Matty asked, bewildered, as the door closed behind her employer.

"Cousin Grace has invited us to call this afternoon," Susan said gleefully. "*All* of us—including Pup!"

"I hope she has no other callers," Catherine said.

Adrian grinned. "I hope she does."

"When are you to go?" Matty asked.

"When are *we* to go," Catherine corrected. "At two of the clock. You must know Mama will not take the children and Pup without you!"

Thank God the invitation had not come yesterday, or she would have been incapable of keeping anyone in order. "Then, girls, go and change into your best dresses and brush your hair. I shall be along directly. Adrian, something without grass stains, if you please. And *with* a neckcloth!"

The Doves' town carriage, a recent acquisition since Viola's marriage into the Gorse family, was reluctantly rejected by Mrs. Dove since she wanted everyone together under her eye. Or at least under Matty's. So, they walked to Mount Street. Fortunately, Pup, having had a walk and a run in the park so recently, was on his best behavior and committed no greater sin than trying to make friends with passersby, who mostly looked terrified.

"Now, children," Mrs. Dove said, frowning particularly in Adrian's direction as they walked along Mount Street. "Her ladyship is not at all high in the instep, as you know, but that does not mean you take advantage. Best manners, please, especially the dog's!"

She turned up the steps and knocked briskly while the others clustered about her. Matty brought up the rear, placing herself tactically on the other side of Pup while Adrian held his leash.

A footman bowed them in at once, and the butler, greeting Mrs. Dove by name, led them upstairs. A set of double doors stood open, and the hum of voices drifted to Matty's ears. *Oh dear,* she thought in dismay. *There are other guests. Pup may be a problem…* He was already wheeling with excitement at all the new smells in the hall and staircase.

The butler did lead them to the open doors. "Mrs. Dove and her family, my lady," the butler said clearly, and Lady Wenning came toward them, smiling.

"Ah, here you are! You're very welcome. I expect you'll know everyone, but Oliver will make any introductions."

Matty halted at the door, one hand on Adrian's arm to detain him. "Your ladyship, perhaps I should take the dog to the garden? Or for a walk?"

"Nonsense, you are required company, Miss Mather," the countess said with a glimmering smile."

On your own head be it, Matty thought fatalistically, following Adrian and the dog into the room.

It was, of course, a large, gracious apartment furnished with elegance and taste. Spring sunshine beamed through the windows on a blur of guests. Pup barked, pulling Adrian at the run to Viola and Lord Dominic, who made a big fuss of him before he rushed at the man standing beside Dominic. Francisco.

Her heart gave one enormous leap and then pattered like rain. Francisco glanced up from ruffling the dog's head and smiled at Adrian. Then with odd deliberation, his gaze shifted and met hers.

Warm, mischievous, and yet…soothing. She hoped the moment hadn't suffused her face with color, at least not beyond what might be expected in a mere governess thrust into the company of the powerful.

She would not for the world betray her relationship with Francisco, for one of the things she had decided in her clear-headed wakening this morning was that she would never hold him to his promises of the night of the ball. They had both been over-emotional, recovering from a shared danger. So, although she did not for a moment doubt her own feelings or regret what she had done, she allowed that in the cold light of day, Francisco might. It would break her heart, but she loved him too much to trap him by *clinging*.

"Come and sit down," Lord Wenning offered, kindly, indicating a chair, while Adrian dragged the dog around the rest of the guests, a good tactic to prevent him lunging from curiosity at an inconvenient moment.

To her surprise, Matty found herself sitting on a large sofa, between the Duke of Dearham and the Earl of Calton, both of whom grinned at her as they hemmed her in as if it was perfectly natural for an obvious governess to be treated with such courtesy. And it was clear they recognized her from the ball.

Her head spinning, Matty took in the other guests—the Duchess of Dearham sat with Ludovic Dunne and his wife. Archie Holles had made himself comfortable on the arm of Catherine's chair. Two other handsome gentlemen, one large, restless, and with a hint of carelessness about his dress and ruffled hair, the other somehow quieter, with more refined features.

"That's Christopher Halland, the member of parliament," Dearham said, nodding at the larger man. "And beside him, Stephen Dornan, the artist."

From sight, Matty recognized the Marquess of Sedgemoor, Lord Dominic's father, who glowered at Pup before surreptitiously scratching him under the chin. It was an odd mix of guests, but at first, the gathering seemed like any other in society, if perhaps a little more relaxed by the presence of the Dove children and Pup.

Lady Wenning's sister Hope distributed cups of tea while the Dove daughters were pressed into offering elegant sandwiches and dainty cakes.

Pup licked his lips and let out a whine. He was straining against Adrian's grip of his collar while Adrian eyed the cakes with resigned longing because he couldn't let go of Pup long enough to actually eat one.

"I could feed you," Susan offered kindly, and Arabella giggled.

"Unfair for you, Adrian," Lady Wenning said, laughing. "Hope, why don't you take your cousins and Pup to the dining room? The servants will lay out more cakes and tea or whatever else you'd like to drink."

Matty made to rise. "Shall I…?"

"No, no, Miss Mather," Lord Wenning said amiably. "Hope will manage."

Inevitably, Catherine rose to go with her friend, and Archie Holles clearly meant to follow.

"We'd like you to stay, Holles," Francisco said, and Archie was so surprised he sat back down again with a bump.

"I suppose you're about to explain this very odd gathering to us, Wenning." The irritable voice belonged to Lord Sedgemoor.

"I am," Wenning said imperturbably, seating himself beside his wife. "At least, I am with the aid of Mr. Francis, here. For those of you not so well acquainted with Francis as I, he is highly respected by the Prime Minister, the Foreign Secretary, and all concerned at the highest echelons of government. I tell you this so that you will not dismiss what he is about to tell you as some bizarre fantasy."

All eyes swiveled to Francisco. Matty almost expected him to stand and bow. He didn't.

He raised his teacup, sipped, and set it back in its saucer. "I have to thank Lord and Lady Wenning for inviting us all here—undercover, you might say, of an eccentric at home. Before I begin, I need to ask whether or not you decide to join my proposed endeavor for your discretion. I truly believe it could be fatal if word about what I am about to say reached the wrong quarters."

Lord Sedgemoor groaned. "Not more cloak and dagger nonsense!"

"On the contrary," Francisco said mildly. "My plan is to bring everything into the light where it can be dealt with safely and according to the law. You will notice that we have here some noted members of both houses of parliament, a respected representative of the legal profession, and an artist."

"I'm pleased to see him, of course, but why *is* Dornan here?" Lord Dominic asked. "Come that, why am *I* here? I'm no politician."

"Dornan's here because he couldn't get Lord Tamar," Dearham said irrepressibly.

"I asked Lord Tamar, too," Francisco retorted. "But he has rushed off to his lady's lying-in. I wanted an artist to...record certain events. It may or may not turn out to be important, but I understand Mr. Dornan can sketch with extraordinary speed and accuracy and specializes in portraits."

"He does," Dearham admitted.

"Though it pains us to admit it," Lord Calton drawled.

"Just because he has drawn you after too many brandies the night before," the Duchess of Dearham said unexpectedly.

This drew a wave of slightly shocked laughter. Dornan smiled faintly but said nothing.

Francisco said, "Lord Dominic, I wanted as a foot soldier and guardian, not least because we may need the help and observation of the ladies present. Miss Mather has already helped me considerably, and she is, moreover, connected to those I am investigating."

"Am I a foot soldier also?" Holles inquired.

"Yes, but you also hold useful information and could play a vital role in this, if you will."

"In what?" Dearham asked curiously. "Who and what are you investigating?"

Francisco took another sip of tea. "I had better go back to the beginning. It had come to the attention of my superiors that political meetings advocating reform and radical ideas had proliferated recently. Moreover, from various sources, they had noted that increasingly, these meetings happened at more or less the same times of the same days, and not just within London, but all over the country."

"You're going after such meetings?" Holles scowled. "I told you, I'll have nothing to do with it."

"Hear me out," Francis said mildly. "One of our informants provided the fact that word of the next meeting—presumably the timing of it—was to be passed at a Maida Gardens masquerade, with slightly ridiculous dramatics. A masked lady wearing red flowers would receive this information secretly from a gentleman wearing a red mask, who would seek her out."

Francis gave a crooked smile. "This is where I come into the story, and I found it as foolish as you clearly do. I will confess that I was annoyed to be sent on the wild goose chase of intercepting this information. I will further confess to a certain sympathy for those trying to win reform. Neither are an excuse for my failure. I allowed myself to be misled." His gaze swept briefly over Matty. "And by pursuing the wrong red flowers, let the information escape me. It was only when I realized my error that I remembered who else had been present at the masquerade and wearing red flowers."

"Who?" Lord Dominic demanded. "Don't keep us in suspense."

"A lady known to all of us and whose scandalous connection to a gentleman other than her husband is only whispered in polite company."

"Emma, Lady Carntree," Viola said flatly. "I thought you were bringing matters into the light?"

Francisco inclined his head. "A fair point, and I suppose this is not the time for gentlemanly discretion. So you'll understand why I looked into her connection with Sir Anthony Thorne."

Mr. Halland, one of the most radical members of parliament, laughed. "Thorne is no radical! He's more reactionary than Lord Sedgemoor!"

"Proud to be a reactionary," growled Sedgemoor.

"The point is," Francisco intervened, "everyone here may be justifiably proud of their opinions and their stances on principle within our political and legal system. Whichever side of the divide they fall."

"Hear, hear," Halland said. "But Thorne would not be seen dead at the kind of meeting you describe."

"As a matter of fact, you're wrong," Francis said. "Though I agree he would not wish to be recognized. But he was seen. Largely because he possesses all the contempt of the south country gentleman for the industrial northerner. He was observed at just such a meeting in Manchester and recognized by a very dedicated and intelligent young man who was as baffled as you by his presence. He assumed Thorne was there to gather information. And he probably was, though not quite for the uses my friend imagined."

"So Thorne is attending radical meetings?" Dearham said with considerable doubt.

"No, I think he's organizing them," Francisco said. "With the help of a few people like Emma Carntree and some devoted servants who maintain the distance between Thorne and the ground-level organizers such as my Manchester friend."

"Seems a bit of a leap to me," Calton said.

"It does," Francisco agreed. "But I have been looking into him quite carefully. For one thing, he quickly ran through his first wife's fortune getting elected to the House of Commons and getting noticed. He is now in debt, living off the expectations of his forthcoming marriage to another heiress—Miss Mather's sister. That is background, and he needs money now in order to make more from a position of power."

"He's likely to advance quickly," Halland allowed. "Unless *we* get into power at the next election."

Sedgemoor snorted.

Francisco said, "That may be part of his hurry. The other is he cannot afford to wait for advancement until he is old. Being Prime Minster does not bring him wealth, of course, but someone like him would find ways to make such power work for him financially. So, he cannot wait. He means to force the pace. He needs to."

"How?" Dearham demanded.

Francisco let out a breath. "By bringing people onto the street en masse in coordinated marches, creating unrest and fear of revolution. From which he will emerge as savior of the country."

"It couldn't happen," Halland said impatiently. "Even if such marches were successful in changing the government, it wouldn't be to put *Thorne* in charge!"

"Of course not," Francisco said. "He doesn't mean the marches to be successful. He wants them squashed by the army, at his command, after which, his army cronies will put him at the head of the country."

This was greeted by stunned silence. Matty's jaw was not the only one dropping.

"A military coup d'etat," Ludovic Dunne said slowly. "Almost like Napoleon Bonaparte in France."

"With a few obvious differences," Francis said.

"The chief one being this is *England*," Sedgemoor snapped.

"It is indeed. But as I've said, I have been studying Thorne, and he has drawn about him several important military allies here in London and the militias stationed throughout the whole country. And I include not only Scotland but Ireland. Holles, perhaps you will tell everyone what you have been asked to do?"

Holles swallowed. "Raise a band of radical-minded students, intellectuals, and young people ready for a fight. To march on Westminster on Thursday afternoon."

"You see what this will do?" Francisco said with more urgency. "With Thorne prepared, he alone will not shilly-shally about, asking protesters to disperse and waiting to see if things will calm down. He will order the troops—already riled-up by him to fear revolution—to fire on the protesters. Among the inevitable dead are likely be all the leaders of popular opposition, including the young men of good family—like Holles here—who might have success in opposing him. He is wiping out the opposition in advance of taking power."

Again, silence fell. And then everyone started talking at once.

It was Lord Wenning who raised a hand for silence, which he was given, reluctantly, since no one could be heard in any case.

Like everyone else, Matty was stunned. And yet, for Sir Anthony Thorne, so ambitious, so self-obsessed, it made a perverse kind of sense. Dread formed in the pit of her stomach.

"It's a theory," Wenning observed. "One we cannot prove but have to take seriously because if we don't, it may be too late."

"So, without this all-important proof," Dunne said, "what the devil can we do about it?"

"*Get* the proof," Francisco said. "And bring it into the light."

Everyone regarded him with consternation.

"How?" Holles demanded. "If he has been this clever so far, he's not going to risk giving himself away now."

"Not if he knows he's doing it," Francisco agreed. "We need to trick him, and I was hoping that between us, we could all come up with a plan that would prove him either guilty or innocent. But we have to be quick, for there's not much time left before Thursday afternoon's march."

"We could just arrest all the ringleaders we know of," Sedgemoor suggested. "Surely it wouldn't go ahead without them."

"I hope you don't include me," Holles retorted.

"And in any case," Dunne pointed out, "no one has yet broken the law. I suspect such arrests would inflame rather than calm the situation."

"He's a slippery customer," Halland said. "I can't see how we would get him to show his hand. Unless we somehow convince him that he needs to stiffen the backs of the protesters, and we're all hiding in a basement, ready to burst in when he says the wrong thing."

"It would have to be *something* like that," Wenning said. "But we'd have to see his face as well as hear the words, and I don't see quite how—"

"Masked," Matty said suddenly.

Everyone turned to stare at her, and she flushed uncomfortably.

Francisco began to smile. "Somewhere he and we could be masked and not out of place, where people of all classes and backgrounds can gather unnoticed, with space enough to slope off and hold meetings."

"Maida Gardens!" Lady Wenning cried, and the Duchess of Dearham began to laugh.

CHAPTER TWENTY-ONE

WHILE CONVERSATION BURST out, Matty happened to be looking at Lady Wenning, mainly so that she didn't gaze too adoringly at Francisco. For an instant, her ladyship stared at the laughing duchess, her eyes widening in something like shock. Her lips formed words which might have been, "So *that* is…" And then she closed her mouth, looking bemused.

Intriguing, but not of vital importance at the moment.

Without rising from his chair, Francisco bowed to Lady Wenning, and the talk around the room fell away to silence. Somehow, he held the attention of all these titled and powerful people without obvious effort.

"Maida is perfect. Saturday's masked ball is our best chance. Holles, I will need you to communicate with your contacts as soon as possible. Suggest the necessity of a secret meeting of group leaders with the men at the top to keep everyone rallied together. Suggest courage might fail without a word of encouragement from your respected leader, or whatever nonsense you think will spread among your fellow radicals and ensure Thorne will turn up."

"*If* it's Thorne who turns up," Sedgemoor muttered. "I don't like the man. He's a jumped-up nobody and far too confident for his own good. But damn, I can't see him having the gall to attempt something like this!"

"Holles could just sew doubt among the radicals so that no one turns up for the march," Lord Dominic said. "Then there is no problem."

"Then we wouldn't know who was behind it, and he would not be stopped," Ludovic Dunne said quietly. "He could try the same thing later on and succeed."

Francisco nodded. "Whoever he is, he must be exposed and punished."

"This works for London," Lord Wenning commented. "But what of the rest of the country, which you say is being likewise led to disaster?"

"Newspapers," Francisco replied. "And pamphlets. Which is where Mr. Dornan comes in. Sketches of our man unmasked with news of the plot should keep everyone off the streets, both protesters and soldiers. Though it will be a close-run thing to print and distribute them as far as Scotland and Ireland between Saturday night and Thursday. I'll have the pieces written so that they're ready to go with only small changes as soon as we have Dornan's sketches to go with them."

"And the rest of us?" Dearham asked.

Francisco considered. "Perhaps, if you can do so discreetly, inform colleagues you trust and bring them to Maida, too. My superiors will ensure the military has observers, too. But we need all of you to lend an air of innocent fun to the whole thing. Thorne, or whoever our puppeteer is, must suspect nothing, or he will simply bolt. I'll be in touch with all of you before Saturday, but Holles, your contribution is vital in the first stages, so we need to talk about your notes and conversations with your fellow organizers."

"I'm free now," Holles said, jumping to his feet. He looked quite incensed that he and his principles were being abused so cynically. And being Archie, he probably felt more for those poorer men with everything to lose.

Catherine, Matty thought, *could do a lot worse than that young man.*

"Feel free to use the library," Lord Wenning said, rising to his feet. "I'll show you the way."

"More tea, anyone?" Lady Wenning offered brightly, and sudden laughter caught in Matty's throat. There was an element of hysteria to it, for her heart already ached for Marion and for the damage Thorne's exposure would do to her already precarious relationship with her sister.

"I suppose your task will be to keep an eye on Thorne's activities through your sister," the Duke of Dearham said as Francisco left the room without glancing at her.

"In so far as I can."

"You are in a difficult position," he observed.

She glanced at him in surprise, for his reputation was not one of great compassion and understanding. But then, reputation frequently lied. "It is not easy. But my sister's position is worse."

"I HAVE NO idea what is going on," Mrs. Dove confided to Matty as the meeting slid back into a kind of extended tea party. "This reminds me only too much of another tea with the Gorses when they all set out to prove Dominic's innocence. Then, my purpose was merely to bring Viola."

"And today you brought Catherine," Matty said vaguely, for she was fighting disappointment in having no chance to speak to Francisco.

Mrs. Dove cast her a look that was surprisingly shrewd. "I brought you." She set down her cup. "We should think about going. I have to take Catherine to a musical evening. Perhaps you would be so good as to fetch the children? Not with the dog!" she added fervently as Matty rose at once to obey.

She found the children by the simple expedient of following the noise. In the dining room, under the anxious eyes of a nurse, they had clearly introduced the Wennings' gleeful heir to Pup. The child was not much more than a year, and Arabella was holding him over Pup's back as though he were riding him. The chortling child held handfuls of the dog's fur while Adrian led him around the table by the collar.

Pup made occasional lunges toward the tabletop for food but otherwise was perfectly good-natured about his role.

"Look, Miss Matty, our new cousin!" Susan exclaimed. "And he likes Pup."

"Fortunately, *Pup* seems to like him," the nurse muttered.

"He is a ridiculously good-natured dog," Matty assured her before turning to her charges. Catherine and Hope were gossiping at one end of the table, occasionally pausing to laugh at the antics of Pup and the baby. "Sadly, it's time to restore his little lordship to his nurse, for your mama is ready to leave. You must go and thank Lady Wenning for her hospitality."

"With Pup?" Adrian asked, a gleam in his eyes, while Arabella swung the child off the dog's back to make him laugh rather than cry to be parted from his steed.

"Sadly, no," Matty said firmly. "*I* shall take Pup downstairs."

Fortunately, Pup seemed happy enough to stay with her as everyone filed out, and the nurse bore her charge back to his nursery for a well-earned nap. Even Pup had need of occasional quiet.

Matty ruffled his great head. "You are a good dog, sometimes," she assured him and received a tail wag and a casual lick on her wrist. "Well done. Shall we go downstairs? Fortunately, you don't seem to have the strength left to pull me off my feet."

Pup wagged his tail again, and Matty led him to the door just as someone strode inside and closed it. There was barely time for the delighted lurch of her heart before she was seized in Francisco's arms and soundly, thoroughly kissed. A tiny sob of relief and happiness escaped her, lost in his mouth. She clutched his shoulder, his nape in an effort to get closer to him.

Until she felt the hard nudge of Pup's head between them. Clearly, he was scandalized. Francisco's lips loosened enough to smile against hers.

"I have missed you," he whispered.

"I was afraid you would not," she said honestly.

His arms tightened. "Someone will pay for your lost confidence, along with everything else..." His lips slid around to her ear. "You are beautiful and fascinating, brave, kind, and clever..."

"And any man would die happy in my basilisk stare."

He let out a breath of laughter. "He would. *I* would. I have set about acquiring a special license. Because it's quicker than banns. But say if you don't like the idea. After all, you have not known me for very long, and I am not a conventional sort of husband."

"I love the idea." She buried her face in his neck, breathing in the scent of his skin and all the sensual memories it inspired. "You are *my* sort of husband."

"Good," he said, kissing her again. This time, Pup nudged him with unmistakable warning, and he released her with a reluctant laugh. "Come, I'll manage your brute."

"Are you not supposed to be closeted with Mr. Holles?"

"He's composing notes, which I'll check over."

His energy was almost frightening. And in amongst everything he'd taken on, he was applying to the archbishop for a special license to marry her.

They made it to the foot of the stairs before the sounds of approaching Doves excited Pup. So Francisco continued to hold him until Matty and the Doves had all donned their outerwear, after which he handed the lead to Adrian, bowed to the ladies, and ran back upstairs while the footman showed them out.

That amazing, brave man is my lover, Matty thought in a fresh burst of wonder and happiness. *He is going to be my husband.*

A COUPLE OF days later, a maid brought a note to the schoolroom for Matty, just as her pupils were finishing off the afternoon's efforts in watercolors. Since they were busy, and she recognized the brisk, bold hand as Francisco's, she unfolded the note at once with a fast-beating heart.

It was not a love letter, merely stating that he had obtained a special license and asking her to meet him in the usual place to discuss times and places for the ceremony. A rush of emotion paralyzed her. She was going to be married. To him. Soon. And before that, she was going to see him again, in just a couple of hours…

"Would this do, Miss Matty?" Susan asked doubtfully.

Hastily, Matty stuffed the note in the pocket of her serviceable dress and went to examine Susan's work. She had no real aptitude for sketching or painting, but her colors were always a refreshing surprise. Matty complimented her on the latter, though added that the perspective needed work—the orange was the same size as the window beyond it—and turned to Arabella's painting, which was more correct. In music, they were the opposite, with Arabella showing the flare but having to be reined in on technical matters.

Matty hoped fervently that her replacement would help them both flourish, bring them on without squashing their spirits and talents.

"I think we have finished for the day," she said. "Clear up, and we'll leave them to dry for now."

"We're having tea in the cellar," Susan informed her. "You're welcome, Miss Matty. Mama and Catherine are out."

"Thank you," Matty said, touched. The cellar had been their place of refuge since they had come to London. In fact, Viola had once hidden Lord Dominic there when he had escaped from prison. She was distracted from the memory by the unexpected sight of her sister walking into the schoolroom.

"Marion!" Matty went to greet her. "Is everything well? Where is Mama?"

"Laid upon her bed in exhaustion," Marion replied with the ghost of a smile. "We have spent the last three evenings at ton parties, and she is not used to the hours."

"Neither are you," Matty pointed out, noting her sister's wan pallor and the faint worry lines about her eyes. "Arabella, would you ask them to send tea up here for us?"

"Of course, though the cellar is more comfortable."

Marion looked understandably startled by this confidence, though she smiled as the girls skipped off. "They are rather sweet children. I can see why you don't want to leave them."

That reduced Matty to silence. She hadn't wanted to live in Thorne's household rather more. And now she *was* going to leave the Dove household to marry Francisco.

"So, Sir Anthony has been squiring you to parties?" she said, reverting to the previous topic as they settled at the table.

"Well, he takes us there and then vanishes. We don't see him again until we leave."

"He seemed attentive enough at the Wennings' ball."

Marion drew in her breath. "He didn't want us in London, you know. He wanted me to wait in the country until he came home in the summer to be married. He didn't seem to understand that I might want some excitement, elegant new clothes, a sight of the townhouse where we are to live when parliament sits."

"To say nothing of spending time with him," Matty murmured. "And he with you."

"Exactly," Marion said. "And he did obtain us the invitation to Lady Wenning's ball, from which all our acquaintance in London has stemmed, but…" She broke off as the footman entered with a tray and set out the tea things on the table.

Matty poured the tea and indicated Marion help herself to sandwiches, scones, or cakes.

"He is always so busy," Marion said. "Even when he takes us to parties, he spends his time with important friends and leaves us quite to our own devices. Once, I'm sure he even *left* and came back to fetch us."

"And this," Matty asked carefully, "makes you discontented?"

"It's a bit like being taken by your parent to play with other children for an afternoon."

Matty sipped her tea. "What does Mama say?" she asked at

last.

Marion shrugged. "That I knew he was a busy man when I agreed to marry him."

"And you are wondering now if this is enough?"

Marion nodded miserably. "You told me, and I knew in my heart, that he would never have offered for me if I had not inherited a fortune. And I knew he had not treated you well. But I thought it wouldn't matter. That I would like to be Lady Thorne, with an important husband, a house in town, respected and sought after. That I would not miss him so much if I was busy, too, especially if you were with me. But when I compare his neglect to…"

"To what?"

"To Lord Danvers's attentiveness," Marion said with a touch of defiance. "He has walked with us in the park. He makes a point of dancing with me or talking to me when we meet at parties. And he dotes on his little daughters, who are delightful."

With an effort, Matty managed not to dive into the fray with both feet. "And so, you have begun to wonder if you would not prefer a husband who is a little more of a partner? Who supported you, as well as expected your support?"

Marion nodded. "I agreed to marry Sir Anthony."

"But no contracts or settlements have yet been signed?"

"No. What should I do, Matty?"

Matty considered. "What you *are* doing. You have been immured in the country all your adult life, knowing only the same people you grew up with. Make friends and see where it takes you."

"But I am engaged to Sir Anthony!"

"It sounds to me as if you no longer wish to be."

"I don't think I do," Marion whispered.

Matty drew in her breath. "Tell him. Sooner rather than later. And then tell the biggest gossip you know."

Marion stared at her, the teacup hovering at her lips. "Why?"

"Because I would not be surprised if Sir Anthony came in for a fall," Matty said, "and I would not like you to be associated with him when it happened. If it happened."

Marion frowned, searching her eyes. "You are warning me."

"I have been warning you since you engaged yourself to him."

Marion was silent. She stared down into her teacup. "You were the brave one, the one who went away and made sure we did not starve after Papa died. I told myself I had to stay, to look after Mama, that my role was equally as vital as yours. But I envied you that courage. Part of me, at least, was ashamed that I did not at least try to do the same. And then I did one better. I, not you, inherited the money, and suddenly everything was different. I was rich, looking after Mama and the house. I had attracted the suitor who had already rejected you. In fact, *you* were the disapproved of sister because you would not leave your post to help me." She paused, shaking her head. "Sibling jealousy is not a pretty emotion. Even at the time, I did not like it."

Marion set down her cup with an upward quirk of her lips. "Funnily enough, since we came to London, I have been remembering our childhood more, the fun and the secrets… It's a shame we grow up."

"No," Matty said. "There's just a different kind of fun to be had."

Marion reached across the table and took her hand. Matty squeezed it and felt tears well behind her eyes.

"SHE'S GOING TO tell him tonight," Matty told Francisco when they met in the disused coach house on the Bernard Street mews. "Which I can't help thinking is a good thing, not just for her, but for our plans. Without Marion's money, he *has* to stick to his scheme, whatever the difficulties raised by Holles and the others. Otherwise, his creditors will descend on him like all the fiends of hell."

"That is true. Providing he takes his conge like a gentleman."

Matty frowned with fresh worry. "I had not thought of that. I just thought she would be safe from association with him if the word spreads beforehand that their engagement is ended."

"It is certainly best. Did you tell Marion about our engagement?"

Matty flushed and shook her head. "It didn't seem right while she was ending her own. There's a world of sisterly grudges and jealousies I never took the time to deal with."

"It is not all your responsibility," he pointed out, taking her hands.

"Nor all hers." She stepped into Francisco's arms and, with a little sigh of contentment, rested her head on his chest. "And your own arrangements for Thorne?"

"Well in hand. We should have a large crowd at Maida, of the highest and the lowest in the city. When will you marry me?"

She smiled into his coat. "Whenever you like. Tonight, if you wish. When this all over if you prefer."

"I have run an old university friend to earth. He is in holy orders and prepared to perform the marriage where and when we wish. Tonight might be a stretch, but we could arrange it for Saturday afternoon."

Her breath caught. "So I will be your wife when we go to Maida?"

"If you would like to be."

She took his face between her hands. "Oh, I would, Francisco. I would."

Their lips met in a sweet, satisfying kiss, one of promise rather than arousal.

"I have to go," he said reluctantly. "Two o'clock on Saturday, at Grillon's."

"Grillon's?" she repeated, startled.

"I thought you would like your family to be there."

"Actually, I would," she said, surprised by the discovery.

"And ask whoever else you wish." He stepped back and raised each of her hands to his lips. "Until Saturday."

CHAPTER TWENTY-TWO

SIR ANTHONY THORNE strode furiously away from Grillon's Hotel. How dare she? The little country nobody thought *she* could jilt *him*? She would soon find out her mistake, for he was not the man to let a fortune slip through his fingers. Or allow himself to be a laughing stock at this critical juncture.

He would allow her tonight and perhaps tomorrow to regret her words. It was pique, after all, and she had a point. He had not been as attentive as he should. She had a right, as his betrothed, to expect more. And as soon as this business at Maida was done, he would live in her damned pocket until Thursday, when the fireworks would begin. By a week tomorrow, he would be Prime Minister or going by whatever title was considered appropriate to a more autocratic ruler. And she would be overwhelmed.

In fact, he could easily nip her intent to jilt him in the bud. He should have thought of it before. Let her wretched mother discover them in a compromising position, and they would be down the aisle tomorrow. For the moment, though, he couldn't really trust himself to manage it properly. He was more angry and flustered than he could recall since he came of age, and having to deal with the last-minute jitters of people who had been eating out of his hand—unknowingly, of course—for months.

This was something else he had not foreseen. Several sources over the last few days had brought him notes and words of worry. They wanted his word the troops would not be turned loose on them, that their voices would be heard with impunity. He had been at a loss as to how to calm these unexpected last-minute nerves, which was part of what had kept him from the side of his betrothed. But then young Holles had come up with the perfect solution. If discretion was so vital to their leader until the march, why didn't he speak, masked, to some of the leaders at Maida Gardens?

There, everyone would be masked for the public masquerade ball. The other patrons would be drunk and dancing, and no one would pay a blind bit of attention to a group of more serious people in a quiet part of the garden. Thorne was something of an orator. He did not doubt his ability to twist the doubters around his little finger, and with less effort that it would take to bring Marion Mather back to heel. The only trouble was, it took more arranging. He would need more bodyguards, a speedy exit, clothes that would not give him away, a thick mask, and practice at disguising his voice.

At this point, he realized his steps were taking him to Bruton Street, which was just what he needed. He would catch Emma before she went out for the evening, restore his male pride and equilibrium to where they should be by means of brisk, physical pleasure. And then go about his business.

The butler, as usual, admitted him without comment, merely remarking that her ladyship was in her boudoir.

"Then I'll just step up," Thorne said and ascended the stairs in his usual stately manner.

Emma was not in her sitting room, though he could hear movement in the bedchamber beyond. He found her sitting on the bed, throwing piles of clothes into a trunk. She looked up at his entrance but didn't pause in her activity.

"Good Lord, are you leaving with the Season in full swing?" he asked, amused. "Don't tell me Carntree has finally stuck his spoon in the wall?"

"No, though he isn't well. I'm going to join him."

"You stun me. When?"

"In the morning."

"Then you have time for a farewell favor?"

She cast him a glance of dislike. "No. I do not. If you have anything to say, Anthony, say it and go away. I'm busy."

"So it would appear," he said acidly, disliking her attitude. "What has put you in such a filthy humor? It is quite unbecoming in a mistress."

"So it is. Consider our arrangement, if there ever was one, at an end."

His eyes narrowed, and he sat on an empty edge of the bed. Two conges in one hour was something of a shock. "You are in the dismals. What has brought all this about?"

"*I* have. I saw myself through another's eyes, and I did not like what I saw. Do you know, I tried to ruin a complete stranger just because someone danced with her rather than with me?"

"Quite right, too," Thorne said. "Ruining her, I mean. If you didn't succeed, we can try again. I am happy to oblige you in such a service."

She threw some hairbrushes into the trunk. "You haven't been listening, have you? I don't *like* who I am, who I've become. I don't blame you, but you are not good for me. We are not good for each other. So I'm going home to my husband. Perhaps I can do better."

"After a little pleasure," Thorne said, knocking her backward across the bed and looming over her. At the last minute, she reached up and grasped the bell pull by the headboard, dragging it with her in a definite tug. The room would soon be full of servants.

"Goodbye, Anthony," she said clearly.

He threw her arm away like an offensive piece of litter and rose to his feet. "Goodbye, my dear. Let us pray you do not regret such rudeness."

ON FRIDAY EVENING, Matty had a slightly disturbing chat with Catherine. The girl had worn a distracted look for some time, but since it appeared to be happy distraction, Matty had not tried to interfere.

From her bedchamber, Matty heard Mrs. Dove and Catherine return from the theatre. Over the years she had worked for the Doves, Matty had got into the habit of leaving her chamber door open a crack when she was prepared to receive visitors. She had always rather liked when any of the Doves brought her their problems or sought her advice.

Tonight, Matty herself was distracted from her nighttime preparation. She lay on top of the bed, still fully dressed, thinking, *Tomorrow by this time, I will be married. I shall be a wife. I could be alone with my husband.* Such thrilling imaginings alternated with *Tomorrow, at Maida, we have to prevent disaster.*

The scratch on her door was both an annoyance and a welcome distraction. She sat up, saying, "Come in."

Catherine slipped inside, closed the door, and rustled over in her evening finery to sit beside Matty on the bed. "Am I keeping you up?"

"I seem to be keeping myself up." There was a frown of anxiety on the girl's face that Matty did not like. "Have you got into another scrape?"

"Oh, no, rest easy on that score."

"Then what troubles you?"

Catherine appeared to be absorbed in making tiny pleats in the gauzy layer of her gown.

"Mr. Holles?" Matty guessed.

Catherine's frown vanished, and she smiled. "Oh, no. Well, partly, I suppose. I like Mr. Holles. He has made me rethink everything."

"Change—improvements—never happen as quickly as young

people would like," Matty warned.

"Oh, I know that. So does Archie, but that should not prevent us from trying, should it?"

"Not within the law," Matty said warily, but Matty had moved on.

"I'm so comfortable with Archie, it's rather like being with a brother—only, of course, he's nothing like Adrian, thank God—or a friend. Only...not quite. I think... Do you remember, only two or three weeks ago, I fancied myself in love with Mr. Granton?"

"I do."

"I was always concerned with what he thought of me, of my effect on him, without really thinking of anything beyond his handsome face and how I would be envied—I, the mocked bluestocking of the family—for catching so eligible a husband so early in the Season."

"Understandable," Matty allowed. "But not, perhaps, very healthy."

"Exactly," Catherine said. "An older, more experienced man had cachet, but you know, he had nothing to say beyond flirtation. Perhaps because he regarded me as that silly, or because *he* is."

Matty let her cogitate that for a little. Then said encouragingly, "Does it matter?"

"Not now. I think a person nearer one's own age is more...appealing."

"Like Mr. Holles."

Catherine smiled a secretive, conspiratorial smile. "I have been wondering if I love him. He is so interesting to me... He kissed me at Lady Wenning's ball."

"Did he?" Matty could hardly scold her as she recalled her own delicious embraces at the same event. "Did you—er... like it?"

Another smile flitted across the girl's face, though she dropped her eyes. "Yes. That is what made me wonder if I love him."

"You do know if he tries to do more than kiss you, you must not let him?" *Yes, I am that hypocritical, but the girl is not yet eighteen years old!* And they had discussed such matters and their consequences before since Matty was sure Mrs. Dove never would.

"Oh, no, he doesn't."

"And yet, it troubles you to imagine you might be in love with him?"

"Oh, no, that does not trouble me. If I am in love, I rather like it. I was thinking more of Hope."

"Hope." Matty wrenched her tired mind around. "How does Archie Holles make you think of Hope?"

Catherine gave a gurgle of laughter. "Well, he doesn't, of course! But *love* does. You see, one of the reasons I was so eager to imagine myself in love with Mr. Granton was because Hope is hope*less*ly in love with someone of around the same age."

A twinge of anxiety twisted through Matty. Hope was not her responsibility, but she had grown fond of the girl. "Dare I ask with whom?"

"I'm sworn to secrecy."

A scene at Lady Wenning's ball came back to her. Hope Darblay arriving out of the blue, apparently to talk to her when she was in company with the recently married Duke of Dearham and…

"Lord Calton," Matty said.

Catherine's eyes widened. "How did you know?" she gasped.

"I didn't. Something just made sense. She does know how unsuitable Calton is? I imagine women have been setting their caps at him for the last ten years. He is a friend of Dearham's, and even, probably, Hope's own brother, although Rollo is probably a little younger."

"I think half the attraction is his wickedness," Catherine confided. "But I can't think he is very comfortable to be around and certainly not to have for one's husband."

"I suspect you are right. And you have this insight because

you are contemplating Mr. Holles as your husband."

Catherine flushed. "Well, yes, it entered my mind, but I am in no rush."

"You really are the most intelligent of all my pupils," Matty said warmly. "And as for Hope... I don't think Calton even notices her. Not very pleasant for her, perhaps, but a lot safer. I expect she will grow out of it soon, meet an Archie of her own."

"Oh, I do hope so. And now that Cousin Grace is home, she will surely take Hope in hand and distract her!" Catherine smiled with happy relief and stood up. "I'm for bed! Good night, Miss Matty!"

THE FOLLOWING MORNING, feeling something of a traitor, Matty took a deep breath, marched up to her employer's bedchamber door, and knocked.

"Come in," said Mrs. Dove's amiable voice, and Matty entered to discover the lady sitting up in bed, surrounded by pillows, wearing a froth of old lace and a fetching nightcap She clutched a cup of hot chocolate and held a piece of buttered toast half-way to her mouth. "Oh! Miss Mather, what a surprise. Surely one of the children is not ill?"

"No, no, nothing like that," Matty assured her. "I... I wanted to give you some news... You have been so kind to me, and I am so fond of all your children that I hate to let you down, but I'm afraid I really will be leaving when my notice is served or maybe even sooner. But I do know of a replacement who might suit."

"Oh, no!" Mrs. Dove, in clear dismay, dropped her toast onto the plate without noticing. "You are not giving in and going to live with your sister, are you? Because I cannot advise you strongly enough against it! Not because of your sister, of course, she seems very pleasant, and she *is* your sister, though I did hear a rumor that the engagement is over—that may well be fustian, of course. But Sir *Anthony*… You must not tell her I said so because no one likes to hear ill of their husband, but he seems to me the kind of man who is so amiable and righteous in public while pinching the maids in private, which will be awful for your sister, of course, but at least she will be his *wife*. But for *you* to be in the power of such a man…"

"Mrs. Dove, I am not going to live with my sister," Matty broke in as soon as Mrs. Dove paused for breath.

The lady closed her mouth and peered at Matty. "You're not? Well, that is good news, at all events. I shall give you a glowing character, of course, but I wish you will tell me if your salary is insufficient because I'm sure I can find a way to increase—"

"Dear ma'am, it is not the salary," Matty broke in desperately, unsure whether she was going to laugh or cry. "It is more than adequate, and I assure you I never hoped to have such contentment, such pleasure, in any post as I have had in your house. The truth is, ma'am, that I am about to be married."

The cup of chocolate sagged in Mrs. Dove's fingers, splashing rich, brown chocolate on the tray. Mrs. Dove set it down hastily.

"Married?" she exclaimed. "But to whom? Does your mama know? Oh, and Miss Matty, I *hope* you are not doing this just to escape Thorne and your sister, for *that* wouldn't answer either, even if…!"

"To Mr. Francis, ma'am. And no, this has nothing to do with anyone but the two of us. My mother does *not* know, but I am on my way to tell her and also," Matty pursued relentlessly as her employer's mouth opened once more, "I wished to invite you and the children—yes, and even Pup!—to my mother's rooms at Grillon's where we shall be married at half-past two this afternoon. If you would like to come. Anyway, I'm sorry and happy and…" She flapped one hand and fled from the room before tears engulfed her. She still didn't know if she was weeping or laughing.

A LITTLE AFTER midday, Sir Anthony Thorne left his house and strolled around to Grillon's Hotel.

Everything was in hand for his appearance at Maida this evening, and after that, all would be ready for the marches on Thursday. By Friday, he expected all power to be his. So, he had the time to spend petting Marion back into line.

He was sure that was all she would need, though he also had the time for more drastic measures, to begin his life in power he needed at least the appearance of money. Rumors of the rift between him and his intended had already reached the most nervous of his creditors, and he wanted such talk nipped in the bud, largely for the sake of appearances which, as he well knew, were so important.

Of course, Emma Carntree's departure for the country did him no harm either. Like everyone else, Marion would no doubt have heard the rumors that Thorne had dismissed her to keep his betrothed happy. She was no schoolroom miss, after all.

And surely, by the time anyone noticed Matilda Mather after next Thursday, she would have given up her ridiculous post as governess. Everything was looking up. One simply had to attend to details.

However, it would not do to enter his wife-to-be's rooms with too much of a swagger. Imposing a contrite, hopeful expression on his face, he knocked on the door and was admitted by the maid, who curtseyed as usual. "Sir Anthony. The ladies are in the sitting room."

They were indeed, although he could not pretend their reaction to his arrival was unalloyed joy. In fact, they looked up from a hat they had been admiring with almost matching expressions of astonishment.

Marion blushed a fiery red while her mother rose from her chair with all the regality of a middle-aged woman whose thoroughly ordinary daughter had unexpectedly inherited a fortune. "Sir Anthony, we were not expecting you. To what do we owe the honor?"

"Why, my desire to apologize to my affianced bride and to crave the favor of an interview with her, even if it is to be our last." That was a good speech. He had practiced it in front of the mirror, in between his rallying cries to arms for this evening's audience.

And he seemed to have found just the right tone, for mother and daughter exchanged glances, and eventually Marion said, "Very well, sir. Would you permit us a moment, Mama?"

"Very well. I shall be in my bedchamber." She stalked across the room into one beyond, not quite closing the door behind her.

Thorne came and sat beside his bride, twirling his hat between his fingers. "Dear Marion, I owe you so many apologies. I don't know where to begin. For my unforgivable anger at our last meeting, most certainly. For my neglect of you since your arrival in London, also. I should have explained from the outset that my commitments would keep me from you far more than I would like. To be honest, this was why I was not in favor of you coming to London until after the wedding."

"When your commitments would somehow be less?" she asked with polite disbelief.

He concealed his irritation, saying merely, "I certainly have the time to make them so. I want to ask your forgiveness, Marion. And I want you to understand that everything I am doing, everything that keeps me away from you, I do for you. For the life you and I deserve together."

"I must ask you to stop, sir," she said, a little shakily. "Although I thank you for your explanation, it comes too late. For I have come to realize I do not want the distant yet public marriage ours would be. I could not be your political hostess. We would not suit, Sir Anthony. I think you know that."

Casting his hat aside, he took both her hands. He was glad to feel the trembling of her fingers. "Come, my dear, there is no need for such talk. We have already agreed we suit admirably. We have already agreed to marry."

"I'm afraid I have changed my mind." She tried to tug her hands free. "I no longer wish to marry you and must ask you to respect my word as final."

He smiled into her nervous eyes. "But I don't," he said softly, much too softly for her mother to hear in the next room as more than an unthreatening hum. "You *will* marry me, for all the reasons we discussed before, but also because you have no choice."

With one swift, hard movement, he pushed her onto her back and rammed his body over hers. Her hands scrabbled against his shoulders, her mouth open wide to scream before he was ready. It was a necessary part of his plan to have Mrs. Mather see them like this, but not until Marion's bodice and skirts were a little more disordered.

He shut the little fool up by covering her open mouth with his and dragging at her skirts. He wondered how far he would get before they were discovered in flagrante. *Damn*, was that her already?

Something hard struck him across the shoulders, the sheer unexpectedness knocking him off Marion and the sofa and onto the carpet. He rolled, springing to his feet to face the fists or worse of whoever dared interfere—and saw Matilda seated on the sofa, smoothing out her sister's skirts with one hand, while in the other, she grasped an umbrella.

Her face was ice cold, and in her fine eyes, the angry contempt that must have reduced her most arrogant pupils to abject apology.

"No need to get on your high horse, Matilda," he mocked, dropping his fists to his sides. "Marion and I are betrothed, remember?"

"I remember she broke the engagement, and I suspect her patience with you has reached its limit?" She glanced at her sister for confirmation, and Marion nodded once, her eyes almost as furious as her sister's.

Their mother chose that moment to appear at the door to her bedchamber. "Oh, Matilda, dear, I did not hear you come in!"

"Neither did we," Thorne said, smiling as wolfishly as he had ever wished to. "I'm afraid Matilda found us in rather a compromising position."

Marion's whole face crumpled in shock and fear. Mrs. Mather strode across the room. Thorne almost laughed. Really, despite the pain in his shoulder, it was perfect, and he smiled mockingly at Matilda so that she would understand that, too.

But Matilda smiled back at him. "Nonsense, Sir Anthony. I was here the whole time."

The blatant lie dropped his jaw. The other women turned their attention to her, too. They both knew she was lying. Well, damnation, it might be clever, but he would not have it.

"If that's the way you want to play it, carry on," he said with vicious amusement. "We'll see how far that gets after a whisper in my favorite club. You will be begging for my protection. I might even give it."

"A man who attacks and compromises an unwilling young lady is no gentleman," Matilda pointed out. "Even before he starts his contemptible boasting. I wonder how long his reputation would stand that?"

"Longer than hers," Thorne snarled.

Matilda only smiled with such utter contempt that he wanted to hit her. "Goodbye, Sir Anthony."

The damned maid was even there by the outer door. There was nothing for him to do but clap his hat on his head and walk out without so much as a bow.

I'll fix this. Tomorrow, after Maida, I will fix this, too.

CHAPTER TWENTY-THREE

WHEN THE DOOR closed behind Thorne, Marion collapsed against Matty. "Oh, thank God! I couldn't get him *off* me, Matty!"

"I'm sure he was hoping Mama would catch you and insist on marriage," Matty said bracingly, patting her sister's shoulder.

"I'm not sure I shouldn't," Mama said, sinking onto the chair opposite them. "I was never so taken in by anyone in my life, but he could do a lot of damage to Marion, to both of you. In such situations, it is always the females who suffer."

Marion looked so appalled that Matty said hastily, "I wouldn't worry about that. He has other things on his mind, and after tonight, no one will believe a word he says. Marion, the world knows he was after your money, and I think you have much truer admirers now. Now, don't cry because I particularly want you to smile this afternoon. There is to be a wedding here—unless you object, in which case, we shall just have to take it to another room. I'm sure Grillon—"

"Wedding?" her mother interrupted in astonishment. "Whose wedding?"

"Mine," Matty said, coloring under her mother's and sister's stares. At least it was an effective distraction. "We have a special license, and in an hour—"

"Who?" It was Marion's turn to interrupt. "Matty, who are

you marrying?"

"Mr. Francis. At least, that is how he is generally known, but his real name is Francisco de Salgado y Goya. He was born in Spain."

"You are not going to Spain!" Mama wailed.

"No, no, not to live at least."

"But who is this man to you, Matty?" Marion demanded. "You cannot have known him long!"

"I believe you met him at Lady Wenning's ball. He is a gentleman, Mama, so you—"

"A gentleman would not court my daughter behind my back!" Mama said.

"We met before you came to London, and I am of age, Mama. Now, are you happy to receive Francisco and the clergyman, Mr. and Mrs. Dunne, and the Dove family? Say now, if you please, for I will have to speak to the hotel—"

"Of course it must be here!" Mama exclaimed. "If anywhere. But Mathilda, why are you in such a hurry over this?" Her face darkened. "Has he behaved ill to you, because—"

Matty, who knew exactly what her mother meant, blushed from memory of her intimacy with Francisco, though she interrupted her mother briskly. "Don't be silly, Mama. Had he behaved ill to me, there is no way I would even consider marrying him."

"An hour?" Mama said, scowling as she recalled the previous part of the conversation. "Marion, don't just sit there, take the hats away! Matty, plump the cushions and make the room respectable, at least! Oh, my dear, you are not planning to be married in that awful dress, are you?"

"Actually, I thought I would wear the evening gown Marion bought for me. It is not too ornate, and we are going out in the evening straight from here."

"Wedding breakfast!" Marion shrieked, her arms full of hats Matty had not even noticed.

"I believe Mr. Dunne is arranging something private," Matty

soothed. "Mama, will you help me to change?"

It was the right thing to say, making her mother feel useful and distracting her from worry. Only once, as she fastened the tiny loops at the back of the gown, she said, "Are you sure about this, Matty? Quite sure?"

"Entirely sure, Mama."

Her mother gave her a quick, hard hug from behind and then let her go. "Now, your hair—where is that dratted girl?"

While her hair was being dressed, Marion came into the room. "Your Mr. Francis is here with the clergyman and lots of fresh flowers. A hotel maid is putting them in water, and I must say they brighten up the room. Matty, you look lovely!"

Matty hung on to that in the nerve-wracking few minutes that followed. It was ridiculously hard to leave the bedchamber, to show herself to Francisco. He had been all over the world, known beautiful, fascinating women in every sense imaginable. The impossibility of dull, sharp-tongued governess Matty Mather ever living up to, let alone surpassing them, weighed her down in sudden panic.

Her mother and sister were gazing at her expectantly. Only pride allowed her to stride across the room, throw open the door, and emerge into the flower-filled sitting room.

And there was Francisco, darkly handsome in formal dress, his gaze seeking and finding her. He smiled, his eyes warm, admiring, delighted, even relieved, as if he had imagined she might yet back out. And suddenly, all her doubts fell away, like a winter cloak cast off before a fire.

She went to him, hands held out because they had chosen each other and nothing else in the past mattered. The bond had always been there, right from the first bizarre meeting in Maida Gardens. They were only formalizing it.

In a happy daze, she smiled her way through Francisco's introduction to his friend, the Reverend Mr. John Warren, and returned the Dunnes' greetings. She laughed as Pup, straining at the leash, yanked Adrian and the other Doves into the room, and almost cried when they were followed by Lord and Lady Dominic Gorse.

Only moments later, she got lost in Francisco's amazing eyes as they made their vows. A gold ring, engraved with entwined leaves, was pushed onto her finger, fitting perfectly, and then they were pronounced man and wife.

Marion was smiling with trembling lips and swimming eyes. Mama looked stunned but prided herself on being the perfect hostess, never even batting an eyelid when a hotel servant led them to the apartment next door, where an impressive spread had been laid out.

Champagne was opened, and formality, such as it had been, was dropped altogether. Pup was tied to the massive central table leg and lay down on people's feet.

The party broke up just before five o'clock, shortly after the arrival of a surprised Lord Danvers, who had come to take Marion for a drive in the park. On being informed of the event, he offered his congratulations and allowed himself to be persuaded to a glass of champagne and a toast to the bride and groom.

"Ladies and gentlemen, young people and canines," Ludovic declaimed. "Join me in a toast to the health and happiness of our friends, the Count and Countess de Salgado y Goya de Valdecara!"

"Count?" Matty repeated, staring at him.

"That was my father's title. I don't use it," Francisco said, though he sounded more amused than angry. "I think Ludo is puffing me up in case your family still has doubts."

"Oh, dear. I shall be, *my daughter, the countess*!"

"Do you hate it? I can tell everyone Ludo is joking."

She shook her head, smiling again. "It's a small price to pay for their happiness. My own couldn't be greater."

His eyes changed, burning her with their heat. "I would like to challenge that," he said softly, and desire flamed through her.

Helpfully, everyone seemed to be leaving. Marion went off with Lord Danvers. The Doves adopted Mama, sweeping her into her own sitting room for a cup of tea. Viola and Rebecca hugged Matty, and Viola promised to see her later.

And then, at last, the door was closed, and they were alone. Suddenly nervous, Matty paced about the room, examining ornaments, opening an inner door that led to an ornate bedchamber. Part of her wanted to slam the door shut again. But her heart beat too fast, and she turned slowly to face Francisco, who had come up behind her and stood so close she could smell his skin, his warmth.

Gently, he placed a finger under her chin and tipped up her face for a long, tender kiss.

"Forgive me," he whispered against her lips. "I am asking myself if we have time for a quick, marital tumble before we go to Maida."

"And have we?" she asked breathlessly.

"Oh yes. Trust me, it needn't take long." He pushed her against the wall to let her feel the proof against her abdomen, and she gasped. He traced kisses along her jaw to her ear. "I want more for you than that," he whispered. "A long, unhurried wedding night when I can shower you with pleasure, not plunder like a pirate."

"I rather like you as a pirate," she managed.

He moved, catching her mouth with his once more. "Don't tempt me, wife of my heart. Shall we go to Maida?"

She closed her eyes, hugged him harder, and then stood back. "Yes. Let us go to Maida."

THE SUN WAS just beginning to set as Matty and Francisco walked arm-in-arm up the path to Maida Gardens. Francisco had bought tickets from the uninterested young man at the gates, but it was too early for there to be many people about.

"The first time I came here, did you follow me down to the

hackney stand?" Matty asked.

"I did. It was the next best thing to escorting you home."

"A white knight in piratical garb."

He cast her a sardonic look. "Don't count on it."

When they arrived at the pavilion, which Francisco told her would be empty at this hour, the first person Matty saw was the Duchess of Dearham, her mask hanging from her fingers, while she danced boisterously without music, arm-in-arm with two young men who looked more like waiters than aristocrats.

They were all laughing, although the young men quickly disengaged themselves when they caught sight of Matty and Francisco. They looked guilty. The Duke of Dearham sat at a nearby table, apparently quite unconcerned by his wife's overly familiar behavior. Deep in conversation with a middle-aged, coatless man, he broke off to smile and rise to greet Matty and Francisco.

"I hear congratulations are in order."

"Who told you that?" Matty asked, mystified.

"Dunne. He's around somewhere. We'd bear a grudge about not being invited, except I understand the Wennings weren't either. Do I get to kiss the bride?"

Matty offered her cheek just as the duchess came over to join them.

"Don't be shocked," she said bluntly. "I was brought up by Mr. Renwick here, along with his sons."

"Kitty is a distant relative of His Grace," Mr. Renwick said severely, "lost to the family for some years and now restored. It's not a connection that's good for either of Their Graces, so we keep it quiet."

There may have been a threat in the blunt voice, though Francisco didn't rise to it.

"Mr. Francis is the most discreet of men," Ludovic Dunne commented, arriving through another door next to the table. "And therefore, so is his lady. As you know, Renwick has been approached by people we think are working for Thorne, to keep free an area of the gardens for his private use. They even asked for Renwick's staff to keep away the curious once his party begins."

"That's us," said one of the young men the duchess had been dancing with. He and his brother grinned. "But never doubt we're on your side."

"The ground is perfect," Mr. Dunne said. "It's the land behind the rose garden, where the children play in the daytime. It slopes up at the back, so everyone will be able to see and hear our speaker. We intend to flood it with light to give Dornan the best chance to draw a recognizable picture. My clerk will take notes verbatim—he's very good."

"Excellent," Dearham said. "But how do we get the mask off him? He'll have his bully-boys near him to fend off the rabble."

Francisco smiled. "As it happens, I have a plan for that. Now, I suggest we don masks and dominoes, for I think the orchestra is about to set up. Keep in touch with each other throughout the evening, but discreetly." As everyone began tying on their own or each other's masks, he lowered his voice. "I don't expect any fights or violence—"

"Good," Mr. Renwick growled.

"Neither," Francisco continued, "do I expect to be obeyed if I forbid the ladies from attending. All I ask is that you keep your distance and avoid Thorne and his bullies. Cornered, our rat may turn."

IT WAS, MATTY supposed, an odd wedding party, but at least she got to waltz with her husband while she watched the various parties of allies arrive. They were not always easy to spot, and sometimes it took a wink or impudent grin to identify them.

The Wennings arrived with Rollo Darblay and a few couples she didn't know.

"A junior foreign office minister and two generals," Francisco murmured. "One of my lot, too."

"And their wives?"

"I think they would have to be. Given Lady Wenning's presence, they would hardly bring their ladybirds."

Lord Calton strolled in with a bachelor party that included Mr. Dornan the artist, and several lords of all ages. Christopher Halland had brought his wife and several members of parliament with theirs, though Matty needed Francisco to point them out.

Archie Holles sauntered in, looking as discontented as ever. Matty thanked God that Catherine was not with him, which had been a serious worry. Instead, he was with three other expensively but unconventionally dressed young men—the representatives of his little band of radical students and intellectuals.

"There are too many of the ton here," Matty worried. "Surely Thorne will smell a rat and flee."

"There are plenty of the other sort, too. Those working men over there are with us. And those entering now. And you only notice the aristocratic ones because you're looking for them. When everyone dances, it's harder to tell who is who."

Thorne's meeting was scheduled for ten of the clock, but as the hands drew nearer, Matty's stomach clenched harder.

"He isn't here."

Francisco shrugged. "He doesn't need to be. Why would he show his face in the pavilion? Shall we walk around to the garden?"

"What if we're wrong?" she countered, squeezing Francisco's arm as they walked. "What if it isn't Thorne?" *Or he sends someone else.* Would he trust anyone else with this speech?

"Then we'll catch whoever it is, and then I'll deal with Thorne in my own way."

Matty shivered, though she knew she would do nothing to prevent whatever he had in mind. Whether or not Thorne was responsible for this treason, he was a greedy, amoral, pest of a man, whose wings had to be clipped.

"I suppose it's no use," Francisco said as they strolled through the rose garden where a few buds had formed in the lantern light, "asking you to return to the pavilion with Lady Wenning?"

"No," Matty agreed. "*There* is Lady Wenning." She and her husband's party were strolling toward the back gate that led to the meeting place. "As we agreed, the presence of women will reassure him that all is well. Otherwise, he will ignore them."

"I love your curiosity." He bent and pressed a brief hard kiss to her mouth. "And I hate it."

Some of the working men were already there, scattered across the slope. Behind those at the front and to one side, Dornan sat on the ground, chewing the end of his pencil. Masked and cloaked, he could have been of any class.

Matty's heart gave a little bump, half of triumph, half of revulsion as she saw another cloaked and masked figure strolling between two large, similarly dressed men. She had known Anthony Thorne most of her life, and she knew his proud, not quite strutting walk. He had grace, she allowed, though it was a contrived grace, learned in his late teens to impress.

"It's him," she murmured.

"I know."

CHAPTER TWENTY-FOUR

THORNE HAD ARRIVED at Maida still furious with Marion Mather and her dreadful, interfering sister. How dare the woman look him in the eye and *lie*? Surely, she had been brought up better than that, and what was more, the mother did not dispute it, although she must have known!

He silenced the voice that told him such barefaced lying was no more or less than he had done himself, and the one that told him he had been thoroughly trounced by three women. Nor could he devote the time right now to detailed plans of revenge. But after Thursday, heiresses would be lining up to marry him, and he could take his time over punishing the Mather women. Tonight was necessary to get to Thursday's marches, and so he forced back his anger and turned his mind to his prepared speeches, his disguised voice, and conjuring up the right attitude to rouse people to a proper sense of the injustices perpetrated against them.

Which was nothing to the injustices that would be perpetrated on Thursday, but there, those were the prices paid for remaining poor and unimportant.

The proprietor of the Gardens, a stout and not very obsequious person called Renwick, showed Thorne's men to the garden set aside for them and introduced them to his sons, who, he said, would be glad to take care of any trouble. If they had to summon the Watch, Renwick said direly, someone would pay.

"Insolent buffoon," Thorne muttered as Renwick stalked away. As people began to arrive in their private bit of garden, hemmed in by the hill and by trees and bushes, and the wall to the rose garden, Thorne let himself draw more attention, puffing out his chest as he walked from side to side. With each turn, the hill sprouted more men and even a scattering of women who had, presumably, come to support their menfolk.

Since he hadn't actually met any of them that he could recall, he did not recognize anyone. Except Archie Holles with a bunch of discontented-looking young men. Although Holles was masked, the sneer on his lips remained.

Thorne was glad to see a couple of men with notebooks and pencils out, ready to take note of his words to pass on to their fellows in persuasion of his ends.

Thorne fully recognized the importance of tonight, for without it, Thursday's marches were not guaranteed to go ahead in numbers enough to work. But looking at the motley crowd, ready to hang on his words, he did not doubt his ability to convince them. It was just a matter of adjusting his oratory to radical phrases rather than reactionary ones.

He flapped his arms, dismissing his burly bodyguards to a greater distance. They moved a few feet behind him and a yard or so to either side, giving him space to speak. The faint hum of his audience's talk died away, and they faced him in silence. They were, he thought, scanning their masked faces and tense posture, more anxious than adoring.

"My friends," he began in a voice pitched to reach all of them and yet to give an illusion of intimacy, to show they shared the same aims and the same dangers. "Thank you for coming to talk to me here tonight. Why don't I begin by telling you how our marches will work and what I hope we will gain with so bold a move.

"Thousands of you, from all over the city, will begin your marches in different places and close in on the seat of our deaf and blind government—and you will not be alone, for all over the country, similar marches will take place, to take over places of local government. But here in the capital, we have the most important role because we have the Houses of Parliament.

"And we will make our grievances known…"

He spent some time on those grievances, which he had learned by heart, although he didn't believe in most of them and didn't care about any. The men began to nod and murmur agreement—really, this was ridiculously easy—and he moved on to the trickier bits, the vital role they would play in history, in the changing of actual government.

"So what do we get in its place?" a man called from the hill.

For the first time since he had begun to speak, Thorne noticed that some latecomers lined the sides of the garden, too, not just the hill. For some reason, it made him feel slightly hemmed in, but he still had his bodyguards and Renwick's two ruffians by the gate. Not that anyone would attack him, for they were eating out of his hand.

"In the place of our old, tired, oppressive government? *I* will look after your interests. I and my allies. Until you, the people of this great country, the country that defeated Bonaparte and paid the price, can choose your own representatives. Things will change because they must, and you, by marching, will make it so."

"What if they send the soldiers against us?" someone asked.

"My plan is that it will be too late by the time anyone thinks to summon them. I will hold them back as long as possible."

"But *if* they come?" another voice demanded. "If they *shoot*?"

Thorne swept his gaze around them and made his voice triumphant. "Then we *fight*, my friends! We have the numbers to overwhelm them, and we are prepared to die for our cause, are we not? Nothing will change if we are not brave and bold and unafraid."

"And where will you be?" someone asked. "While we are being so brave and bold?"

Thorne did not quite like the tone of this, though he answered at once with earnest certainty. "With you, of course, leading the march and the fight."

"And if *you* are shot?"

"Then our allies take my place," Thorne said impatiently. "My friends, this event is bigger than one man, this endeavor to bring down a government elected by a few rich men, who care nothing for you and your children, and replace it with one that truly represents you, that will end your poverty and powerlessness, find work for all and pensions for those like our forgotten, crippled soldiers."

"Seems to me," someone said into the hum of excitement, "we're depending entirely on the word of one man we don't know. Who are you? What's your name?"

Thorne was ready for this one. "If the authorities hear my name, I shall be arrested and unable to lead you."

A man near the foot of the hill stood up. "Enough of secrecy!" he declared. "If we are all friends here, why are we all masked like the fools at the ball or highway robbers?" In one quick movement, he tore off his mask. "Shall we?"

Several others sprang up, removing their masks, too. Thorne knew a moment of fear, as if the crowd was getting away from him. But even as the others unmasked, those who had stood sat back down again.

"Brave, honest men," Thorne applauded, desperately trying to come up with a reason for retaining his own mask. Damn it, the masks were the reason he'd chosen this ridiculous spot.

"Aye, we are," someone shouted, "and now it's your turn."

"When we march, you will see me. My friends!" He raised his voice above the murmur of protest sweeping about the garden. "If just one whisper of my identity comes out before then, we are *all* lost!"

"Don't seem fair," someone to the right of the hill complained.

And from the left came determined footsteps. Thorne's bodyguards stepped closer to him, and he glanced warily to his left. The approaching man began to run, straight at him. The bodyguards lunged in front of Thorne, blocking him from attack.

"My friends!" Thorne shouted, trying to keep the desperation from his voice. He had completely forgotten about disguising it. "This moment—" He broke off, gasping, as he was seized from behind and his mask ripped off.

At the same, awful moment, he saw his bodyguards both sprinting toward the gate after the first attacker, who was damned light on his feet. And the arm across Thorne's throat prevented him from even choking out the order to come back.

It was too late. His mask lay on the ground. People bearing lanterns were closing in on all sides, and yet the silence in the garden was profound. From beyond the gate, he heard a few muffled thuds, which he prayed meant his bodyguard had dealt with the first man and would be returning for the second.

But the damage was already done. Unless he could be more convincing than he had ever been in his life before. Bizarrely, he could hear the distant strains of a waltz.

Everything else was still and silent, including him.

"Do you recognize this man?" asked a voice Thorne knew but could not place.

"I do." Two men were strolling toward him, elegant domino cloaks swung back to reveal correct evening dress. Christopher Halland, the radical member of parliament. And…dear God, the Duke of Dearham. And it was the latter who spoke. "Sir Anthony Thorne. Not usually the friend of reform, eh, Mr. Halland?"

"Never."

"But a man can see the error of his ways, perhaps," said the voice behind him. The arm loosened.

"Oh, trust me, he will!" snarled a military voice. "Send a mob to fight with my men, would you? Threaten a sitting parliament?"

"No, no," Thorne said feebly. Blood was ringing in his ears, an impossible weight bearing down on his shoulders—that of failure. And disgrace. "You misunderstand!"

"Oh, I think we understand perfectly," said the hatefully mocking voice behind him. "Rile up a mob of men with genuine grievances, a mob larger than any we have ever seen—and all over the country, too. Send them to fight for their cause so suddenly that those in charge freeze and dither as to what to do. Then you would step forward, order out the troops, squash the mob, and as hero of the hour, with the generals behind you, declare some kind of interim martial law to deal with the emergency. Only the emergency never ends. Sir Anthony Thorne remains in power, a dictator more autocratic than Bonaparte, only without the good intentions."

Dear God, how had he found this all out? *Who the devil…?* He jerked around, staring at his former captor while the mob on the hill, muttering angrily, began to advance.

"Francis?" he said incredulously.

Francis's lips curved, though it was not a smile. "I have friends in higher places than you. I believe you are under arrest."

Oh, no I'm bloody not. Sheer terror lent him power as he bolted between Halland and Dearham and ran for the gate at breakneck speed, well ahead of the mob bearing down on him. He had a carriage waiting—if he could just make the hidden path without being seen. And then to the continent to lick his wounds. *Damn it all to hell!*

There was only a woman seated on the grass, just to one side of the gate. No threat. Until, just as he thought he was home and free, he tripped over her foot, which had not been there an instant before.

He fell on his face with a cry of rage. But two men were hauling him to his feet. Renwick's men. He breathed a sigh of relief. "Get me out of here," he commanded grimly.

"Certainly, sir," came the cheerful reply. "Captain, your prisoner, I believe?"

A man appeared in front of him, shedding his domino cloak to reveal a red military uniform. Thorne stared at him, breathing through his mouth. And then, movement on the ground distracted his attention as Francis raised to her feet the woman who had tripped him.

Matilda Mather.

"SO MUCH FOR staying away from any fighting," Francis said.

"I knew he would run," she replied. He always had, even in his teens, leaving others to take the blame. Why on earth had she ever found his apparent admiration flattering? She kept hold of her husband's hand, squeezing it tightly. "Your plan worked, and your timing was perfect."

"Lord Dominic certainly ran like the wind before Thorne's bullies. We should make sure he is unhurt."

"I'm fine," Lord Dominic said cheerfully from the gate, where the soldiers were waiting to haul off the bewildered Thorne. "Managed a rather clever throw of one of them, though I say it myself, and then Renwick's other fellows were on them. My only regret is I didn't see your great unmasking, Francis."

"It was superb," Lord Wenning murmured as he strolled up, kissing his fingers. "Perfect in every way. You could have heard a pin drop when they saw his face. Although the subsequent fury weaving through the crowd was downright alarming. Halland and young Holles are calming them down, and Dearham's reassuring them that the soldiers are not interested in arresting them. For one thing, there aren't enough of them."

"*Dearham* is?" Lord Dominic said, amused, and Wenning stood aside to give him a view of the scene. "Well, well, who would have thought our Loose Fish would turn into such a responsible pillar of respectability?"

"I would," said Ludovic Dunne, joining them. "My compliments, Mrs. Francis! An excellently aimed and most elegant foot."

"It did the trick," Matty said modestly.

Dominic said, "The charges against Thorne *will* stick, will they not?"

Ludovic exchanged glances with Francisco.

"Truthfully," Francis said ruefully, "they will probably cover it up. Force him to retire abroad with an excuse about his health and hold a bi-election."

"I'll push for even a closed trial and prison," Ludovic said, "but I doubt the powers that be will want all this laundry aired. Francis is probably right."

"Either way," Francis said to Matty seriously, "he won't bother you or your family again. And now, I believe, we shall bid you gentlemen goodnight."

Wenning blinked. "Don't you want to stay until all is cleared up and the crowd disperses?"

"Lord, no," said Francisco. "I just create the chaos and leave the clearing up to others. Protects my anonymity, don't you know?" He bowed sardonically and placed Matty's hand in his arm as they walked away to the laughter of their friends.

"After tonight, your anonymity may well have gone for good," Matty warned. "Dornan draws what he sees, and you did play a vital role in revealing Thorne's face. Yours will be right beside it."

"It doesn't matter," Francisco said. "I'm retiring, remember? My superiors already know."

Matty felt a pang of guilt leaving the others to do the calming and dispersing. But in truth, it also felt good to walk away, to realize they had brought down a bad man and prevented disaster, and that now she could walk in sweetly scented gardens with her husband.

It was, indeed, their wedding night.

She hugged his arm to her. "What would you like to do now?"

He glanced down at her, smiling. "I would like to waltz with you once more and then take you to bed."

She had no quarrel with that and smiled back, just a little shyly. He paused, though not to kiss her—there were, she thought irritably, too many people around—but to retie her mask and whisk the domino round to cover the luxurious blue of her evening gown.

Back in the pavilion, it was as if they had never been away. Dancing and drinking, flirting, and not very surreptitious fondling all carried on as before. The orchestra still played waltzes. Francisco led her to the dance floor and took her in his arms once more.

She sighed, relaxing into the dance and into him. Contentment began to steal over her, a sort of pleasurable exhaustion.

"You kissed me on this dance floor," she recalled, smiling. "In public. I was outraged."

"So you should have been, though you weren't. Not entirely."

"Sadly, that is true," honesty compelled her to admit. Who cared? They were masked. "You could do it again. If you wished."

"With half of our friends watching, I would not be so crude. I have a better idea. Let me take you to bed, and we can do all the kissing we want in private."

"Suddenly, it seems a long way back to Covent Garden."

"We're not going to my rooms in Covent Garden. We have much closer rooms bespoken at Renwick's Hotel."

Of course, there was a new hotel here, catering largely to the wealthier traveler. "That is very clever of you," she said, "only Mrs. Dove sent my things on to Covent Garden."

"No, she didn't. I had them brought here instead, along with a few others that are my wedding gifts to you."

"Francisco, when did you have the time to arrange *any* of this?" she said weakly.

"There is always time for the important things."

She smiled as the music stopped. Her contentment had developed an edge of excitement.

"Shall we?" he asked, releasing her and offering his arm.

She took it. "We shall."

They left the dance floor, Matty lost in the look in his eyes.

Somewhere, she had the impression that the path to the nearest door was lined by masked, smiling faces that were strangely familiar, but her attention was too fixed on her husband to be sure. Together, they walked along a pleasant path and up the hill to a gate that led to the hotel entrance.

"Good evening, sir, madam," the liveried porter greeted them, opening the heavy door to the wide, gracious entrance hall. A smart young man at the desk also bade them a civil good evening by name, so clearly Francis was known here.

He conducted her up a flight of wide stairs and along a carpeted passage to the room at the end. He unlocked the door with a key taken from his pocket, and she walked inside. A single lamp burned low in a sitting room.

The door closed behind her. She heard the key turn and listened to her fast-beating heart. Over it, she imagined she could hear, very faintly, the continued music of the pavilion orchestra. Francisco brushed past her, turning up the lamp, before coming back and removing her domino. He dropped both their cloaks over a chair and set about lighting the other lamps.

As he progressed into the room beyond, she followed at a distance, stripping off her gloves while she watched him light the lamps in the bedchamber, which was dominated by a huge, canopied bed with a step reaching up to it.

He turned and pulled back the curtains on one window, then held out his hand to her. "Come."

She went to him, taking his warm, familiar hand as though to remind herself who he was. Only then did she look out on the view from the hill over the sweep of countryside beyond. With the light from the moon and the glow of the torches and lanterns from the Gardens, it looked almost like a painting.

"It's pretty," she murmured. "I didn't expect that."

"We can make our stay as long or as short as you would like. We can arrange our wedding journey from here or go back to London first."

"Can we decide tomorrow?"

"Or the day after. We need do nothing at all until we wish to. Are you hungry?"

The magnificent wedding breakfast had not been so long ago, although she had been too excited to eat much of it. Nevertheless, there seemed to be no room in her for food.

She shook her head. "Are you?"

He bent his head nearer. "Yes. But only for you." His mouth covered hers, hot and tender and sweet, and she raised her arms to hold him, to caress his cheek and run her fingers through his hair.

The kiss deepened, but still, he did not rush her, merely stroked her back and her hair, causing pins to tumble to the floor. It was she who impatiently untied his cravat and tugged at his coat. But as he shrugged off the latter, she realized her gown was partially loose.

He smiled, throwing his waistcoat after the coat and, in one swift movement that had her heart racing, jerked his shirt up over his head and took her back into his arms. She kissed the hot, velvet skin of his chest, running her hands over the muscles corded in his arms and shoulders.

He lifted her, and somehow, her clothes slid away, and she was naked beneath him on the huge bed.

"Tonight," he whispered, "we give a whole new meaning to *pleasure garden*."

A sound escaped her, half laughter, half desperate need, as she arched up, pulling him into her. "*Love* garden," she corrected huskily as they began to move together. "After all, how much pleasure can a woman take?"

He smiled, bringing her deliberately to an astonished wave of joy. "Lots," he promised. "Lots and lots." And for the rest of the night, he proceeded to prove it to her. And she to him.

EPILOGUE

SIX MONTHS LATER, Francisco walked across the courtyard of his hacienda in southern Spain, until, from the archway, they could see out over the vineyards. The grapes were all in for the year, but the sight was still beautiful, the sun still warm, and the woman pressed to his side more precious than ever.

"We have laid a few ghosts here," he said at last. "Thank you for that."

They had come for a week and stayed nearly two months.

She rested her head against his shoulder. "If you are at peace with your home, then I am content."

He *was* at peace. Of course, he could never forget what had happened here in the past, but now it was Matty's face he saw everywhere, in his mind as well as in every room and garden. He had come to realize that he had let the past define him, who he was and what he was prepared to do.

But between them, there had to be honesty.

"Thorne is dead," he said casually.

"I know. I read it in the English newspaper in Lisbon."

She did not ask if he had anything to do with it. That alone proved she knew he had. The authorities would never have allowed Thorne to live. But it did not trouble her. She believed in Francisco. She trusted him. And he would spend his life making sure he lived up to that trust.

"Is it time to leave?" he asked.

She considered, then laid his hand against her abdomen. "That rather depends on where you would like your child to be born."

She caught at his breath in so many delightful ways, this bright, wonderful woman. When he realized he was in danger of crushing her, he loosened his arm and pressed his lips to her temple instead.

"Then you are pleased?" she asked anxiously.

"Oh, my love, how could I not be pleased? I am ecstatic! And I think we should go home to have the child closer to your family."

She stood on tiptoes to kiss him. "Thank you. I am sure Marion will be expecting soon, too, if she isn't already."

Marion had married the gentle Lord Danvers, much to Mrs. Mather's joy. Francisco knew Matty was missing them and was anxious to look in on the Doves, too. Francisco also looked forward to returning to England. It had been a wonderful half-year abroad with her. Seeing the world afresh through her awed eyes gave him new appreciation, feeding his continual happiness.

Of course, in six months, there had been low points, too. One of them had been when they heard about the massacre the newspapers were calling "Peterloo." In August, the cavalry had charged protesters in Manchester and killed and maimed many people. The disaster they had prevented in the spring had happened on a smaller scale anyway.

While Matty had mourned the unknown dead, Francisco had wondered if he could not have prevented the slaughter. If he had stayed in England, in touch with events, could he not have turned this around, too? Was it selfish and plain wrong of him to reject the work for which he was so well suited?

Matty, putting her arms around him, had convinced him otherwise. Understanding without any need of explanation, she had said simply, "You are not that man anymore. And the responsibility was never yours."

And she was right. She was nearly always right.

"Come then," she said, lifting his hand to her lips and kissing it. "Let us go home."

About Mary Lancaster

Mary Lancaster lives in Scotland with her husband, three mostly grown-up kids and a small, crazy dog.

Her first literary love was historical fiction, a genre which she relishes mixing up with romance and adventure in her own writing. Her most recent books are light, fun Regency romances written for Dragonblade Publishing: *The Imperial Season* series set at the Congress of Vienna; and the popular *Blackhaven Brides* series, which is set in a fashionable English spa town frequented by the great and the bad of Regency society.

Connect with Mary on-line – she loves to hear from readers:

Email Mary:
Mary@MaryLancaster.com

Website:
www.MaryLancaster.com

Newsletter sign-up:
http://eepurl.com/b4Xoif

Facebook:
facebook.com/mary.lancaster.1656

Facebook Author Page:
facebook.com/MaryLancasterNovelist

Twitter:
@MaryLancNovels

Amazon Author Page:
amazon.com/Mary-Lancaster/e/B00DJ5IACI

Bookbub:
bookbub.com/profile/mary-lancaster

CPSIA information can be obtained
at www.ICGtesting.com
Printed in the USA
LVHW051258200422
716609LV00014B/1268